4

Drawing Close

BARBARA HINSKE

Also by BARBARA HINSKE:

Coming to Rosemont, the first novel in the *Rosemont* series
Weaving the Strands, the second novel in the *Rosemont* series
Uncovering Secrets, the third novel in the *Rosemont* series
Bringing Them Home, the fifth novel in the *Rosemont* series
Shelving Doubts, the sixth novel in the *Rosemont* series
The Night Train
And Now on The Hallmark Channel…
The Christmas Club
Available at Amazon in print, audio, and for Kindle.

UPCOMING IN 2020

Guiding Emily, the first novel in a new series by Barbara Hinske
The seventh novel in the Rosemont series

I'd love to hear from you! Connect with me online:

Visit **BarbaraHinske.com** and sign up for my newsletter to receive your Free
Gift, plus Inside Scoops, Amazing Offers, Bedtime Stories & Inspirations from
Home.
Facebook.com/BHinske
Twitter.com/BarbaraHinske
Instagram/barbarahinskeauthor
Search for **Barbara Hinske on YouTube** for tours inside my own historic home
plus tips and tricks for busy women!
Find photos of fictional Rosemont, Westbury, and things related to the Rosemont
series at **Pinterest.com/BarbaraHinske**.
bhinske@gmail.com

Library of Congress Control Number: 2016936739
ISBN-13: 978-0-9962747-1-5
ISBN-10: 0-9962747-1-5

Casa del Northern Publishing
Phoenix, Arizona

Dedication

To Judy Angulo, whose wit, grace, and courage are an inspiration. I'm a better person for knowing you.

Chapter 1

Maggie Martin stared until the image was seared in her brain. She recognized the eyes of the child in the photo; the tilt of her chin. Even sick and in a hospital bed, Nicole Nash bore an unmistakable resemblance to her father. The little girl was Paul's daughter. Her late husband's mistress must have been pregnant when the cheating bastard had died.

She dragged her eyes from the photo and looked at the man she had married not more than twenty-four hours ago. John Allen held her gaze, and smiled. She opened her mouth to speak but the announcement from the gate agent drowned her out. "Flight 722 to Cornwall will begin boarding in fifteen minutes."

Maggie stood abruptly. "I'm going to the ladies' room." She was moving away from him, through the crowd, before he had a chance to reply.

Maggie strode down the concourse, weaving through the horde of travelers rushing to make their connections. All she knew was that she had to move, to process this revelation of yet another of Paul's betrayals, before she embarked on her honeymoon. How was it that Paul always managed to cast a shadow on her happiness—even from the grave?

She passed the women's restroom, then turned back and made her way to a sink. She put her hands in the basin. The water was far too hot for a public restroom, but the stinging heat was therapeutic. She looked at herself in the mirror as the water ran over her hands.

So Loretta Nash may have been pregnant when Paul died of a heart attack. Why was this throwing her for a loop now? She was starting a new life with Dr. John Allen, DVM. What was wrong with her? She needed to get hold of herself.

She walked to the automatic towel dispenser and attempted to dry her hands on the six inches of paper towel it provided. She checked her watch and gasped. She had been away far too long—their departure was in ten minutes. They couldn't miss their flight. She wouldn't spoil the beginning of her new marriage.

Maggie shoved her way through the line of women waiting to get into the restroom and broke into a run as soon as she got free of them. She could see John, standing at the gate, looking anxiously in her direction. She raised one hand over her head and waved at him. It took a moment, but he finally saw her and smiled.

She pushed past a young couple trying to corral a couple of toddlers into strollers, and rushed into the gate's now-deserted waiting area. John came forward to meet her as the gate agent announced, "Last call for passengers of Flight 722 to Cornwall."

"There was a long line. Sorry," she said breathlessly as she picked up her purse and carry-on.

"I was getting worried. I tried to call you, but you left your purse here."

Maggie nodded in the direction of the gate. "We'd better hurry."

They handed their boarding passes to the gate agent and walked down the ramp to the plane.

"I thought maybe you had second thoughts," he said.

"Now you're talking crazy, Dr. Allen. Nothing of the kind. You know very well that there are never enough stalls in a ladies' room." She stood on tiptoes and kissed him squarely on the lips. "This will have to hold you until Cornwall."

Maggie pulled up the blanket the flight attendant had given her and nestled against her new husband. John was a proficient sleeper and being on an airplane was no exception. He was reclined in his seat, sound asleep.

Maggie, however, was wide awake. Even though she was exhausted from their wedding the day before, she couldn't force her mind to be quiet. Constantly thinking she needed to get to sleep wasn't helping her, either. They'd land at Heathrow at six a.m. local time, after the overnight flight from the States. If she didn't sleep on the plane, she'd be miserable on the train ride from the airport to Cornwall.

She glanced at her husband. What a gem he was, surprising her with this trip. Penzance. She'd wanted to go there since she'd read *The Shell Seekers* more than twenty years ago.

Maggie closed her eyes and her mind seized on the unwelcome revelation of a few hours before. Before she and John boarded their flight, they'd been happily sipping coffee, scrolling through her tablet, looking at the photos her kids had sent her of the events leading up to and during the wedding. Susan had snapped a photo at Mercy Hospital, where she'd taken her nieces and their new friend Marissa Nash to visit Marissa's very sick little sister. Their friend's mother was also in the picture.

Maggie threw off the blanket.

Marissa's mother was none other than Loretta Nash. *The* Loretta Nash from Scottsdale, Arizona. The woman her late husband, Paul Martin, had been having an affair with. The one he had been supporting in lavish style—probably the reason he'd started embezzling from the college where he'd been the "esteemed" president for years.

Maggie released her seat belt and gingerly crawled over John, taking care not to wake him. She needed to move, stretch her legs, go to the bathroom—do something. Why does this bother me so much? Hadn't she accepted all of these betrayals by Paul and moved on? Hadn't she just married the love of her life on the lawn of Rosemont?

Maggie paced in the dim aisle, passengers on either side sleeping or reading quietly.

What could she do about this now? Nothing. She owed it to John and herself to put this aside. She'd deal with it all when she got home, at Rosemont.

Maggie returned to her seat, fished the natural supplement out of her purse that Judy Young insisted would help her sleep like a baby on the plane, and put it to the test.

Chapter 2

Chuck Delgado roused himself when he heard the garage door open at the other end of the house—Frank Haynes' house. Although he and Haynes were both successful businessmen and members of the Westbury Town Council, his visit tonight was occasioned by their clandestine dealings. Specifically, he wanted to discuss their mutual involvement in the infamous fraud that had almost bankrupted Westbury. Delgado checked his watch in the thin moonlight filtering through the closed plantation shutters. Midnight. He'd been sitting in the massive leather chair in Haynes' home office for more than two hours. He'd thought about leaning back and propping his feet on the teakwood desk, but decided against it. He'd have fallen asleep. Better to let Haynes find him waiting patiently—alert and upright—in the dark room.

The back door opened and Haynes whistled to his border collie, Sally, to join him outside for her last comfort break of the day before he headed to bed. *Some watchdog,* Delgado thought. The mutt grabbed the bone out of his hand the minute he jimmied the door open and hadn't made a sound since. Delgado smiled. He hadn't done any breaking and entering for decades, but he still had the knack. Like riding a bicycle— once you learned how, you never forgot.

Footsteps along the hallway told him he wouldn't have long to wait. He took a deep breath. Haynes moved swiftly across the dark room and tossed a stack of papers onto the desk before turning to retrace his steps to the door. Delgado waited until Haynes was silhouetted in the door frame before he spoke.

"Workin' late again, Frankie?"

Haynes tripped on the rug and caught himself on the mahogany molding framing the door. He spun to face the speaker.

"You been doin' a lot of that, lately. Spendin' too much time whimpering over that 'financial analyst' of yours with the sick kid. Or are you busy covering your tracks so you don't get arrested for fraud, too?"

"How in the hell did you get in here, Charles?" Haynes sputtered as he regained his footing and approached the desk.

"It was easy, Frankie. Haven't lost my touch. And that dog of yours is worthless," he said, gesturing to Sally who was waiting for her master in the hallway.

Haynes came around the side of desk and perched on the corner, facing his partner in crime. The cliché about regret leaving a bitter taste in one's mouth was true; his mouth had tasted like bile for months. He should have known better than to get involved with the Delgado brothers in this scheme that Ron Delgado convinced him was a legitimate loan from the town's pension fund. *Some financial advisor and upstanding member of the community Ron Delgado turned out to be,* Haynes thought.

The minute he learned that Chuck was involved, he should have backed out. The fact that Chuck was a member of the Westbury Town Council lent him an air of credibility he didn't deserve. Rumors had circulated for years that Chuck Delgado was connected to the Chicago mob. And now he, Frank Haynes, was up to his eyeballs in this thing.

"Why are you here? We decided to lay low and avoid each other, except for council meetings, until this investigation is over."

Delgado nodded. "That's why I'm visiting you here, in the middle of the night."

"Go on."

"I got some very distressing news, Frankie." Delgado rose and stood nose to nose with Haynes. "Distressing for both of us. I think maybe you set me up."

Haynes swallowed hard. Delgado's breath was stale but without the customary aroma of alcohol. Delgado had come to deliver his message sober.

"That Smith kid—the young attorney that's on loan from Stetson and Graham to help Scanlon—the one that we own? I met with him and he gave me copies of all of the incriminating documents that the town subpoenaed from the offshore banks."

Haynes nodded.

"They mention me and our esteemed former Mayor William Wheeler—may he rest in peace." Delgado leaned in. "Not one word about you. Anywhere." Delgado scrutinized Haynes' face. "Do you know how that happened, Frankie? You're in this as deep as Wheeler and me. How in the hell did you arrange that?"

"Is that what this is about?" Haynes pushed himself from the desk and began to pace. "Why do you think I'm not implicated?"

"Your name isn't on any of the documents Smith gave me."

"And you think that ends the matter?" Haynes turned away. He didn't dare show his relief that his Miami contact had removed any reference to himself or his bank accounts from the records of the offshore banks. It had cost him an arm and a leg and been worth every penny. "Smith wouldn't give you everything. For all you know, the remaining documents mention me. I could now be alone in their crosshairs. You may have extricated yourself at my expense, Charles."

A slow smile spread across Delgado's face. "Hadn't thought of that, Frankie boy. You may be screwed."

"Your concern is heartwarming." Haynes paused and regarded Delgado thoughtfully. "What did the documents show about you and Wheeler?"

"I'll give you a copy. Mainly just our signatures on paperwork opening the bank accounts and authorizing wire transfers."

"That may be too thin for them to prosecute on. I'll bet they're trying to build their case with new evidence. This whole thing is being orchestrated to induce us to do something stupid. Like this," he said, pointing to Delgado. "We don't want to play into their hands. We need to stick to our plan."

Delgado shifted his portly frame from one foot to the other. "You could be right about that."

"I know I am. We've dodged the bullet this long and I think we can continue to do so. If they had anything on us, we'd already be in jail."

Delgado nodded. Haynes took him by the elbow and steered him to the back door. "Go home. Lay low, and don't do anything stupid. Leave the Smith kid alone." He swung Delgado to face him. "And don't ever break into my home or anywhere else associated with me again. I can promise you I won't be the gracious host next time."

Delgado straightened and pulled his arms free. "You might want to get yourself an alarm system, Frankie boy. You and that mutt of yours are easy prey."

Chapter 3

John and Maggie walked hand-in-hand along the causeway at low tide, back to Penzance. The abbey-fortress atop St. Michael's Mount filled the sky behind them. "Breathtaking view from the chapel," John remarked. "Well worth the climb up to it." He glanced over his shoulder. "Did you read that plaque about Jack and the Beanstalk? Legend has it that the giant lived there."

Maggie nodded, brushing a strand of hair off of her face and attempting to secure it behind her ear. He eyed her closely.

"Do you want to talk about it?"

"I don't know. What's there to say? I feel certain that Nicole Nash is Paul's daughter. Susan and Mike's half-sister, born after Paul died."

"Loretta's made no mention of it. Don't you think she would have tried to get child support from Paul's estate after he died if Nicole were his daughter?"

"I hadn't thought of that," Maggie said. "Now that you mention it, I suppose she would have. It makes sense." They continued to stroll in silence.

"Unless she's not sure who the father is." Maggie stopped and looked up at John.

"I guess that's possible," he conceded. "But I wouldn't think it likely." He took her in his arms. "I hate to see you unhappy. You've been consumed by that mess at Town Hall. You act like you're personally responsible for everyone that lost money from the pension fund even though you didn't even live in Westbury when it all went down. Don't add this to your worries."

"You're right. Whether Nicole is Paul's daughter isn't my issue, one way or the other." She sighed heavily and leaned her head against his chest. "It's just unsettling, that's all. What else am I going to learn about

Paul? Haven't I had enough? How will Susan and Mike feel if they ever find out about all of the bad stuff that their dad did?"

John looked into her eyes. "Do you ever plan to tell them?"

"Not if I don't have to. At least not yet. Maybe someday. Or I could write it down for them to read when I die."

"Wouldn't that be harder on them? To learn about it when you're not there to answer questions?"

"Good point. I'm just not ready."

"Fair enough. Some advice?" John asked. Maggie nodded. "Leave it alone for a while longer. Get past this fraud business and get used to having me underfoot."

Maggie laughed. "That last bit will be easy. I'm going to love having you underfoot. What about my suspicions about Nicole Nash? Should I say something to Loretta?"

"I wouldn't," John replied. "What would you say? I think my late husband is your daughter's father? What's she supposed to say to that? If your suspicion is true—and I'm not saying it is because lots of unrelated people bear a striking resemblance to one another—Loretta knows, and she'll make it public if and when she wants to."

"I guess you're right." She pulled her sweater close around her as the breeze picked up. "The poor child has some serious health issues, according to Susan. I still can't stand Loretta Nash, but I wouldn't wish a sick child on anyone. If I'm correct, this is her secret to reveal. Not mine."

Maggie's phone began to ring as they resumed their walk to the safety of the shore. "It's Susan," she said, pulling the phone out of her purse. "What's up, honey? Is everything okay?"

"Hi, Mom. Yes—everything's fine here. Sorry to bother you on your honeymoon. Are you having fun? How's Cornwall?"

"We're having a marvelous time. Exactly what we hoped for. It's simply beautiful here. You'll have to visit, one day."

"I'd like to. And I'll want to hear every detail when you get home. The reason I'm calling is to tell you Aaron and I are coming to the party and to let you know we'll be staying with you through the sixth. If that's all right."

"What are you talking about? What party?"

"Alex's surprise party. He'll be forty on August fourth. Didn't Marc email you?"

"I haven't been checking emails on my honeymoon. We promised each other we'd totally unplug."

"Good for you. Proud of you for sticking to it. I'm not sure I could." Susan took a deep breath and continued. "Marc's renting a private dining room at The Mill. There'll be dinner, music, and fireworks over the Shawnee River."

"Sounds like quite the party."

"Aaron and I will fly in on the first and home on the sixth. I know you won't be able to take time off of work. Don't worry about meals or entertaining us. We can wing it on all of that. In fact, Marc doesn't want Alex to know his brother is in town until the party. He's afraid Aaron's being here will give it away."

"He might be right about that. How is Marc planning to get Alex to The Mill on his birthday without him being suspicious?"

"Marc's booked to play for an event there the night before. He's going to tell Alex that he forgot the cord for his amp and get him to ride out there with him to pick it up."

"Sounds plausible. So what will the two of you do when you're in Westbury before anyone can know you're there?"

"I'm looking forward to spending time with Aaron. I don't care if we just hang out at Rosemont and read or binge-watch TV. As it is, he's either studying for his boards or working. We barely talk and have only had dinner together twice during the last month."

"Has anything changed between you or is he just in the final crunch before boards? I remember that you lived like a hermit the month before the bar exam."

"I think it's that he's busy, but I'm wondering whether his feelings for me have cooled. This trip will be right after he's taken his boards, so I'll be able to tell then."

"Sounds like it will be exactly what you need. You'll have lots of time together because John and I will both be busy at work. We can have dinner together; but the rest of the time, the two of you can be on your own."

"Perfect. And you don't mind if we stay with you?"

"Of course not! Where else would you stay?"

"I can't wait, Mom. I'm going to let you go. Give that husband of yours a hug from me. And remember—this is a surprise party. Don't spill the beans to Alex!"

Chapter 4

"I'm leaving to take the deposit to the bank," Loretta Nash said as she paused in the door to Frank Haynes' office. "Would you mind if I cut my day short and went home after that?'

"Sure. That'll be fine," Frank said, without taking his eyes off of his computer screen.

"It's just that I need to get Sean and Marissa some clothes and supplies for church camp," she said.

Haynes waved his hand dismissively. "Fine."

"I could wait until tomorrow, if you'd prefer," she continued.

Haynes looked up. "Go now." She turned on her heel.

Frank Haynes watched until Loretta Nash pulled out of the parking lot, then locked the door to Haynes Enterprises and removed the painting by his office door that concealed the wall safe. He opened the safe and withdrew a folder labeled *F.H./Rosemont*, leaving the only other thing in the safe—a jump drive—undisturbed. Haynes glanced at the jump drive and stopped short. Had it been moved?

He took a deep breath. That was impossible. No one else had access to the safe. He was letting his imagination run away with him. Maintaining the secrecy of the information on that jump drive was crucial. It was his insurance if the fraud investigation ever got close to him. He had enough evidence on that drive to put Delgado in jail for decades. The jump drive was his ticket into the Witness Protection Program.

Frank Haynes returned to his desk and leaned back in his generous leather chair. He paged through the thin file until he came to an original copy of his mother's birth certificate, listing his grandmother and Hector Martin as her parents. Hector Martin, town patriarch and former owner of Rosemont, was his grandfather. His grandmother had been employed as a maid at Rosemont when she got pregnant. She never married

Hector. Instead, his grandmother wed a local tradesman—the man that raised his mother as his own child—seven months before his mother's birth.

None of this mattered, except that this birth certificate established his ownership of a half-interest in Rosemont. A sly smile crept across his face. Hector had left his estate to his "living heirs." When Hector died, the only known living heir was Paul Martin, Hector's great-nephew. If Paul had attempted to conceal the existence of this birth certificate and Haynes' inheritance in Rosemont, Hector Martin's estate could be reopened and Frank Haynes would own half of Rosemont. His lifelong dream of owning the grand home might come to fruition after all.

Haynes pulled his wallet out of his back pocket. He carefully withdrew a scrap of paper bearing the telephone number of the retired Vital Records Clerk. He'd taken her to dinner following her retirement in March and, after encouraging her in her third glass of wine, been rewarded with information that would prove crucial.

The retired clerk had confided her suspicions that the fire at the Vital Records Office shortly after Hector Martin's death in 2000 had been deliberately set. She remembered the attorney for Hector's estate and his hasty visit to the Vital Records Office the afternoon before the fire. He'd been an odd one, for sure; nervous and looking, for all the world, like a man with something to hide. She'd accused the attorney of setting the fire and had plenty to say about the fire marshal's lackluster investigation into the blaze. According to the clerk, nothing before 1951 had been entered into the computer database and all of the older records had been lost, including his own mother's birth certificate.

If Haynes could prove that Paul Martin had bribed the estate's attorney to set the fire that destroyed the old records, his inheritance of a half-interest in Rosemont could be established.

Haynes chuckled. He could just imagine Maggie Martin's face when she got the news that she wasn't the sole owner of Rosemont after all. Haynes rested his chin on steepled fingers. The usual solution in such situations was for one owner to buy out the other. Rosemont was worth a small fortune. The acreage alone would be worth close to two million.

He might be wrong, but he didn't think Maggie and her new husband had that kind of money. He, on the other hand, had enough cash in the bank to buy out her interest. He could toss her out and look like the good guy doing it.

Frank Haynes grasped the dusty files that the court clerk passed to him across the counter. "You can take these to one of those cubbies on the far wall," he said. "And that's not all of them. Hector Martin's probate is seven files thick."

Haynes nodded. "I'll want to see all of them." He traversed the room and placed the files on a shallow desk. "Is there anywhere I can have more room to spread out?" he asked the clerk as he returned for the final load.

"Nope," the clerk answered with a malicious gleam in his eye.

Damn these self-satisfied government employees, Haynes thought. "I'm Councilman Frank Haynes," he said, drawing himself to his full height. "Surely you can let me bring them into a conference room."

"Since you're on the council, sir," the man stared down his nose at Haynes, "you'll want me to follow the rules. And the rules are that the public can review documents right over there." He jerked his thumb to where Haynes had stacked the files. "So it's real handy for you to ask us to make a copy of anything you might need from the files. They're twelve cents a copy. Some people might be tempted to take a document right out of the file if we aren't watching."

Haynes suppressed his irritation and retraced his steps to the cramped work space. At least he knew what he was searching for. He turned to the first file on top of the stack. Although the estate of Hector Martin was large, its administration had been fairly straightforward. The bulk of his liquid assets had been bequeathed to a mix of a few local charities and the American Red Cross. Rosemont—and enough money to maintain it in perpetuity—had been left to Hector's living heirs.

Haynes leaned back in his chair. He had to prove that he was a living heir and that Paul Martin had concealed that fact.

He struck gold in the fourth file he went through. The file contained an affidavit from the first attorney to administer the estate—one Roger Spenser—attesting to the fact that he had personally made a thorough search of the public records and found no evidence of any other living heirs of Hector Martin. The date recited in the affidavit was the day after the fire.

Haynes pulled out the affidavit and went to the counter to secure a copy. He now knew what his next move would be. He would arrange a face-to-face meeting with Spenser. He needed the attorney's written statement that Paul Martin paid him to remove his mother's birth certificate from the public records so that Martin could establish his claim as the only living relative of Hector Martin.

Chapter 5

Maggie and John ambled along Chapel Street, admiring the architecture and enjoying the balmy day. After yesterday's expedition to Land's End and hike along the wind-swept cliffs, it was nice to mosey along at a leisurely pace. They'd spent the morning poking in and out of shops and galleries along Market Jew Street.

John pointed to the small storefront of a quaint tea shop just ahead. "Are you game? Or are you going to point to my waistline and recommend we pass?"

"Your waistline? I need to be worried about mine. I'm beyond caring at this point. We're on our honeymoon. When will we ever get real Devon cream again?"

"Exactly." He held the door open for her.

A pretty young woman showed them to a table next to the window. They placed their order for a full cream tea and sank into plush armchairs that showed the right amount of wear to be inviting without being down-at-heel. They scooted themselves close to a round table dressed in a crisp linen cloth.

Penzance was busy during the summer holiday and they watched tourists and tradespeople pass by the window. The waitress brought their sandwiches, scones, and sweets on a tiered china server.

Maggie studied the flowered pattern of the china as she placed a sandwich on John's plate and selected one for herself.

"I know that look, Mrs. Allen," John said. "You'll be wanting to know the name of that pattern, and we'll be searching for one of these thingies," he said, tapping the server, "as soon as we get out of here."

Maggie smiled at him. Even though she had decided not to change her name, she loved hearing "Mrs. Allen" on his lips. She pointed to the divided porcelain dish that held jam on one side and thick Devon cream on the other. "We'll be needing one of these, too."

"I'd better fortify myself," he said as he tucked into the food. "I'm not complaining, but I don't think you can call these tiny things sandwiches." He consumed a small round of fresh white bread topped with cucumber and cheese in one bite.

"You were expecting a sandwich like you would get at a deli?"

John shrugged. "All I'm saying is that if you're really hungry and want a sandwich, afternoon tea isn't your best bet."

"Fair enough," Maggie replied. She placed a silver tea strainer onto his cup and poured strong black tea from the delicate china teapot. She followed suit with her own cup and reached for a blueberry scone. "What is it they told us? In Devon they put the cream on first and then the jam, but in Cornwall they start with strawberry jam and finish with clotted cream?"

"I think we should try it each way to see if it makes any difference. In the interest of science."

They were hungrier than they thought and ordered a second round of scones—to fully test the cream versus jam issue, they told each other.

"I'd never given Cornwall any thought before you mentioned it. Wasn't on my bucket list to come here, but I've enjoyed it immensely." John squeezed her hand. "The company of my charming wife has everything to do with it, I'm sure."

"I'm so glad. I'd have felt very guilty if you were disappointed. It's so hard to clear our schedules to get away, not to mention the time and expense to get here."

"I'd like to take back something to remind us of our honeymoon."

"We've got lots of souvenirs already. Like that pottery I bought this morning that they're shipping to us. But that's more for me. We need something for you. What do you have in mind?"

"I'm struck by the paintings we've seen. By the Newlyn School artists. They're absolutely beautiful."

Maggie nodded. "The contemporary works or the older stuff? They call the turn-of-the-century works English impressionism."

"The older ones, for sure. I never thought I'd want to own a real painting. But I do now." He arched an eyebrow. "What do you think about buying a piece of art for Rosemont? Almost everything there is from prior owners. Maybe it's time we made our mark on the place."

"I think it's a grand idea. I'm not fond of that dreary landscape over the mantel in the living room." She slid forward on her chair and leaned toward him. "What do you think about replacing it? Or should we go for something smaller and more affordable that we can hang in our bedroom?"

"I was hoping you'd say that. Of all the things in Rosemont, that large painting is my least favorite."

"Then its days are numbered," Maggie replied. "When Gordon Mortimer comes back to appraise the furniture in the attic, we'll ask him if it's worth anything. If it is, we can sell it."

John grinned. "I thought you'd put up a fight."

"Of course not. It's your home now, too. Is there anything else that you'd like to get rid of?"

He shook his head. "The only other change I would make would be to add more TVs."

"So you can watch football in every room? Not a chance, mister."

"It was worth a try."

"Shall we start shopping for our painting?"

John nodded and motioned to their server for the check.

＊＊＊

Maggie and John spent the remainder of the afternoon going between two antique stores they'd visited earlier that morning. One had a large collection of paintings with famous signatures and hefty price tags; the other offered a sole canvas.

"It's hard to narrow it down, isn't it?" Maggie asked.

"You like the women on horseback, don't you?"

"I do. The clothes on the women, sitting regally on their side saddles, are beautifully detailed. The colors the artist used are glorious. And they'd look terrific over the mantel. Very in keeping with our decor."

She drew a deep breath. "But I'm drawn to the one of the mother and children picking blackberries in the sunshine. You can feel the warm breeze just by looking at that painting. Like the breeze we're feeling now," she said holding her hands in the air. "I feel happy looking at it, and it'll always bring me back here when I do."

John wrapped his arms around her. "That's my favorite, too. I don't have the vocabulary to talk about paintings, but I've liked that one since the first time I laid eyes on it. None of the others come close."

She tilted her face to his. "Why didn't you say so earlier?"

"I wanted to look at everything. Just to make sure. We're about to spend a lot of money."

"Good point. Let's go talk to the shop owner. He only has the one painting. Maybe it won't be too pricey."

They retraced their steps to the tiny antique shop that featured nautical bric-a-brac and fishing items. One large canvas hung prominently on the back wall.

"You've come back for her," the owner smiled. "I could tell that she was talking to you." He gestured to the painting.

"It's interesting," Maggie said, trying to sound noncommittal.

"Who's the artist?" John asked.

"It's unsigned," the man replied. They walked up to the painting and he pointed to the lower left. "The artist wasn't finished with it. The grass on the right side is more detailed than the grass on the left. Same thing with the sky. See what I mean?"

John nodded. "What happened? Do you think the artist died before he could finish it?"

"We don't know, of course, since we don't know who painted it, but I don't think that's likely. This would have been done by one of the early members of the Newlyn School. Possibly Elizabeth Forbes or Dame Laura Knight. That would be my best guess. They might have gotten a commission to do something else or been working on other projects and forgotten about it."

Maggie gulped. She'd read enough about the Newlyn artists to know that these were big names. She held her breath. "We're here on our honeymoon and are looking for something to take home as a keepsake."

The man smiled. "I think this would be a perfect choice. Where are you from?"

"We're Americans," John supplied. The man nodded. "I guess you knew that already. We live in a small Midwestern town that feels a bit like Penzance. The people in Westbury are warm and friendly, just like all of you."

"I think she'd be happy there," he said gazing up at the painting. "She's been here a long time. I haven't been terribly interested in selling her."

This will be expensive, Maggie thought. "What are you asking for it?"

The man quoted a figure that was near the top of the price range they'd set when they'd left the tea room. "If you include the tax and shipping with it, we'll take it," John replied.

The man nodded. Maggie threw her arms around John and hugged him hard before they headed to the counter to complete the paperwork. As John supplied the necessary details to the shop owner, Maggie turned back to look at their purchase. Was it her imagination or had the little girl with the basket on her arm waved at her?

Chapter 6

Loretta Nash pushed through the door of Haynes Enterprises shortly before eight o'clock. She hung her purse on the back of her chair and stepped into the doorway of Frank Haynes' office. He was hunched over his computer monitor, and she was surprised to see that he wasn't concentrating on a spreadsheet. She knocked lightly on the doorjamb.

"Good morning, sir."

"It's Frank. You don't need to call me sir," he said gruffly, but then looked up at her and smiled. "How's Miss Nicole today?"

"She's doing much better, sir ... Frank. I was just going to make coffee. Would you like some?"

Haynes stretched. "That would be great. I need something."

"What are you working on?" she asked tentatively, half expecting him to bite her head off for poking around in his business.

"I'm trying to get in touch with an attorney."

"That shouldn't be too hard," she ventured.

"He retired and moved out of the country more than a decade ago."

"That might be a different story," she conceded. "Do you know if he's still alive?"

"I don't. I found his bar association records, and he retired at the very young age of forty-three, so it's reasonable to think so."

"Lucky him," Loretta remarked. "Do you know where he moved to?"

"No. I've been searching on the Internet. I thought you could find anything on the Internet. But I'm coming up empty-handed."

"Would you like me to help? I'm pretty good at Internet searches, and there are paid services that you can use to help, too. Genealogy and skip trace websites. Stuff like that, if you don't mind spending the money."

Frank Haynes beamed at her. "Loretta, you're brilliant. That would be super."

Loretta turned aside before he could see her blush. One thing was certain; she could never predict the moods of her boss.

Frank Haynes stood in front of Loretta's desk as she bundled the day's receipts for deposit at the bank. "Any luck finding Roger Spenser?" he asked.

Loretta shook her head. "Sorry. We've been so busy here. Once I get through posting last month's expenses, I'll have more time."

Haynes frowned. "When will that be?"

"Not until next week, I'm afraid. Are you in a hurry to find him?"

"I might be."

"I'll work on it tonight, at home."

"I'd appreciate it—very much." He moved toward his office and turned back. "Keep track of your hours. I'll pay you overtime."

"You don't need to do that. You were so understanding about my time out of the office when Nicole was sick. I'm happy to do this for you."

Haynes nodded and a smile flickered on his lips. "Even so, I'm going to pay you. When do you think you can start?"

"Tonight. Sean and Marissa are away at church camp, and Nicole goes to bed early. I'll work on it every night this week, if necessary."

"Call me the minute you find anything, okay?"

"Sure. You really want to find this guy, don't you?"

Haynes ignored her question and returned to his office.

Loretta tuned to a Disney movie on the television and opened her laptop while Nicole snuggled next to her, drowsily watching the tale of a prince and princess that she'd seen dozens of times before. Roger Spenser was a common name, and Loretta unearthed a lot of entries to sort through. Knowing his age and that he had been an attorney in Chicago helped narrow her search.

The movie was nearing its inevitable conclusion when one entry on the third page of results caught her attention. There was a Roger Spenser who had made a name for himself as a birdwatcher. As she scrolled through the links, she learned that he was referred to as a "birder" rather than a "birdwatcher" because of his more serious pursuit of the hobby. He'd even lead international excursions and written a blog on the topic.

Loretta brushed the hair off of Nicole's forehead as the movie credits rolled on the screen. "Let's get you to bed," she whispered as she clicked the remote to turn off the TV.

Nicole slowly lowered one foot to the floor.

"Are you feeling okay, sweetheart?" Loretta asked, placing her hand under her daughter's chin and raising her face to look at her carefully.

Nicole nodded.

"Just tired?"

Nicole nodded again.

Loretta put her arm around her daughter's shoulders and steered her into the bathroom and then into bed. She tucked Nicole's favorite blanket around her and watched as her youngest child fell quickly asleep. Loretta said a prayer of thanks that her little girl's kidneys were responding to the medication and working properly. She never wanted to see Nicole hooked up to a dialysis machine again.

Despite staying up until after midnight researching noted birder Roger Spenser and making a record of her findings, Loretta was waiting at Haynes Enterprises when Frank Haynes arrived at seven thirty the next morning.

"Sorry to keep you standing out here," he said as he hurried up the steps and inserted his key. "Why are you here so early?"

"I have some things to attend to," she said cryptically.

"Find anything about Spenser last night?" he asked as he held the door open for her.

"Yes. That's actually why I came in so early. I want to make a couple of calls before the phones start ringing off the hook around here."

Haynes turned to her. "Tell me."

Loretta arched a brow and smiled. "Not yet."

"When?"

"I should be finished this afternoon."

"I've got meetings out of the office from lunchtime on," he said, frowning.

"It'll keep until tomorrow."

Haynes shook his head. "Can I call you at home, tonight?" His head came up. "Better yet, why don't I take you and your daughter out to dinner and you can tell me then?"

Loretta stared. Frank Haynes never ceased to surprise her.

"Where would you like to go? What does Nicole like?"

"With Nicole in tow, we'll need to go to a place with a play area. One of your restaurants would be fine."

"Ahhh …" Frank rubbed his hand over his chin. "Can you get a babysitter? Would you like to go to The Mill?"

Did Frank Haynes just ask her on a date? No, get over yourself, Loretta. He just doesn't want Nicole to interrupt. Haynes was looking at her, waiting for her reply. She cleared her throat. "I'd love to. Let me see what I can do."

"Good, it's settled. I'll pick you up at six thirty. Can you make a reservation?" He tossed the office key on her desk. "And make yourself a copy of this key. It's ridiculous that I have to always be here to open and lock up."

Would wonders never cease? Loretta thought. Frank Haynes was taking her to the nicest place in town for dinner, and he was finally giving her a key to the office. Maybe she was making progress with him after all.

Loretta locked up Haynes Enterprises at four o'clock and attached her new key to her key chain. She wanted to have enough time to get Nicole fed and over to Mrs. Walters, the babysitter, so she'd be home by five thirty. She'd like to touch up her makeup and change her clothes before Frank picked her up. *This isn't a date,* she reminded herself. She hadn't been on a date in years—not since before Paul died. This was a business dinner, but she wanted to look her best.

When she stepped into her closet an hour and a half later, she pulled out the strapless red dress that had been Paul's favorite. Loretta pulled it over her head and turned side to side, scrutinizing herself in her full-length mirror. It still fit perfectly, and she looked like a million bucks, if she did say so herself. But it didn't suit her anymore. It was a dress for a carefree, fun-loving, seductive woman. Loretta wasn't that person anymore. She pulled the dress down around her ankles and kicked it aside. It was time to put it in her donation box.

Loretta stepped to her closet and worked her way through the hangers, passing over the scores of expensive garments that Paul had bought for her. It was time to put all of this behind her. High time. Loretta swept the clothes onto her arm and carried them to her kitchen table. She'd bag them up when she got home and donate them on the way to work the next morning. Before she lost her nerve.

With a lightness that was palpable, she returned to her now much-depleted closet. Shoved into the far corner, one shoulder perilously close to slipping off the hanger, was a plain black sheath. She'd had the dress for more than a decade. It was the first "good" dress she'd ever bought herself. The fabric was lovely, with a soft sheen that glowed in candlelight. Loretta had balked at the price, but the saleslady had insisted that this was a dress that she could be proud to wear for the rest of her life. Loretta pulled it off the hanger. She was going to see about that, right now.

From the admiring look in Frank Haynes' eyes when she opened her door to him precisely at six thirty, the saleslady had been right. Loretta looked beautiful, and she knew it. She was also sure that Frank thought so, too.

"We'd better get going," he said after an awkward silence in her doorway.

They drove through the midsummer countryside to the old sawmill, now repurposed as an inn, restaurant, and spa, as the last rays of sun slanted through the thick canopy of trees lining the route. Frank expertly navigated the twists and turns of the country road while Loretta relaxed and enjoyed the unexpected treat of being a passenger and not a driver.

Not more than twenty minutes later, the courteous hostess ushered them to a table by the window. "As requested," she said.

Loretta turned to the woman. "I didn't request a window table when I made the reservation. This must be meant for someone else."

"I called to arrange it," Haynes said.

Loretta turned to him in surprise. "Thank you."

"The sunset over the river should be spectacular tonight." He pointed to the sky as he held her chair for her. "Clouds always magnify the colors of a setting sun."

Loretta placed her purse on her lap and began removing a small stack of papers.

"I'm anxious to hear what you've found," Haynes said as he sat down, "but let's order, first."

Loretta laid the papers aside and picked up her menu.

The waiter approached and offered to take their drink order. Loretta shook her head. "I'm fine with water."

"You like red wine, don't you? Malbec?"

"You've got a good memory," she replied.

Haynes studied the extensive wine list and pointed to one of the offerings. "That's an extremely nice choice, sir," the waiter said. "You have very good taste. I'll get it right out."

"I remember your penchant for salads, but they're known for their steaks. The fillet is superb."

Loretta perused the menu. It was the most expensive thing listed.

"That's what I'm having," Frank said, folding his menu and putting it on the table.

"All right," Loretta said. "Sounds good."

"Why don't you pick out the sides? You're more interested in vegetables than I am."

Loretta smiled. "What do you like?"

Haynes shrugged. "Whatever you pick will be fine."

Loretta looked at him over the top of her menu. Frank Hayes actually had "game," as Loretta and her girlfriends in Arizona used to say about the men they dated who knew how to flirt. *That was such a long time ago,* she thought.

The waiter approached and made a dignified show of displaying the bottle to Frank, uncorking it, and waiting for him to approve the sample. He poured them each a glass and took their orders.

"Garlic mashed potatoes and roasted asparagus to your liking?" Loretta asked as the waiter retreated.

"The potatoes, yes. I'm sorry to say I've never tried asparagus."

"What? Why didn't you tell me?" She turned in her chair to summon the waiter back to them.

Frank leaned toward her. "It's fine. High time I tried new things. And if I don't like it, I don't think they'll make me clean my plate." He smiled at her and she smiled back.

He leaned back into his chair and Loretta felt an invisible curtain fall between them. "So. Tell me. What did you find?"

Loretta drew a deep breath and gathered her notes. "Roger Spenser is a fairly common name, so this took a bit of time. And I'm not certain I've found the one you want."

Haynes nodded, impatient for her to proceed.

"I found a Roger Spenser who was an attorney in Chicago. The Illinois bar records show he retired from the practice in 2001. So the timing of that is good. He's an avid birdwatcher and moved to the Lake District in England to pursue his hobby. His wife was even more serious about it than he was." She looked up at him. "Did you know that if you just like to look at birds, you're a birdwatcher, if you're really serious

31

about it, you're known as a birder, and if you're studying them for scientific purposes, you're called an ornithologist? Who knew ..."

Haynes shifted in his chair and resisted the urge to make a rolling motion with his finger, telling her to move her story along.

"Anyway, both of the Spensers were considered birders. They went bird-watching all over the globe for the next ten years, and his wife even led birding expeditions. When she died in 2011, he took over and continued to lead at least two trips a year. He even wrote a monthly blog called *On a Wing and a Prayer.*"

"He's still in the Lake District, leading folks with huge binoculars slung around their necks through field and forest and writing about it?" Haynes could hardly believe his good luck.

"Not really. That's what I found last night, but his blog abruptly stopped six months ago, and the website where his tours were booked doesn't list any to be led by him. The trail came to a screeching halt."

Haynes shoulders sank. "So that's the end of the line?"

"No. That's why I came in early today. I called the tour company."

"And?"

"They were reluctant to give me any information at first—kept trying to sell me on one of their other tours. I made up a story about being particularly interested in one type of bird that I knew, from his blog, he was obsessed with. I insisted that there would be no point in my going out with another guide." Loretta beamed, pleased with her resourcefulness.

"Well done," Haynes supplied, willing her to continue.

"They finally told me that Spenser had fallen ill and moved back to the States to be near his sister's family. Apparently he and his wife had no kids of their own. The last time anyone talked to Spenser, he was in chemotherapy and holding his own. The prognosis wasn't very good, however."

Haynes leaned forward, resting his elbows on the table. "Did you find out where the sister lives?"

Loretta looked triumphant. "She lives in Richmond, Indiana, and her married name is Gina Gallagher."

Frank Haynes reached across the table to squeeze her hand. "Perfect. Thank you so much for all of this. Good work," he said, releasing her hand. "Extraordinary."

"Glad I could help. You're pleased?"

"Very pleased," he replied.

They finished the evening with small talk about Loretta's children and Frank's plans to expand his restaurant empire.

"This was a real treat, Frank. Thank you very much. And the wine was superb. You must not have liked it, though. You only had one glass."

"I'm driving, remember?" he replied as he signed the credit card receipt, folded it carefully, and placed it in his wallet.

She nodded and pointed to the bottle. "In that case, I'm afraid I've consumed the rest of it. Boy, it was smooth and went down easy." She attempted to stand but quickly sat back down.

Haynes looked at her questioningly.

"Oh my gosh, Frank. I think I'm tipsy. I'm definitely a little unsteady on my feet." She turned to him and tears rimmed her eyes. "I'm so sorry. I know this is a business dinner. I never meant to do this."

Haynes moved quickly to her side. "Nonsense, my dear. This was my fault. If I hadn't been driving, I'd be in the same boat. That wine is irresistible." He pulled back her chair and extended his arm.

Loretta looped her arm through his and took a few tentative steps, conscious of the other restaurant patrons' eyes on them. "I think I'll need your arm around my waist, sir," she said in a whisper.

Frank Haynes found he was delighted to oblige.

They stopped for coffee at the drive-thru window of the first fast-food restaurant they passed on the way home. Loretta was marginally steadier on her feet when they got out of his car in the parking lot of her apartment complex. "Do we need to go get Nicole?" Haynes asked.

Loretta shook her head. "She's spending the night at the sitter's."

"Let me help you get up the stairs and into your apartment," Haynes said.

Loretta steeled herself for what she assumed, from experience, would come next. He'd get her inside, offer to help her make her way to her bed, get her shoes off, and proceed from there. And, truth be told, she didn't think she was interested in fighting him off. She was surprised, then, when he took her key, opened the door, and remained on the threshold as she stepped across it. Loretta turned to face him.

"Will you be all right from here?" he asked.

Loretta tried to read his expression, but his face was obscured by shadows. She nodded slowly. "Yes. I'll be fine."

"Good. And thank you for all of your help with this, Loretta. You've been invaluable."

"You're welcome."

He took a step back. "Don't worry about being at Haynes Enterprises bright and early tomorrow. You may need to get some extra sleep," he said, and she was certain she heard kindness in his voice. He turned to go.

"Frank," she said, grabbing his elbow and leaning toward him, her breath warm and fragrant against his face. She paused, then placed a gentle kiss on his cheek. "Thank you. For everything." She stepped back into her dark apartment and closed the door.

Frank Haynes pulled out of the parking lot of Loretta Nash's apartment and, instead of proceeding directly home at this late hour, turned toward Rosemont and his familiar perch in the berm of the road that ran below the grand home's back lawn. The house was in complete darkness, its residents—Maggie Martin and John Allen—undoubtedly fast asleep. *Residents for now*, he thought.

He smiled and patted the breast pocket of his jacket, where he'd secured Loretta's notes about Roger Spenser. He knew what his next move would be. He'd find Spenser and get him to confess to removing the evidence that established Haynes' ownership of a half-interest in Rosemont, probably for a hefty sum that he received from Paul Martin. Enough to allow him to retire at an early age and for him and his wife to live out the remainder of their years indulging their passion for—what did Loretta say they called it—birding? He'd have to think through how he was going to present this to Spenser. If he was really a dying man, he would be immune to threats. He'd appeal to the man's better nature; maybe he'd be concerned about his immortal soul.

Haynes stared at the dark edifice of Rosemont, washed in moonlight. He brought his hand to his cheek and touched the spot where the softness of Loretta's kiss lingered. Happiness—an unfamiliar feeling for Frank Haynes—surged through him. Whether the feeling arose at the prospect of owning Rosemont or over the memory of her kiss, he couldn't say.

Chapter 7

"Alex? What's up?" Maggie said, pressing her phone tightly to her ear to compensate for the poor connection. "Is everyone all right?"

"Yes, fine. Sorry if I alarmed you."

"Two voice mails and four text messages in six hours will do that."

"I wanted to catch you before you left to come home. You leave tomorrow, don't you?"

"We catch the train to London first thing, and we'll be on a red-eye flight home."

"How would you like to extend your honeymoon?"

Maggie snorted. "Nothing I'd like more. Cornwall has been marvelous, and my new husband has been spoiling me rotten," she said, smiling at John. She angled the phone away from her mouth and said, "It's Alex. He wants to know if we'd like to stay here longer." John gave two thumbs up.

"I didn't say stay longer in Cornwall," Alex said. "I said extend your honeymoon. At least, that's what we'd have the outside world think."

"You've got my attention," Maggie replied. "What would we be doing instead?"

"Going through four boxes of the documents that we obtained from the banks in response to our subpoenas. We've segregated the most critical documents, and you need to go through them with a fine-toothed comb, using your expertise as a forensic accountant."

"I see. I'm not so sure that's necessary, Alex. I can return to work on Monday as planned and still get through the documents in the next several months."

"That's why we came up with this plan. We don't have several months to sit on our hands and wait, Maggie. And we don't have the money to hire anyone else."

Alex cleared his throat and Maggie knew he was just getting started. She leaned back into the chair in their hotel room and eased her aching feet out of her shoes.

"Right now, no one knows what we've got in our hands. We want to finish our investigation and take action as soon as we can. We also don't want anyone to get wind of the fact that we're having a forensic accountant review the documents, which won't be a secret once you're spotted coming and going from the document room."

Maggie laughed. "I'm not sure how you avoid that unless you smuggle me into a secret location where you've secured the documents."

"That's exactly what we have in mind," Alex replied and was certain he heard a sharp intake of breathe from the other end of the phone. "We've got use of the basement storage room in my cousin's dental practice in Ferndale. He has a duplex and lives on one side and runs his office out of the other. He takes the last two weeks of June off every year and shuts down his entire practice. No one will be there. You and John can sleep in his guest room, and you can go through the documents in the basement without interruption. He's just outside town, so no one will see you. And it won't cost the taxpayers a dime. It's the perfect scenario."

Maggie sighed heavily. Having an uninterrupted block of time to cull through the documents would be ideal. Once she set foot in Town Hall, she was sure she'd be swamped with her duties as mayor of Westbury. She leaned forward, sitting on the edge of her chair. "I don't think it's a very practical suggestion. John has to get back to his veterinary practice. What would we say?"

"We've thought of that. If John is okay with it, say that you've contacted John's elderly second-cousins in London. They've invited you to stay with them for a week so they can show you the sights, and you'd both like to oblige. Everyone will think you're gadding about London when you'll really be slaving away in a basement in Ferndale."

"Seems pretty iffy. What if someone sees us arrive at the airport?"

"Change your flight and come into Chicago. Forest Smith can pick you up and drive you to my cousin's house. When you're done, Forest can take you to the original airport and you can take the same shuttle service home—just a week later."

"You've thought this through very carefully, haven't you?"

"I have. It's important, Maggie, and it's our best shot." She heard the pleading in his voice.

"Let me discuss this with John, and I'll call you back within the hour."

Chapter 8

Alex Scanlon and Forest Smith approached the duplex on the outskirts of Ferndale from different directions that Saturday night and arrived within five minutes of each other. They pulled around the building and into the deserted parking lot of the dental practice.

Both men got quietly out of their cars and approached the house. The back door opened before they could knock. John Allen stepped to one side and motioned them in. "You weren't followed?"

"I'm sure I wasn't," Alex said.

"I wasn't either, Dr. Allen," Forest said.

John nodded. "Good. And please, it's John. Come on through. Maggie's still downstairs, finishing her report."

John turned, leading them through the kitchen and down a hallway to the basement door.

"How was your honeymoon?" Alex asked.

"The first part was glorious. Cornwall is almost as charming and beautiful as my new wife. This last week, however, has been rather odd. I've watched so many sports on TV that I'm sick of them."

Alex stopped and caught John's arm. "I'm sorry to intrude like this. I—we," he said, motioning to Forest, "thought this was our best option. We're at our wits' end here, John. We've got to find some way to get these guys who have stolen the pension funds and wrecked the retirements of so many people. I know it must have been hard for you to get someone to cover your veterinary practice for another week. We're grateful to you."

John shrugged dismissively. "The young vet that's been filling in for me hasn't found a permanent position yet, so he was glad for the extra work. To tell you the truth, I've been thinking of hiring someone to help me. I can keep up if I work sixty hours a week, but I don't want to do that now that I've got someone to go home to. If I like how he's handled things while we've been gone, I may offer him a job. So this all worked out fine for me, too."

"I thought I heard voices," Maggie said as she came up the steps. The three men turned in her direction. "I've just finished. Come on down."

Maggie spent the next three and a half hours taking Special Counsel Alex Scanlon and his co-counsel, Forest Smith, through each document that established the paper trail that led to perpetrators William Wheeler and Charles Delgado. Wheeler had been identified early in the process, stripped of his position as mayor of Westbury, and thrown into jail. While in jail, Wheeler had conveniently—too conveniently—committed suicide, leaving his wife, Jackie, and teenaged son, David, destitute and heartbroken.

The fraud and embezzlement from the town's general fund and the town workers' pension fund was a complex criminal enterprise. It was unlikely to have been the effort of only one person. But they had been unable to unearth evidence against anyone else. Until now.

Maggie pointed to a handful of papers. "Based upon my examination, these are the only ones that haven't been altered. They point to Wheeler and Chuck Delgado. Nobody else."

Alex riffled through the stack of papers. "It's weak, Maggie. Very weak." He cradled his head in his hands. "We know Wheeler had to have help, and we know Delgado isn't smart enough to have come up with this scheme on his own. It would be unethical to use any of the evidence that we suspect has been altered—Delgado's defense team would get it thrown out in a heartbeat, anyway. Probably strip me of my license to practice law along with it."

Maggie turned to Forest Smith. "I agree with Alex, ma'am. There's not enough here to go forward."

"Finding out who altered these documents would be nigh unto impossible," she said, resting her hand on another stack. "I've seen this before in fraud cases I've worked on. Once you subpoena records from outside the borders of the United States, like these records from offshore banks in the Caribbean, your chances of success diminish precipitously." She leaned toward them. "What if we went forward anyway? What's the worst that could happen?"

"The case gets thrown out, and we're the laughing stock of the community," Alex answered.

"Then we're right back where we are now. No difference. We're already considered to be completely incompetent by most of the constituents, thanks to the fine editorial work of the *Westbury Gazette*," Maggie said bitterly. "What could we accomplish if we arrest Chuck Delgado?"

"He'll be off the streets for a while," Forest said.

"For a matter of hours," Alex cut in. "He'll make whatever bail is set for him."

"Would he offer to talk in exchange for a lighter sentence?" Maggie asked.

"Not likely," Alex scoffed. "Our evidence won't get us that far."

"At the very least, it will make him furious. Delgado is prone to doing stupid things even at the best of times. If we make him mad enough, he might slip up and give us something to go on," Maggie suggested.

Alex cocked his head to one side, thinking, and caught Forest's eye. Forest nodded. "You might have something, there, Maggie," Alex said. "But we could be unleashing some new evil that we can't control. Remember the arson fires in my home and office and the suspicious car accident that almost killed Marc and me?"

"Believe me, I haven't forgotten. If we decide to arrest Delgado, I'll have Chief Thomas put round-the-clock security details on both of you," Maggie replied.

"You'll need one, too, Maggie," Alex said. "Don't look at me like that—you're in as much danger as we are."

Maggie shrugged. "If you really think so."

Both men nodded their agreement.

It was close to one in the morning when Maggie led Alex and Forest back upstairs.

"So we're agreed," Alex said as they headed to the back door. "Some of the significant documents have been altered. Someone is trying to cover something up. We've got just enough evidence in the unaltered documents that Maggie's set aside to arrest Delgado, without using any of the tainted documents. We'll arrest him and hope we get him stirred up enough to do something stupid. Who knows—maybe he'll even lead us to his cronies."

"He mentioned Frank Haynes when I gave him the copies of the documents that fingered him. That was when he thought I was in his hip pocket," Forest said.

"If Haynes got himself involved in this mess, he's not the kingpin we're after. He's a sharp businessman, always looking for an easy way to make a buck, but I don't think he's got mob connections," Alex said. "Chuck Delgado, on the other hand, has been in bed with the mob since he was old enough to walk. His brother, Ron, maintains a legitimate facade, but I'd bet my paycheck that he's dirty, too. Haynes isn't our top target. We're after the mob bosses at the heart of this. That's where I want Delgado to lead us."

Maggie nodded. "I agree. Let's take our best shot and put pressure on Delgado."

Alex looked from Maggie to Forest and nodded. "We'll have Delgado arrested first thing Monday morning." He smiled a mirthless smile. "By the time you get to Town Hall, he should be in custody."

Alex turned to Forest. "Delgado is going to assume that you reneged on your promise to keep these documents hidden from me. The first thing he'll do is lash out at you."

"I'm not worried …" Forest began.

Alex held up a hand to silence him. "I am. I'm very worried. Keep your eyes open and don't take any lonely drives in the country."

Smith remained silent. "We're all in danger here," Maggie said quietly. "The fact that they haven't succeeded in killing anyone, yet, doesn't mean that they won't the next time they try." She put her hand on the doorknob. "We'll be back in Westbury by midafternoon tomorrow." She nodded at Smith. "Forest is dropping us at the airport at noon, and we'll be on the next shuttle to Westbury. I'll text you when we get home. I'll be in my office by eight on Monday morning. Time is on their side, not ours. They think this will be a battle of attrition—that we'll be gridlocked by mountains of documents. We're going to show them differently."

Alex smiled. "Thanks, coach!"

"Be careful getting home tonight and from here on out." She opened the door and watched until their taillights disappeared around the side of the house and out of sight.

Chapter 9

The receptionist buzzed Susan Martin's private line for the second time in under a minute. The call must be important. The woman knew she didn't want to be interrupted. Susan extended an arm awkwardly toward her phone, all the while keeping her eyes trained on her computer screen, and found the speaker button.

"I'm sorry to disturb you, Susan," the woman rushed to say, "but there's a man here that insists he needs to see you."

Susan opened her calendar on her computer screen. "I don't have anyone scheduled," she said.

"That's what I told him." The receptionist sounded pleased with herself. "Told him he'd have to make an appointment and come back. But he says you know him, and you'll want to see him."

"Who is it?" Susan tried to keep the irritation out of her voice. If her visitor was a salesman, she'd send him packing in a heartbeat.

"Says his name is Aaron Scanlon. Dr. Aaron Scanlon."

Susan was on her feet and headed to the law firm's lobby before the woman finished speaking.

"What in the world?" Susan gasped as she approached Aaron and gave him a quick kiss on the cheek. He reached out to pull her to him, but she took his hand to divert him. The receptionist would have enough fodder for office gossip with just that kiss on the cheek. "Come on back to my office," she said quickly, leading him away from the receptionist's prying eyes.

"Is everything all right?" she asked, shutting the door to her office behind them.

"Everything's fine, except that I'm missing you." Aaron swept her into his arms. "I got off work unexpectedly and came straight here. Can I buy you lunch?"

"I ate at my desk. It's almost three."

"A cup of coffee, then? Are you in the middle of some big motion?" he pointed to her computer screen.

"I am, actually. But I could use a short break. If you haven't eaten, I'll go with you to keep you company." She leaned into his embrace. "I'm surprised you came here instead of racing home to your books."

Aaron winced. "I know I've been going overboard studying. I'm a compulsive over-preparer. But today is just too beautiful to spend inside—either studying or drafting motions." He rocked back on his heels. "Why don't we jump in my car and drive up the coast? Find someplace along the beach for an early dinner and take a stroll on the sand at dusk. Can you afford to leave that for tomorrow? You're always advising me to lighten up, so I'm challenging you to do the same."

Susan smiled up at him. "All right, Ferris Bueller. You're on. Let me log off and grab my purse."

The afternoon was Chamber of Commerce perfect. They took the Pacific Coast Highway and headed north, meandering through the beachy communities, packed with summer visitors. They were inching through Carlsbad when Susan sighted a parking spot not more than twenty yards ahead.

"Can we?" she asked as Aaron deftly maneuvered his car into the tight spot. "I love the shops here. I haven't wandered through them in ages."

"Then that's what m'lady should do," he replied.

"There's the best spot for ice cream here, too. If it's still there."

They found the ice cream parlor and most of her old favorite shops. She was in her element, weaving through colorful displays, comparing items, weighing the wisdom of her purchases. By the time they headed back to Aaron's car to feed the parking meter, he was loaded down with shopping bags, which he insisted on carrying for her.

"I really could have taken some of those," she remarked as he loaded them into the trunk of his car.

"Do you want to make another round?" he asked, smiling at her.

Susan shook her head. "That's about all my credit card can take for one afternoon. Why don't we head back—maybe stop in Del Mar for dinner?"

Aaron opened the car door for her. "I Googled things to do while you were in that dress shop. There's a performance tonight of *Les Misérables* at the La Jolla Playhouse. If we can get tickets, would you like to go?"

Susan turned to him, wide-eyed in amazement. "You know that's my favorite musical. I'd love to. It runs almost three hours—are you sure you're up for it?"

He sensed she was holding her breath, waiting for his answer. He passed his phone to her. "See if we can get tickets," he replied. "All I want to do today is treat the best girlfriend in the world to a special day."

Les Misérables had been sold out for weeks, the ticket agent told Susan, but they were in luck as a season ticket holder had just turned in two seats for that evening's performance. They were in the third row, center, and could be hers if she'd give the agent her credit card number to hold them. Susan fumbled in her purse, but Aaron shook his head and handed her his wallet. "This one's on me."

With the tickets secured, they drove into La Jolla and found a quaint seafood restaurant near the beach. It was fully booked for dinner, the maître d' advised, but they could sit in the bar and enjoy the full menu. They perched on chairs at a high-topped table in the most secluded corner and followed their server's suggestions for appetizers and entrees. By the time they finished their calamari and sea bass with risotto, they were stuffed.

"We ate like mad dogs," Susan observed.

"I was starved. Being outside all afternoon gave me quite an appetite."

"Delicious." Susan smiled at the waiter. When he asked if they'd like to see the dessert menu, they both shook their heads.

"Let's walk along the beach," Aaron suggested. "Work off this dinner before the play. I don't want to fall asleep in my seat."

Aaron took Susan's hand to steady her as she slipped her shoes off before stepping onto the beach. They walked along, into the light wind, holding their shoes and swinging their clasped hands. Aaron turned to her. "This has been the perfect day. Thank you so much for putting your work aside."

She smiled up at him. "I'll pay for it tomorrow, but it'll be worth it. Even if I have to work all night tomorrow."

Aaron stopped and looked into her eyes. "I want us to have a lifetime of these kinds of days. There's nothing I want more, Susan Martin."

The La Jolla Playhouse did a masterful job with the ambitious production of *Les Misérables*, and the audience was on its feet for a standing ovation at the final curtain. Susan waited in the long ladies' room line before they undertook the drive home. The parking lot was almost empty by the time they made their way to the car. Aaron was closing Susan's door when she reached out and stopped him.

"Listen," she said. "Do you hear that?"

Aaron straightened and paused, then shook his head.

"That!" she cried, stepping back out of the car.

He looked at her quizzically.

"I hear meowing," she insisted. "Can't you hear it?" She put her hand on his arm. "There!"

This time, Aaron nodded.

"It's coming from over there," she pointed to the dumpster in the corner of the parking lot. "It sounds like a kitten. I'll bet someone's abandoned it in there and left it to die. "

Aaron began to shake his head. "I don't know, sweetheart. Stray cats eat out of dumpsters all the time."

Susan was already halfway to the dumpster. "We have to rescue it."

"It's probably feral and doesn't want to be rescued."

She stood next to the dumpster and waited. The plaintive sounds were muffled but distinct. "We have to get it out of here."

Aaron studied this woman whose kind heart and generous spirit were so endearing to him. He knew there was no way he could dissuade her.

"There's a milk crate over there," Susan said, pointing to the fence behind the dumpster. "I can stand on it and look inside."

"I'll stand on the crate," he said, retrieving it and placing it next to the dumpster.

"Do you see any signs of her?" Susan asked after Aaron had been on his perch for several minutes.

He shook his head. "I think we were mistaken. I don't think there's anything in there." He waited another two full minutes before stepping off the crate.

Susan nodded and reluctantly retraced their steps to the car. They were headed to the exit of the now empty lot when Susan unhooked her seat belt. "I need to get up on that crate and see for myself. I know she's in there, Aaron. I can feel it. She'll come to me."

He thought about protesting the futility of the effort and the lateness of the hour, but turned the car and drove slowly to the dumpster.

"Stay back," Susan urged. "Let me go alone. She's frightened. Both of us will scare her off."

"You don't even know if there's a cat in there, let alone that it's a girl," he remarked.

Susan was out of the car. "She's there, and it's a girl," she turned and whispered.

Susan climbed onto the milk crate and hung over the side of the dumpster, ignoring the fact that she was still dressed in her expensive business suit. She extended her arm and cooed softly. She was beginning to lose hope when she heard a soft meow. She reached in the direction of the sound and two matted ears, followed by two enormous eyes, emerged from the trash and debris.

Susan leaned further into the dumpster, whispering soft assurances to the bedraggled creature. Her efforts were rewarded, and the tiny kitten emerged. Susan scooped her up and brought the filthy animal to nestle under her chin. The kitten made no protest, instinctively understanding that this woman was her salvation. They made their way back to the car.

"Let's take a look at what you've got here," he said.

Susan held the kitten away from her chest but didn't relinquish her.

"She must be only a few days old." He turned on the dome light and leaned in to inspect the kitten. "Her fur is patchy and her eyes are goopy. She's full of fleas." He looked at Susan and knew she would not abandon this animal. "She may not survive, sweetheart," he said gently. "She needs to see a vet right away."

Susan looked into his eyes. "I'll take her to the vet first thing and nurse her back to health. Don't you see? This is a sign—I'm meant to have her. I'm naming her Cozette, after the poor little orphan girl in *Les Mis*."

Aaron ran his finger lightly along the kitten's cheek, and Cozette began to purr. "We'll nurse her back to health. Let's get the two of you home."

Chapter 10

Police Chief Andy Thomas handed a Styrofoam cup to Special Counsel Alex Scanlon. Alex took a swig and winced. "This coffee is lethal."

"It's been on the burner since I came in at four." He turned to face Alex. "We're finally going to get Chuck Delgado. We've had him in our sights for years."

"Don't get your hopes up. The evidence is thin, and we won't convict him unless we can lay our hands on something else. His lawyer will have him out on bail by dinnertime."

The chief blew out a heavy sigh and leaned back against his desk, crossing his ankles. "That may be true, but it'll be good to put the cuffs on him. Lock him up in a cell, even if it's only for a few hours."

Alex nodded. "I plan to stop by the jail to see him in custody. It's been a long time coming."

"What's next?"

"We're hoping he'll talk and cut a plea deal."

"What?" the chief pushed himself to his feet. "After all this, you'll let him off?"

"You, of all people, know that we're after bigger fish."

"I understand that, Alex, but the chances that Delgado will finger anyone in the mob who's higher up the food chain are slim to none. It'd be a death sentence, and he knows it."

"We could offer to put him in the Witness Protection Program."

The chief shook his head. "He'll never go for it. His lawyer will tell him how weak our case is and advise him to lay low and keep his hands clean."

Alex smirked. "You know how likely he is to follow that advice? Delgado's got no self-control at all. That's our best hope—that he'll do something stupid."

The chief shrugged. "You may be right."

"When do you plan to take him into custody?"

"Any time now."

"Arrest him at his home?" Alex asked.

"That was our plan. Except he didn't go home last night. Stayed in that office of his above his liquor store, and he had company."

Alex arched a brow.

"We don't want to increase the drama of this arrest by having his lady friend in the picture. We've got him under surveillance and the minute she leaves, we'll bring him in."

Alex nodded.

"I'm going to put the cuffs on him myself. I'm just waiting for the call. Care to join me?"

For the first time in weeks, a genuine smile spread across Alex Scanlon's face.

Chief Thomas' cell phone rang thirty minutes later and they were underway. Two burly young officers mounted the exterior stairway to Delgado's second-floor office, followed by Chief Thomas. Alex Scanlon brought up the rear. Their footsteps reverberated on the metal stairs, making a racket that would wake the dead. It did not, however, wake Chuck Delgado, who was sprawled across the decrepit sofa in the corner of his office in a state of unconsciousness that was more hangover than sleep.

The first officer knocked loudly. "Police. Open up." He listened at the door, then repeated his summons. This time, he could hear sounds from within. After what seemed like an eternity, Delgado fumbled with the door and opened it a crack.

"To what do I owe the pleasure?" he slurred, running his hand through the few remaining hairs on his greasy pate.

Chief Thomas pushed past his officers and into the office. Surprise and fear raced across Delgado's face.

"You're under arrest." The chief took the list that Alex handed him and read the eighteen counts of fraud and embezzlement. "You have the right to remain silent …" When the chief concluded the Miranda rights, Delgado stepped toward the door. "Bastard," he spat.

"We're not done yet, Delgado." The chief took one of his arms and motioned for Alex to take the other. The chief secured the handcuffs.

"What the … ? You bastards are taking me in in cuffs? Afraid I can get away from Westbury's finest?" he scoffed. "I'm a town council member and an upstandin' businessman. You don't need no cuffs."

The chief grabbed Delgado's arm and pulled him toward the stairs. "Watch your step. We wouldn't want you to fall and break your neck. We're looking forward to providing hospitality to our distinguished guest in the town jail."

Alex punched Maggie's number into his cell phone as soon as he and the chief were back in the patrol car. "He's in custody," he said as soon as Maggie answered.

"Thank goodness. I was getting worried that something had gone wrong. It's almost ten."

"Delgado had a visitor last night, and the chief thought it best to wait for her to leave."

"So you didn't pick him up at his home?"

"Nope. At the liquor store."

"Did anyone see him being taken away?"

"There weren't any customers at this time of day, but the clerk noticed and was on his phone before we got to the car."

"He'll spread the news, and I'm sure it'll be no time before it gets to the highest levels within the mob."

"I suspect you're right about that. I wouldn't be surprised if Delgado's lawyer isn't waiting for him at the station."

Maggie remained silent, digesting this news. "That might not be the worst thing, you know."

"How so?"

"If he won't talk, the next best thing is for him to do something stupid. He can't do something stupid if he isn't out on bail."

Alex laughed. "You're right about that. You always find the silver lining in any black cloud, don't you?"

"I don't always succeed, but I try." She took a deep breath. "Keep me posted. I'm in my office at Town Hall and will stay here. Our phones will light up shortly, and the press will be all over this."

"I'll stay with Delgado until he's in a cell. I'll call you when he's booked. Why don't you schedule a press conference for three this afternoon? We can make the announcement together. That'll give the receptionist something to tell callers."

"Will do."

"I'll come to your office by two thirty."

"Perfect. And Alex—well done. You should be really proud of yourself."

"I'm proud of us. We make a great team."

Maggie leaned back in her chair as she ended the call. Alex was right—they made a great team. What had started as a small group of concerned citizens tackling corruption at Town Hall could end up taking down part of the Chicago mob. With any luck, pairing her expertise as a forensic accountant with Alex's experience as a prosecutor would prove the undoing of those who stole so much from the people of Westbury.

She shook her head. It hadn't been that long ago that she was alone and dealing with the mess left by her philandering, embezzling late husband. And now she was married to the love of her life, mayor of this town, and living at Rosemont. *Never discount the possibility of a happy future,* she thought.

Chapter 11

Tonya Holmes picked up the complimentary toothbrush and sample of floss that her dental hygienist supplied after every cleaning. She pulled her phone out of her purse as she walked the short distance to her car. There were three missed calls from Maggie.

Tonya opened her car door, slung her purse onto the passenger seat, and tapped the Call Back button.

"Thank goodness!" Maggie said, answering on the first ring.

"I was at the dentist. What's so urgent?" She reached for the ignition, then stopped. Something told her to give this call her full attention.

"Delgado's been arrested."

"What?" Tonya gasped. "When?"

"This morning. About five minutes before my first call to you. I wanted you to know before you got here. Town Hall is crawling with reporters."

"I'll bet it is." Tonya leaned back against the headrest. "About time we put that creep behind bars. When will you talk to the press?"

"We've scheduled a news conference today at three in the lobby here at Town Hall. I'd like you to be there, and I need to fill you in."

"On my way. Have you thought about who you'll appoint to fill Delgado's seat while he's awaiting trial?"

"Haven't gotten that far yet. We'll need someone that everyone in town knows and respects. They'll have to be squeaky clean."

"Are you open for a suggestion?"

"I'd be grateful. Who do you have in mind?"

"The perfect candidate. And if you ask him, I'll bet he'll say yes."

"I'm all ears."

"Tim Knudsen. Voted most respected Realtor in the state the last six years."

Tim Knudsen pulled into the lot at Town Hall shortly before noon. Maggie's cryptic call an hour earlier intrigued him. What urgent assistance did the Town of Westbury need from one of its busiest Realtors?

Maggie's assistant rose from her desk as soon as he entered the anteroom to the mayor's office. "Mayor Martin and Council Member Holmes have been waiting for you. I'll take you right in," she said as she knocked lightly, then opened the door.

"Ma'am, Mr. Knudsen is here to see you."

Maggie came around the side of her desk and extended her hand. "Thanks for coming on such short notice. I know you had to juggle your schedule."

"Good to see you, Tim," Tonya said, offering the seat next to her.

"Happy to do anything to help, Maggie. You two know that," he said, taking a seat. "I'm beyond curious. What does the town need from me? Are you planning to sell some of its property?"

Maggie shook her head. "It's much bigger than that." She took a deep breath and launched into her story.

"So, you see, Chuck Delgado's seat on the town council is now vacant, and I'd like you to fill it. The mayor has the authority to appoint a replacement, and I need someone on the council that is experienced, well-respected in the community, and—most importantly—someone I can trust." She looked pointedly at him.

"We think you'd make a strong addition to the council," Tonya added.

"I don't know. I've never aspired to political office. I don't know the first thing about it. You can do a lot better than me."

"I disagree," Maggie replied. "Your business acumen and knowledge of the local real estate market will be invaluable as we dig ourselves out of our current financial mess. And after the arrests of both William Wheeler last year and now Council Member Delgado, the public perception of local government is significantly tarnished. Your presence on the council will restore credibility."

Tim dropped his gaze to his hands.

Maggie scooted to the edge of her chair and leaned toward him. "I know this is sudden. You should be afforded the time to think this through. Being on the town council right now will eat up a lot of your time. The pay is inadequate. But I know you love this town with every fiber of your being. And I am absolutely certain that you are the best person for the job. I can't afford to appoint someone who isn't qualified. The town needs you." Tim raised his eyes to meet hers. "If you need time to think about it, I'm willing to give it to you. But if you know—in your heart—that you'd like to do this, I encourage you to commit right now. If I can announce your appointment at the news conference today at three, it will send a positive message to our constituents."

Maggie leaned back in her chair and regarded him thoughtfully. "We're going to get coffee and leave you alone to think about this." She motioned for Tonya to join her. "Want a cup?"

Tim turned to face them and a smile crept across his face. "Does the mayor serve coffee to the council members in this town? Is that one of your official duties?"

Maggie stopped short, searching his face to make sure she correctly understood the implication of his words. Tim nodded as he stood up. Maggie closed the gap between them and swept him into a quick hug. "This is a very courageous thing you're doing. There may be times when you'll want to strangle me for this, but I know you'll be proud of yourself in the long run."

"Thank you, Tim," Tonya said. "I'll show you the ropes and help you any way I can."

Tim checked his watch. "I'm assuming you're staying put until the news conference?"

Maggie nodded. "And I'd like you there with us when I announce that you'll fill Delgado's seat. Would you like to say a few words?"

Tim rolled his eyes. "Not really, but I think I should. I'll come up with something between now and then. In the meantime," he said, heading to the door, "why don't I go over to Pete's and bring us back some sandwiches? I don't imagine we'll get out of here on time for dinner, either."

"Great idea and much appreciated. Will you get something for Alex as well? He'll be here for the news conference, and I'm sure he won't have eaten lunch."

Alex hurried up the back stairs at Town Hall and into the mayor's office at three fifteen. He didn't try to approach the elevators. The lobby was packed with reporters and curious members of the public as news of Delgado's arrest spread like wildfire through the small town. They were all on hand for the news conference that was now running late. He burst into Maggie's office with an apology on his lips.

Maggie held up her hand to silence him. "Don't worry about it because nobody's going anywhere. Believe me—they'll wait. A few more minutes won't hurt them. Sit down and relax for a minute." She reached into the small refrigerator behind her desk and withdrew a sandwich wrapped in paper. "Here," she said, thrusting it at him. "Eat this. You don't know when you'll get another chance today." She nodded to the far corner of the room. "Council Member Knudsen got it for you."

Alex's head snapped up from his unwrapped sandwich. "I didn't see you there," he said. "Maggie told me she was going to approach you. You're the ideal person to succeed Delgado. Thank you for agreeing to step into this quagmire with us."

"Is that what I'm doing?" Tim joked. "Maggie didn't put it quite that way."

"Now, gentlemen ..." Maggie began.

Tim waved her off. "No worries, Maggie. I know what I'm getting into."

Alex turned to Maggie. "Why don't you run through your presentation for me while I finish this?"

Police Chief Andy Thomas met Mayor Margaret Martin and Special Counsel Alex Scanlon by the rear stairwell on the first floor of Town Hall. Council Members Tim Knudsen and Tonya Holmes brought up the rear.

"Good work, Chief," Maggie said, extending her hand. "Now—let's get this news conference over with. It's quarter to four. The building closes at five. I'll use that as an excuse to end the conference if I have to."

"I think you'll have to, ma'am," Chief Thomas said. "The natives are restless."

"We'd better get started. Follow me." Maggie turned sharply on her heel and made her way through the crowded lobby to the podium. "Members of the press and citizens of Westbury," she began, "as you may have heard, council member and local businessman Charles Delgado was arrested this morning on eighteen counts of fraud, embezzlement, perjury, and conspiracy related to the recent theft of funds from the town's general fund and the town workers' pension fund. Special Counsel Scanlon is with me today, and I'll turn the microphone over to him to give you a detailed recap of the charges."

Hands flew up across the room. "We'll be taking questions after Special Counsel Scanlon concludes his remarks. First, I want to publicly thank Chief Thomas, the Westbury Police Force, Special Counsel Scanlon, and his staff for their hard work and dedication in uncovering the evidence to support this arrest. This case has been extremely complex and everyone involved has worked tirelessly to get to this point. Without—" Maggie was interrupted by a reporter from the crowd.

"Mayor Martin, can you explain to us why it took so long?"

"As I said, we'll be taking your questions after Special Counsel Scanlon's address." Maggie motioned for the smattering of raised hands in the crowd to be lowered. "By operation of state law, Council Member Delgado's arrest suspends his position on the council until he is cleared of all charges. As your mayor, I'm empowered to appoint his replacement. I'm pleased to announce that prominent local Realtor and lifelong Westbury resident Tim Knudsen has graciously agreed to serve out the remainder of Mr. Delgado's term."

A smattering of applause spread through the crowd. "I'll bet every one of you out there knows Tim and shares my belief that he's exactly who we need on the council right now. Born and raised in Westbury, there's not a square inch of this town that he's not familiar with or a person or business that he doesn't know. We're very fortunate that he's willing to take time away from his thriving real estate business to help us restore prosperity to the town and integrity to Town Hall."

The sea of heads in front of her nodded in agreement. "Without further ado, let me present to you Council Member Tim Knudsen. Tim—why don't you say a few words before I turn the podium over to Special Counsel Scanlon and Chief Thomas."

Tim Knudsen approached the microphone. "I'm as surprised to find myself up here as all of you must be. Mayor Martin is right—I'm a born and bred local boy. I know many of you whose futures are now uncertain because your retirement funds have been snatched away from you, through no fault of your own. I'll work tirelessly with the mayor and the other council members to right this wrong. Looking around the room, I see people I went to school with and members of my Kiwanis club, couples I've helped purchase their first home and people I regularly pass on the street. You know where to find me, and my door will always be open to you. I'm honored to be selected to fill this position, and I thank the mayor and all of you." He stepped away to an enthusiastic round of applause.

Maggie nodded to Alex and he came forward, motioning for Chief Thomas to join him. "As Mayor Martin just said, Charles Delgado was arrested at his place of business this morning and taken into custody without incident. This arrest is the culmination of months of detailed police work and Chief Thomas and the Westbury Police Force are to be congratulated for their efforts. I'll now ask Chief Thomas to read the formal charges against Mr. Delgado."

When Chief Thomas finished, Maggie returned to the podium. "We'll take as many of your questions as we can before the building closes in twenty minutes." She pointed to a reporter she recognized from the *Westbury Gazette*.

"Where is Delgado being held?

Maggie deferred the question to Alex, who joined her at the microphone. "He's incarcerated at the town jail."

Maggie pointed to another reporter.

"How strong is the state's case? Why did it take so long to arrest him?"

"The state's case is substantial; our evidence is compelling," Alex answered and launched into a detailed account of the difficulties of subpoenaing documents from the offshore banks.

"Do you expect Delgado to get out on bail?"

"We really couldn't say if Mr. Delgado will post bail or not," Alex replied.

"I can answer that for you," came a booming voice from the back of the room. A tall, stocky man with an expensive suit and a confident swagger addressed the crowd in a voice that needed no amplification. "Ladies and gentlemen, let me introduce myself. You're going to be seeing a lot of me. I'm Phillip Hastings, and I'm Mr. Delgado's attorney. I'm not from these parts. I'm from Chicago. I look forward to getting to know all of you and your lovely town. A town that Mr. Delgado, much like Mr. Knudsen," Hastings turned to glare at the newly appointed council member, "has spent his life working to make a better place. I've reviewed these charges," he continued, flicking a piece of paper he raised over his head, "and can assure you that none of these will hold water. Mr. Delgado will post bail later today and get a good night's sleep in his own bed tonight. And he'll be found not guilty of every single charge on this sheet. I promise you that," he concluded.

"We'll leave this debate for the courtroom," Maggie replied. "It's after five and Town Hall is now closed. Thank you all for coming."

Maggie turned and, flanked by the others, pushed her way to the elevators.

Chapter 12

David Wheeler sat in the waiting room of Westbury Animal Hospital with Dodger sitting like a perfect gentleman at his side. The dog was due for his annual checkup. Dodger had been working as a therapy dog at Mercy Hospital and needed to be up to date on all of his shots. Juan, the senior veterinary technician, knelt to scratch Dodger behind the ears.

"I hear you've been taking the hospital by storm," Juan said, looking up at David.

David shrugged. "Dodger's a natural. Everybody likes him—young and old. He loves visiting people in the hospital and nursing homes."

Juan nodded. "And I hear you're an excellent handler. Weren't the two of you doing agility before he got hurt?"

"We'd just started."

"Have you ever thought about being a vet or a vet tech, like me? I love my job, and you'd be good at it."

"I've thought about it," David said. "I'm not sure I'll have the money to go to college."

"You could get loans. I did. When do you graduate?"

"I'll be a junior this fall."

"You've got plenty of time to figure things out. Think about it. And if you want to spend a day or two here shadowing me to see what I do, I'll ask Dr. Allen about it. I'm sure he wouldn't mind."

David nodded. "That'd be cool."

"Let me see if they're ready for you."

"Hello, David," John said, extending his hand. "How's the talk of the town?" he said, bending to stroke Dodger.

"He's good. We're here to get his shots so we can keep going to the hospital."

"Excellent. Let me have a look at him." John ran practiced hands over the compliant animal. "What are you doing this summer?"

"Dodger and I spend a day a week at the hospital and at Fairview Terraces, and I'm working at Forever Friends."

John nodded. "The folks at the shelter speak very highly of you. You're a natural with animals." He paused and looked at David. "Juan tells me you might be considering studying veterinary medicine and that you'd like to spend time with us to see what we do. We'd be delighted to have you anytime you can make it. Just coordinate with Juan."

David smiled fleetingly. "Thank you. That would be great. But right now I need to get another job."

John turned his attention back to Dodger. "I see. I thought you were full time at Forever Friends."

"I am, but my mom's hours got cut back, and she says we're going to lose the house," he blurted. "I work at the shelter during the day, but I need something on the weekends." David fixed his gaze on his shoes.

John glanced at the boy. "I'm very sorry to hear that, David. The two of you have been through enough." He paused, thinking. "You know, now that Maggie and I are married and I've moved into Rosemont, she's got a honey-do list for me that's a mile long. Can you lend us a hand, like you did last year with the attic?"

"Sure," David replied quickly.

"Sam Torres is installing a safe and building us cabinets for all of that silver. I know he could use some help. Why don't you come by this Saturday about eight? Is that too early for you?"

"Not a bit. I'll be there, for sure." This time, the smile remained on David's lips.

———

Sam Torres was carefully unloading lumber from the back of his pickup truck, parked along the side of Rosemont. Once he got it loaded onto his cart, he'd be fine, but transferring it to the cart was tricky business. As Joan liked to remind him, he wasn't a kid anymore. He'd hoped to enlist John's help, but John had been called to the animal hospital on an emergency earlier that morning.

Sam paused and leaned against the side of his truck, catching his breath. He almost missed the solitary figure walking purposefully up Rosemont's long, winding driveway. He waved when he recognized David Wheeler.

"What brings you out here so early on a Saturday morning? It's not even eight o'clock. I thought all kids your age were asleep at this hour," Sam called.

David grinned. "Maybe so, Mr. Torres, but not me. Dr. Allen said I should come by. I'm here to help with his 'honey-do list,' whatever that is."

"That Dr. Allen is a smart man, David. He's been called out on an emergency, but Maggie's inside. You can go around to the kitchen door and knock. She was in there a minute ago."

"I'm also meant to work with you, Mr. Torres. Can I help you unload your truck? This wood looks heavy."

"I'd be grateful, David."

The pair set to work. "Balance the load evenly on the cart, and we'll have an easier time pushing it," Sam said.

"What are you working on?" David asked.

"Shelves for all of that silver you found in the attic." He winked at the boy. "See what a lot of work you've created? You'll probably have to haul it all downstairs for her to put away, too."

"I hope so. We could use the extra money."

"What do you mean? You're still at Forever Friends, aren't you? Frank Haynes didn't lay you off, did he?'

"No—nothing like that. I've still got my job, and he even gave me a raise. Mr. Haynes has been great to me." The two muscled the cart around the side of the house and stopped by the French doors to the conservatory. "My mom's hours got cut, and she's afraid she'll get laid off and then we'll lose our house. So I'm trying to make extra money this summer. Just in case."

Sam searched the boy's face. "You're being very mature and responsible about the whole thing. I'll bet your mom is very proud of you and your dad would be, too," he said quietly.

David turned aside.

"You know," Sam continued, "I've got more work this summer than I can handle. Joan's been after me to hire someone to help, but I've been resisting the idea. I need someone that I can trust to do a good job and to be on time. I think you'd fit the bill nicely."

David's head snapped up.

"I put in a twelve-hour day most Saturdays, but I never work on Sunday. I'd pay you fifteen dollars an hour. It's hard work and I'm a tough taskmaster. What do you say?"

David pumped the older man's hand. "You've got a deal, sir! That's way more than I make at the shelter. You won't be disappointed. I'll do a good job for you. You can count on me." He took a breath. "My mom's going to be so excited. That's enough for a week's worth of groceries, all in one day."

"Then you're hired, starting now. Let's get this lumber unloaded, and I'll show you how to use a table saw." David turned and began stacking the lumber along the side of the house. Sam shook his head. A sixteen-year-old shouldn't be worrying about grocery money.

Chapter 13

Loretta Nash turned as Frank Haynes exited his office. He hesitated, then locked the door. "You won't need anything in there."

"I shouldn't," she said, returning her attention to her computer screen. She knew all too well why he kept his office locked. There was a safe concealed by a picture hanging right inside the door. She'd found it several months ago while Haynes was in the hospital after a severe kidney stone attack.

Her curiosity, fueled by her repulsion over his connection with that reprobate Chuck Delgado, had compelled her to open the safe. Loretta knew that they sat on the town council together, but she'd never understood why her boss had business dealings with Delgado—especially after Delgado had attempted to rape her. Loretta shuddered. If Haynes hadn't come looking for her that New Year's Eve, Delgado would have succeeded.

The safe contained one solitary item—a computer jump drive. She'd managed to make a copy of it, and that copy remained hidden on the top shelf of her bedroom closet. She wasn't sure what the data stored on that drive meant, but she suspected it related to the fraud and embezzlement from the town. Frank Haynes probably kept it as some sort of insurance for himself—something to turn over to the authorities if he were ever implicated. She'd made the copy in case she ever needed something to hold over Haynes. After their dinner the other night, she wasn't sure she wanted to keep her copy of it any longer. Loretta looked up and realized Haynes was staring at her.

"You know what to do with the suppliers? And you'll get the payroll submitted in time?"

"Of course I will, Frank. You've given me explicit instructions, and I took careful notes," she said, gesturing to a steno pad on the corner of her desk.

Haynes drew a deep breath. "You've got my cell phone?" She nodded. "Call me if you need anything."

"You're acting like a parent leaving a newborn with a babysitter for the first time," she quipped.

Haynes smiled sheepishly. "I guess I am. This company is my baby."

Loretta came around the side of her desk and walked him to the door. "I know it is, Frank. And I take that very seriously. I won't let you down."

He nodded and opened the door.

"Everything was fine here when you were hospitalized last year. It'll be fine again now. When did you say you'd be back?"

"I'm not sure. I'm visiting a dying friend," he said, supplying a partial truth.

"Have a safe trip. I'll be right here the whole time," she replied confidently. "I'm not going anywhere."

Loretta, however, was not "right there" the whole time. Frank Haynes hadn't boarded his flight before she got the call she had been dreading.

"She's sick again, Loretta," came the familiar voice of Mrs. Walters, her babysitter.

"How bad is she?" Loretta asked, eying the mountain of paperwork on her desk.

"She's warm and listless just like she was when this all started."

"But not terrible?" Loretta fought the rising panic inside her.

"No, not yet. That's why I called. Thought you'd want to nip this in the bud."

"I do. I'll call the doctor and see if I can get her in right away."

"I think that's best, honey," the kindly older woman said.

Loretta dialed the number of her daughter's pediatric nephrologist and cradled the phone on her shoulder while she straightened up the piles on her desk. If she had to come back there later that night to finish the payroll, she'd find a way.

Forty-five minutes later, Loretta and Nicole Nash were ushered into an exam room. The nurse took Nicole's temperature and blood pressure, noted them on her chart, and told them the doctor would be right in. Loretta settled Nicole on the exam table where the four-year-old closed her eyes and fell quickly asleep.

Loretta was sifting through a stack of old magazines when the doctor knocked softly and entered the room. "Mrs. Nash," he said, extending his hand. "How's our girl? I was sorry to see her chart on the door. She's been doing so well."

Loretta turned to her daughter. "Nicole was fine this morning when I left her at the babysitter's. Mrs. Walters called me about an hour ago, so this came on suddenly."

The doctor nodded. "Let's take a look," he said. "Can I wake you up for a few minutes, Nicole?" he asked, touching her shoulder gently. The little girl roused herself and sat up.

"Have you been giving her the medication as directed?"

Loretta hesitated, and the doctor looked up at her sharply.

"She's been at half dose for the last few days," she confessed. "I've been waiting to refill it until payday.

"You need to give her the medicine as directed," he replied stiffly.

Loretta twisted her hands. "I know. But she was doing so much better, and you told me that if she continued to do well, you'd wean her off the medicine. So I didn't think it would hurt for a few days …"

"And that may not be it at all," he reassured. "She may need a change in medication." He looked directly at Loretta. "For now, I want her to go back on her medicine—as instructed. Can you afford to get the prescription refilled?"

Loretta flushed and nodded. "I can do that."

"Tonight," he said. "You need to restart her on it right away. I'll call you tomorrow to see how she is. If she gets worse tonight, take her to the emergency room at Mercy Hospital. If she gets better, I'll want to see her back here day after tomorrow."

Loretta nodded, glancing at the clock on the wall. If the pharmacy wasn't too busy, she'd be able to pick up Nicole's medicine and drop her off at the babysitter's in time to return to Haynes Enterprises and make the daily bank deposit. She coaxed her lethargic child out of the doctor's office and into the car.

Loretta was running much later than she'd anticipated. The pharmacy had been busy, and now, after taking her medicine, Nicole was clinging to her at the sitter's. Loretta handed her inconsolable daughter to Mrs. Walters. "I'm sorry, but I really have to get back to work. I've got to finish payroll."

"I don't mind having her, but she wants her mother. Surely Mr. Haynes can get along without you for the rest of the afternoon," Mrs. Walters said, bouncing the crying child on her hip and following Loretta to the door.

"That's just it," Loretta said. "Frank Haynes is out of town, and he's depending on me to run things while he's away." She looked at the sitter and could see that the older woman disapproved. "He's been very good to me, you know," she snapped. "He's let me take time off work to be with Nicole, and he gave me a bonus that allowed me to send Sean and Marissa to the camp they're at now. So I owe him."

"If you say so, dear. I didn't mean to offend you. I know how hard this is on you," she said and patted Loretta's arm. "Just don't overdo. You need to take care of yourself, too."

"I'm not worried about myself," Loretta said. "I may not be able to pick her up until late."

"Not a problem. Nicole will be asleep by then," Mrs. Walters said, smoothing her hand over Nicole's back. "Do you want me to keep her overnight for you?"

Loretta shook her head emphatically. "I'm going to tuck her into bed with me tonight." She kissed Nicole on the forehead. "I'll be back as soon as I can."

Chapter 14

It wasn't quite noon when Frank Haynes took the first exit off of Interstate 70 and headed into Richmond, Indiana. He'd programmed Gina Gallagher's address into the rental car's GPS and was making good time.

He hoped his plan would work. He hadn't phoned ahead and didn't know if Gina Gallagher would be home in the middle of the day, let alone if Roger Spenser was living with her and would be willing to speak to him. Surprise was still his best bet. If Roger Spenser had done what Haynes thought he had, he'd be suspicious of anyone from Westbury. If he had a chance to think about it, Spenser would probably refuse to talk to him.

The GPS took Haynes to a quiet residential street of large two-story brick homes set well back from the tree-lined roadway. *The best of Middle America,* Haynes thought to himself as he slid the car to the curb. He admired the intricate brickwork as he made his way slowly up the steep walkway. Was it his imagination, or did he see someone watching him from a crack in the curtain of a window on the second floor?

Haynes knocked firmly on the front door and composed his expression into what he hoped was a reliable-looking countenance. After a long pause, a woman's voice could be heard through the closed door. "Can I help you?"

"I'm Frank Haynes, ma'am. I believe Roger Spenser is your brother and may be living with you. I'm here to see him on an urgent matter." Haynes tried to sound comforting and respectful. He waited.

The woman finally opened the door and stood, examining him carefully.

"You're Gina Gallagher—Roger Spenser's sister? Might I see him for a moment? I know he's been ill, and I promise I won't wear him out."

"He's beyond all that now, Mr. Haynes. Roger died last week."

"I'm sorry," Haynes replied.

Gina Gallagher nodded. "After months of suffering with this wretched disease, he's now at peace."

Haynes remained awkwardly in place. Gina Gallagher regarded him with an odd expression. "Where are you from?"

"Westbury."

She sighed heavily. "What was your grandmother's maiden name?" she asked curtly.

"Mary Rose Hawkins," he answered, startled by the question.

The woman nodded. "You'd better come inside."

She led him into a tidy living room furnished with an overstuffed sofa and love seat. She did not invite him to sit. Gina Gallagher opened a small drawer in an antique rolltop desk in the corner.

"My brother gave me this when he first came to us; when he was so sick." She handed Haynes a thin business-sized envelope. "He told me not to open it but to keep it in a safe place. Said that someone from Westbury might come looking for him. He told me to ask who their grandmother was and if they answered 'Mary Rose Hawkins,' I was to give them the envelope."

Haynes steadied his hand as he reached for the envelope. "Did he tell you why he left this?" Haynes asked.

Gina Gallagher shook her head. "I was so busy taking care of him that I just stuck it on a shelf and forgot about it." She looked at him closely. "When he gave it to me, I could see he was troubled about something having to do with it. I was reminded of it, again, in his final days."

Haynes arched his brows.

"He was heavily medicated and too incoherent to make sense. But he was very remorseful about something he'd done years ago. Wouldn't be comforted. Kept mumbling about the letter. The only thing that eased his agitation was my assurance that the letter was safely tucked away."

Haynes moved to open the letter, and Gina Gallagher put her hand on his arm. "No. Not here; not in front of me. I can accept that there's

71

something dark in my brother's past, but I don't want to know what it is. Roger was my older brother and very dear to me. He never had children of his own and helped us put braces on our kids' teeth and sent them all through college." She looked at him with red-rimmed eyes. "Leave me with my memories of my brother."

Haynes put his hand over hers and nodded. "Thank you, Mrs. Gallagher. I'm sure you've been a wonderful sister. Now that you've delivered this letter, I hope you can forget about it," he said.

"Me, too," she answered as she ushered him to the door.

Frank Haynes drove to the end of the street, out of view of the Gallagher home, and opened the envelope. It contained one sheet of paper, the final legal document ever drafted by Roger Spenser—an affidavit, signed by him in front of a notary public. In straightforward fashion, Spenser confessed to accepting a bribe of one million dollars from Paul Martin in exchange for removing from the Vital Records Office the original birth certificate of one Mary Rose Hawkins and giving it to Paul Martin. He revealed that the office fire had been his own idea—extra insurance that his perfidy would never be uncovered—and went on to state that he was making this confession before his death not to stir up any trouble after so many years but to assist anyone that might be persistent enough to pursue the truth. He concluded by apologizing for the wrongs he had done and for the disgrace he had brought to his family.

Haynes re-read the affidavit. He'd done it. Unearthed the evidence necessary to secure his claim to Rosemont. He slapped the steering wheel with his hand. Wait until he put this into the hands of the very talented Simon Wilkens, Esq. He punched his attorney's number into his phone and waited while his call was connected.

Chapter 15

Maggie walked down the sloping back lawn of Rosemont toward the low stone wall that separated the lawn from the swath of woods that circled the property. The dew on the grass soaked through the old canvas espadrilles that she kept stationed by the kitchen door as her "garden shoes." Roman raced ahead of her while Eve picked her way judiciously through the wet grass. She smiled at the sight of the unlikely couple before her—Sam, the experienced journeyman and David, the young apprentice—working seamlessly together to restore the corner of the stone wall that had begun to crumble.

"You two look like you could be in a painting of rural England a hundred years ago," Maggie called as she approached.

Sam raised his head but didn't turn. "Joan is always telling me I need to get new work clothes. If I look like someone from a hundred years ago, I guess she's right."

"I didn't mean that." Maggie laughed. "You're repairing a wall in the ancient method." She turned to David. "You don't look like you're from a hundred years ago. You look like a modern young man of today," she hastened to add, realizing she might have offended him.

"I think it's kinda cool. I like this work," he replied, kneeling to accept a profusion of doggy kisses from Roman.

Maggie nodded. "I came down here to see if you'd have time to carry the silver down from the attic and place it on the folding tables I've set up outside the butler's pantry. I'm anxious to start putting it away."

David looked to Sam.

"I think that'll be fine. We'll be finished here by noon, and then I'll send him to you."

"Perfect. You come, too, Sam, and I'll make you both a sandwich."

Sam nodded. "Best job in town, son," he said to David. "See you in a bit, Maggie."

David knocked lightly on the library door in midafternoon. "I've got all the silver downstairs for you, ma'am."

Maggie pushed her chair back and tossed her reading glasses on the thick stack of documents on her desk. "Good. I'm going cross-eyed looking at these spreadsheets, and I need a break. Let's see what you've got for me." She gently dislodged Buttercup from the cat's customary perch on her lap and stood. Maggie motioned for David to follow her down the long paneled hallway to the butler's pantry.

"Well, look at this," she declared. "You've lined everything up by category, and in rows of descending height. Very organized," she said, turning to smile at him. "I didn't ask you to do this, but I appreciate that you took the initiative."

Maggie turned back to the sea of silver spread out on the folding tables. "I need to polish all of this before I put it away. That will be a huge job." She looked at David over her shoulder. "Care to help?"

"I've never polished silver, but I'm willing to learn."

"Next Saturday? Or will you be helping Sam?"

"Neither one, actually." He turned aside. "My mother and I are getting ready to move."

"Oh," Maggie said. "Are you leaving town?" She, of all people, could understand if Jackie Wheeler wanted a fresh start where no one had ever heard of her disgraced husband.

David shook his head. "No. My mom got laid off, and we can't pay the mortgage, so we have to move."

"I'm terribly sorry to hear that," Maggie said. "Where will you go?"

"We're putting our stuff into my uncle's garage, and we'll stay at his house until we find someplace we can afford."

"That's nice of your uncle. Lucky he has a big enough place."

"He doesn't, really. I'm sleeping on the sofa. And he won't let Dodger in the house. I'm going to have to leave him in the garage or chain him up outside." David brushed the back of his hand across his eyes.

Maggie turned to him. "Something will turn up for you, David. You'll see. This seems very bad to you right now, but it may turn out to be a blessing."

Maggie rolled toward John as soon as he turned out the light and rested her head against his shoulder.

"I can tell by your breathing, sweetheart, that you're thinking about something. Your mind is going a mile a minute, and you're not the least bit sleepy," he said.

Maggie pulled her head back and looked at him in the soft moonlight seeping through the shutters. During warm weather, Maggie left the heavy drapes open to hang as sentries to the shuttered windows, only closing them when required to shut out the cold drafts of winter. "You know me so well, don't you?"

"So what's on your mind? Still worrying about that creep Delgado? Or is it the town's financials?"

"Neither, actually. This time it's David Wheeler."

"Why? What's happened to David? I thought he was working with Sam and doing a great job."

"He is. But I talked to him today—asked him if he'd like to polish that blasted silver next Saturday—and he told me he can't. He's getting ready to move."

"I'm sure he can do it another Saturday. Surely there's no real hurry. Or you can get someone else."

"It's not the silver I'm worried about; it's David. He said that his mom lost her job and they have to move because they can't pay their mortgage."

"That's a shame," John agreed.

"The worst part is that they're moving in with his uncle, who doesn't have much space. David seems terribly unhappy about it. He said he'll have to sleep on the sofa and Dodger won't be allowed in the house." Maggie rose on her elbow. "It broke my heart, John. What's wrong with that uncle of his? Can't he see how much David loves that dog? The poor kid's been through enough. He needs to make an exception for Dodger. I've got half a mind to pay his uncle a visit."

John reached to his nightstand and turned on the light. "Don't do that, honey. People don't like strangers poking their noses into their business."

"Then what do you suggest we do to help?"

John rested on his elbows. "We decided to keep my house as an investment rental property, remember? Tim Knudsen said it's ideal for that."

"I remember."

"I just hired Sam to paint it and put in new carpet—touch up a few things—before we put the 'For Rent' sign out. In fact, I'll bet David will help Sam with it. What if we rent to David and his mom?"

"Do you think they can afford it?"

"I own it free and clear. If we don't get market rate out of them, is that the worst thing that could happen?" John asked.

Maggie sprang to her knees and grabbed his face with both of her hands, planting a big kiss on his mouth and knocking him back into his pillow. "Of course not. It's a brilliant idea. You are the sweetest, kindest man in all the world. And I'm the luckiest gal for miles around."

John grasped her waist and reached for the light. "I'll call Sam and Tim in the morning. We'll put our heads together and find a way to make this happen so that they don't feel like they're getting charity from anyone."

"You are both kind and thoughtful in the way you do things."

"Glad you approve."

"I find it terribly sexy, actually."

"Even better," John said as he pulled her toward him.

David Wheeler stumbled as he caught the cuff of his jeans on a loose baseboard in the kitchen. He managed to keep the box he was lugging to his mom's car upright, so its contents didn't cascade to the floor. He turned and gave the baseboard, now jutting into the room, a firm kick.

Instead of going back into place, as he'd intended, the baseboard buckled and broke free, exposing the wall and a sheaf of papers.

David set the box on the kitchen counter and picked up the strange papers that were hidden behind the baseboard. Rows and rows of ten-digit numbers, six columns across, filled three and a half pages. All carefully printed by the same hand.

His father had been the only person in the family with secrets to hide. David was staring at the numbers, trying to discern some meaning from them, when his mother came looking for him.

"David," she said, running her hand through her hair. "What in the world are you doing just standing there? I need to take that stuff to the consignment store before it closes. If we're lucky, we'll get three or four hundred dollars out of it all."

David nodded absently, keeping his attention fixed on the papers in his hands.

"What have you got there?" his mom asked.

David handed them to her. "I don't know. Have you seen these before?"

"Oh, that," Jackie Wheeler said and pushed the papers back at him. "Your father had a bunch of those before he was arrested."

"So they were Dad's?"

She nodded and scanned the room with her eyes. "Is there anything else you think we can sell?" David shook his head. She gestured to the papers he was holding. "That's all gibberish. You may as well throw it away. Grab that box and let's get going. Break time is over."

David crumpled the papers into a ball and was about to send them sailing to the trash bag when something compelled him to stop. He smoothed the papers, folded them into a neat bundle, and carefully tucked them into the back pocket of his jeans. If they had anything to do with his late father, he wanted to find out more about them.

Chapter 16

Frank Haynes slid his Mercedes sedan into the loading zone outside the rear entrance to Forever Friends. He needed to quickly review the week's receipts and approve the payroll records before heading back to Haynes Enterprises. He'd been behind in his work at both places ever since his fruitful meeting with Gina Gallagher. Loretta was busy attending to her sick child, so Haynes had been doing double duty at the office. As he walked to the back door of Forever Friends, he realized that he'd long ago abandoned any thought of firing Loretta for her absenteeism. Whether he was simply accustomed to her or harbored a deeper affection for her, he couldn't say—but he didn't want to work with anyone else. The prospect of hiring temporary help was unthinkable. Better to do the work himself and await her return.

Haynes spotted David Wheeler cleaning the kennels when he walked in. "Hi, David. Walk with me to the office, would you? I'm in a tearing hurry tonight."

"Sure," David said, quickly wiping his hands on a nearby rag and grabbing a sheaf of papers lying next to his backpack on the floor.

He genuinely cared for the boy and was delighted that he was able to give him a job at Forever Friends. The easy friendship they'd established over their common interest in dogs might be the nearest thing Haynes would ever get to a father-son relationship. "How are you and Dodger doing?"

"Great." David fidgeted with the papers in his hand.

"That's good news, son," Haynes said. He found the folder that the bookkeeper routinely left for him on the upper-right corner of her desk and began running his finger across the spreadsheet. He made some marginal calculations on a scrap of paper and, satisfied, pulled the fountain pen out of his pocket and signed the series of documents that the bookkeeper had tabbed for him. He replaced the cap on his pen and was inserting it into his pocket when he realized David was still standing there, watching him.

"Is there something else?" Haynes asked.

David nodded. "I found some old papers when we were moving, and I want to show them to you. Maybe see if you know what they mean."

Haynes rose and headed down the hall. "Sure, maybe sometime next week. Sorry, I'm in such a rush now." Haynes had his hand on the door handle. "Just remind me, okay?" he said as he sailed out the door, fired up his Mercedes, and roared off. He never looked back at David, who stood in the parking lot, shoulders slumped, folding and unfolding the small packet of papers.

—⁂—

"What's got your goat?" Sam Torres asked David Wheeler the next morning as they set about building a new garden gate for Judy Young.

"Nothin', really," David drawled.

"Nonsense," Sam said. "You can't fool me." He glanced at the boy. "You know you can tell me anything."

David nodded. "I know." He pulled the papers out of his back pocket and handed them to Sam.

Sam scanned the top page and glanced at the others. "What's all this?"

"That's just it. I don't know."

"Where did you get them?"

"They were hidden behind a baseboard at our old house. I found them by accident."

"Did you ask your mom about them?"

David nodded. "She said they were my dad's"

"Then we need to get these to the police," Sam said, aware that this was the last thing David would want to hear.

David shook his head emphatically and snatched the papers from Sam's hands. "After what happened to my dad, I'll never go to the police."

"Special Counsel Scanlon, then."

David Wheeler stared at him with a stony gaze. "He's no better."

"Maggie. Mayor Martin. She's in the official channels, and she'll know how to make sense of these and what to do with them."

David looked steadily at Sam, then nodded his assent.

"We're almost done with this gate. Let's finish up, and we'll go see her. How would that be?"

David released the breath he'd been holding. "That would be great."

Chapter 17

John Allen entered Rosemont through the back door and dropped his keys on the counter. He didn't mind the occasional late-night call to attend to a veterinary emergency, but tonight's case had been extraordinarily unsettling. A trucker noticed an animal along the side of the road and stopped to help. The dog had lacerations all over its body and one eye so badly damaged that John had no choice but to remove it. The poor creature had probably been used as a "training dog" for a fighting animal. He'd been able to patch up the injuries on the young dog, so it would survive. But did any animal really survive this type of cruelty?

John opened the refrigerator but nothing looked appealing. He slammed the door shut.

"I thought I heard you come in," Maggie said.

John turned sharply. "What are you doing up? You were sound asleep when I left."

Maggie shook her head. "Not really. I've been tossing and turning every night since Sam and David brought me those lists of numbers. They're handwritten, John. Meticulously so. And were hidden very cleverly. The police didn't find them when they searched the house. They've got to mean something."

John nodded. "I have to agree. And I also know that if anyone can figure this out, it's you."

Maggie slid her arm around his waist. "I appreciate the vote of blind confidence, but so far, I'm batting zero." She turned to him. "You look exhausted. Tough case?"

John nodded.

"Want to tell me about it?" She began massaging his shoulders.

"I don't want to rehash it. Neither of us would get any sleep. Suffice it to say, we've got a terrible problem with animal abuse in this county."

"Maybe I could do something to help."

"You've got enough on your plate. I think I'll give Frank Haynes a call in the morning. This'll be right up his alley."

Maggie rolled her eyes. "If you say so. Let's get to bed. Roman and Eve are already up there, snoring away."

Maggie checked the time when she stepped out of the shower. One minute past seven. She scampered to the fluffy rug in the center of the room. The marble floor was cold under her bare feet, even in summer. She slipped into her chenille robe and punched Alex Scanlon's number into her phone. He answered on the first ring.

"Maggie. What's up? Is everything okay?"

"Yes. Sorry to call so early. Did I wake you?"

Alex snorted. "I haven't slept past six since you appointed me special counsel. I've been at it for hours."

"Thought so. I need some information from you."

"Sure—anything."

"Can you get me a list of all of the bank accounts that we suspect are involved in the fraud, plus each bank's routing number, and the transaction numbers of each wire transfer?"

"That won't be hard to do. We've got all of that for the money being drawn out of the general fund and the pension plan. It's where it goes from there that's the problem."

"I understand. When can I get it?"

"I'll bring it by your office before the end of the day. Why do you want it?"

"I'll explain when I see you. I'll wait in my office."

"I'll text when I'm on my way."

Alex Scanlon walked through the door of Mayor Margaret Martin's office shortly after six o'clock that evening and handed her a spreadsheet containing the information she requested. Maggie flipped quickly through the four-page document and laid it on her desk.

"Why the urgent need for these account numbers?"

Maggie motioned for him to sit down as she opened her bottom desk drawer and withdrew lists of handwritten numbers from her purse and slid them across the desk.

He scanned them, then brought his eyes to hers. "Where'd you get these?" He listened intently to Maggie's story and whistled softly. "This may be the break we need."

Maggie rose with both sets of papers in hand. "Let's see if any of these numbers match the ones on that spreadsheet." Laying out the pages on the conference table in the corner of her office, she and Alex sat to scrutinize the lists.

After several minutes, Alex leaned back in his chair. The spreadsheet and the lists contained identical numbers.

"Wheeler must have been keeping this as some sort of insurance," he said.

Maggie nodded. "If this is really his handwriting."

"We'll need to establish that fact, but it shouldn't be hard to do. We can get a handwriting expert."

"If he were keeping it as some sort of 'insurance,' then why didn't he use it? What was he waiting for?"

"Impossible to say. Maybe he got so much pressure from the mob that he felt his family wouldn't be safe if he talked. Maybe he didn't trust the Witness Protection Program. Who knows? When someone commits suicide, they're not thinking rationally."

Maggie rose and began to pace. "This still doesn't paint the whole picture. It's simply confirmation of what we already know. We need to find out where the money went after it was siphoned out of the town's accounts and into these offshore banks. Who got it after that?"

Alex slapped the table with both palms. They turned to each other.

"Do you think there might be other lists hidden at the Wheeler home?" Maggie asked.

"My thought exactly," he replied.

"I'll have another search warrant by tomorrow morning."

Maggie put her hand on his arm. "Can you hold off on that? You know how public that would be. Even if you tried, you couldn't keep it a secret for long in this town." Maggie held his eye. "What if I can get the Wheelers to allow us to search for additional lists? Would that work?"

"If they'll cooperate, that would be ideal. But we can't run the risk of your tipping them off and their destroying the lists before we get in there. And it has to happen soon."

Maggie nodded. "Understood. Our timing may be perfect. David told me that they're losing their house to foreclosure and moving out this weekend."

"That's rough. They can't catch a break, can they? Where are they going?"

"They plan to move in with her brother, which isn't ideal for David, so John is going to offer to rent them his old house."

Alex arched one brow. "Pretty nice rental, if you ask me. Can they afford it?"

Maggie smiled. "He'll make it affordable. I married a kind man."

Alex nodded. "Do you know when the foreclosure sale will be?"

"I had Tim Knudsen find out for me. It's Monday morning. Right here on the steps of Town Hall."

"We need to get in there this weekend. If we don't, I'll have a search warrant ready to serve on the new owner right after the sale. Investors buy foreclosures to fix and flip, and they get started almost immediately. We need to go through that house with a fine-toothed comb before anyone starts tearing it to pieces."

"I'll drop by the house to talk to Jackie Wheeler. I'll let you know."

Alex rose and pointed to the purse in Maggie's open desk drawer. "Get that thing, and we're out of here."

"I'll be right behind you. I have a few things—" Maggie began and Alex cut her off.

"Not a chance. I'm walking you out. We're both exhausted and need to get home to our significant others while they're still speaking to us."

"When did you become so bossy?" Maggie laughed as she slung her purse across her shoulder and they headed for the elevator.

Chapter 18

Frank Haynes shifted his weight from foot to foot as he stood in the taxi queue at JFK International Airport, his cell phone to his ear. He'd decided to deliver Roger Spenser's affidavit to Simon Wilkens in person. The attorney's reaction to it would tell him volumes about whether the document would successfully advance his claim to Rosemont. He wanted to witness that reaction firsthand. But he would have to wait. His flight to New York City had been delayed in Dayton, and he'd arrived much later than expected. He'd rescheduled his meeting with Simon Wilkens for the following afternoon.

The phone at Haynes Enterprises continued to ring in his ear, but no one picked up. Haynes disconnected before the call went to voice mail. Where was Loretta Nash? *Maybe she's making the bank deposit,* he reasoned with himself. *After all, she's given you no reason not to trust her.*

He replaced his phone in the breast pocket of his jacket as he moved to the front of the line. A driver signaled to him and opened the rear passenger door. As Haynes slid into the leather backseat, he realized he hadn't eaten since breakfast. He'd indulge himself in a pricey meal at one of the city's fine restaurants and check on Haynes Enterprises tomorrow.

Loretta hurried up the steps to Haynes Enterprises and quickly assembled the day's bank deposit. She had just locked the door when the phone started ringing. If it were important, they'd leave a message or call back. She continued on her mission and arrived at the bank at closing time. She could see the head teller approach the glass entry door, keys in hand. She gave him her biggest smile.

The teller hesitated, then swung the door open and held it for her. "Cutting it pretty close today, aren't we?" he said.

"My daughter's been sick, and I've gotten behind," she said as she hurried past him.

"Frank Haynes could make the deposit," he observed as he ushered her to his teller station. She began unbundling the deposit.

"He's out of town and left me in charge," she replied. "I want to do a really good job. Thank you for waiting for me," she said, glancing behind him at the clock on the wall that displayed the time, five minutes after five. She smiled at him again.

The teller looked down quickly. "That's okay," he said. "We can do that for our favorite customers."

"She's out like a light," Mrs. Walters said quietly as she opened the door later that night and led Loretta to the sleeping child.

Loretta scooped up Nicole and carried her to the car. The sitter helped nestle Nicole into her booster seat. "I'm always amazed at how soundly children can sleep," she said. "Envious, actually."

"That's for sure," Loretta agreed. "I'll see you in the morning."

"Why don't you sleep in a bit?" she suggested.

"Nope. Tomorrow will be a busy day. I may even try to get in early."

Fifteen minutes later, Loretta laid Nicole gently into bed and curled up next to her. She placed her hand on her daughter's forehead. Her skin felt cool. Loretta drifted off to sleep, listening to the peaceful rhythm of her daughter's breathing.

Chapter 19

Frank Haynes entered the sleek reception area of the prestigious New York City law firm of Hirim & Wilkens. Unlike his first visit to the firm, he was escorted directly back to the office of his attorney, Simon Wilkens.

"Mr. Haynes," Wilkens said, coming around his desk with an outstretched hand. "Can I get you anything? Coffee? Or something stronger? It seems you have something to celebrate."

Haynes shook his hand and took a seat in one of the client chairs.

"I've been anxiously awaiting this affidavit from the mysterious attorney," Wilkens said.

Haynes nodded and took an envelope out of his attaché case, sliding it across the desk. He sat back and waited while Wilkens studied the document. When the attorney was finished, he looked up and smiled broadly at Haynes.

"This should do it. It'll be more than enough."

"No glitches? No qualifications?"

"Well … not necessarily." Wilkens hedged his bets. "How hard do you think this Martin woman will fight? Does she have the money to wage war with you?"

It was now Haynes' turn to smile. "She'll fight it. She's been around litigation as an expert witness, so she knows the ropes. But I've got a war chest and she's got a piggy bank."

"Doesn't sound like a fair fight." Wilkens smirked.

"What could they do to challenge this?" Haynes asked, pointing to the document lying on the desk between them.

"Question its validity. Authenticity of the signature or his mental capacity at the time he signed it. You said he was very ill when he wrote this. Undergoing chemotherapy?"

Haynes nodded. "Could they say that he wasn't in his right mind?"

"They can try. If this gets heated, they most certainly will allege that this isn't credible—that it shouldn't be admitted into evidence because Spenser is dead and they can't cross examine him."

"How do we handle that?"

"It's acknowledged, of course, so we might need the testimony of the notary. A notary has the duty to make sure that a person knows what they are signing and has the mental capacity to understand its ramifications."

"Can we find this notary?"

"Shouldn't be a problem. They're licensed by each state." Wilkens turned to the computer behind him. "Let me do a quick Google search." He reached for the affidavit and typed in the name of the notary and pressed enter.

"Your good luck continues," Wilkens said. "The notary works for the largest law firm in Richmond. We'll be able to find her, and my guess is that she followed all the rules when she notarized his signature."

For the first time since he'd entered his attorney's office, Haynes allowed himself to relax.

"Congratulations. Something stronger, now?" Wilkens asked, pulling out a bottle of Glenfiddich and two cut crystal glasses from the credenza behind his desk.

"Why not?" Haynes replied. "So what's next?"

"You give me the go-ahead, and we'll start drafting the paperwork to reopen Hector Martin's estate." Wilkens handed a glass to Haynes. "The neat and tidy life of your Mayor Martin is about to come crashing down around her ears."

"I'll drink to that," Haynes said, clinking his glass to Wilkens' and draining it in one gulp.

Chapter 20

Maggie glanced out the mullioned window over her kitchen sink as she finished loading the dishwasher and pressed the start button. The back lawn of Rosemont was in deep shadow at twilight. For the first time in over a week, the evening promised to be clear and dry. She turned as John approached, two leashes in hand.

"Remember how much we enjoyed our evening walks after dinner in Cornwall?" he asked. "And how we swore we'd keep it up when we got home?"

Maggie nodded. "It's been too wet," she replied defensively.

"It's not too wet tonight. I'll saddle up Roman and Eve. Go get your shoes on."

Maggie sighed, and John shook his head, sweeping her into his arms and planting a kiss on the top of her head. "No excuses."

"You're right. Once we get out the door, I'll be glad we went. It's just that I brought a mountain of work home with me," she said, a note of pleading in her voice.

"All the more reason," he replied with mock sternness as he released her and whistled for the dogs.

The four of them set off down the long, sloping driveway through the tunnel of trees that imposed an early dusk. By the time they emerged at the bottom and stepped onto the sidewalk, the spreadsheets and financial statements in Maggie's briefcase didn't seem so pressing anymore.

"Which way?" John asked, as Roman sat to an immediate heel while Eve pulled at her leash.

"Let's make a lap around town square. It'd be fun to window shop. Like we did on our honeymoon."

John stepped out with Roman at his side. Eve cut in front of them. "We're going to have to train Eve to walk on the leash," he said.

"I've never been good at dog training," Maggie replied. She looked over at him. "I guess you knew that before you married me."

John nodded. "Here," he said, handing her Roman's leash. "Let's trade dogs. I'll work with Eve, and Roman can show you how a dog should behave. Unless you want to do this yourself?"

"No. Good idea," Maggie rushed to reply, grateful that she could rely on John to train Eve.

"Speaking of shopping in Cornwall, shouldn't the painting we bought arrive soon?"

"I think so. I've been tracking it online, and it's supposed to arrive in New York next week. I'm planning to have it hung before Gordon Mortimer returns to go through the furniture in the attic."

"Hoping he'll approve of our purchase? We like it, and that's all that matters."

"I know. But he's very knowledgeable about fine art, and it would be fun to see what he thinks."

John eyed her kindly. "Just don't get disappointed if he doesn't rave about it. That painting will always take us back to those windswept green highlands and some of the happiest moments of my life."

Maggie leaned into him. "I'm glad we finally decided to throw caution to the wind and buy it."

They crossed the street and began strolling along the sixteen-block rectangle that surrounded the square.

"I haven't been to Celebrations since we've been back. Let's see what Judy has in her window," Maggie said as she turned in the direction of the card and gift store that was her favorite shop on the square. John and Eve followed slowly in her wake.

Maggie was studying a beach-themed tablescape in the window when she heard John call to someone.

"Jackie. We get to see David quite a bit at Rosemont, but I'm sorry that we haven't seen you," he said, nodding to the boy at her side. John dropped to one knee to greet Dodger. "How are you?" he asked, looking up at her.

"We're all right," she said stiffly.

John stood up as Maggie and Eve walked over to join them. "David's been a great help to us, and Sam Torres raves about him, Mrs. Wheeler. You should be very proud of him," Maggie said, smiling at the widow of the town's discredited mayor. She wanted to reach out to this betrayed woman—to tell her that she understood what she was going through—but knew that she would remain silent.

Jackie Wheeler looked at her shoes.

"We came down to check out places for rent behind the candy store," David said, pointing in the direction of Candy Alley. His mother reached up and pulled his hand down.

"I lost my job. We're losing our home to foreclosure." Jackie made an effort to keep her voice even. "We're moving in with my brother for a while, but we can't stay there forever."

"Those places behind the square are pretty small and won't have a yard for Dodger," John said, all the while thinking of how hard it would be for mother and son to move from their lovely home to a shabby apartment behind the square. "We're putting my house up for rent," he continued. "The yard is fenced, and it already has a doggie door. Sam and David have painted it on the inside, so it's ready to go. Why don't you look at it?"

David beamed. "It would be perfect." He turned to his mother. "You'll love it, Mom. You should see the kitchen. Mr. Torres and I put in granite counter tops. It's close to my school, and Dodger would have a yard."

Jackie Wheeler turned to her son. "I'm sure we couldn't afford it, David. Everyone in this town thinks I knew that William was embezzling. They think I have a ton of money hidden somewhere." Jackie turned to John and Maggie. "I assure you I don't, and we're broke. I've found a job, but it pays half of what I used to make."

"We'll work something out so you can afford it," John said. "I want a tenant I can count on that won't tear the place up. You and David would be ideal. And if anything needs to be repaired, I know David can fix it," he said, clapping David on the back. "Tim Knudsen has the key. Call him tomorrow, and he'll show it to you."

Jackie Wheeler nodded slowly. "We will." She looked at John. "Thank you. You've always been kind."

"I think this will work out for all of us," Maggie interjected. "I'm so glad we ran into you."

Jackie Wheeler ignored her and turned on her heel.

"Thank you, Mayor Martin," David said quickly over his shoulder as he followed his mother.

"What did I ever do to her?" Maggie huffed.

"You replaced her husband as mayor," John replied. "She may blame you for his demise."

"That's ridiculous. I didn't even live here at the time the fraud and embezzlement took place."

"I know, but it looks like she's holding you responsible. Would you like me to change my mind about renting my place to them?"

"C'mon, Roman," Maggie said as they resumed their walk. "Of course not. I feel sorry for both of them. I believe her when she says she didn't know what her husband was up to. I certainly didn't know Paul was embezzling from Windsor College or that he supported Loretta Nash and her kids. I was lucky that I was able to quietly settle the college's claim. Jackie Wheeler hasn't been so fortunate. I don't think she's sitting on piles of money anywhere. And David is a really nice kid. I want you to be kind to them. I don't care how much you charge them in rent."

"That's the woman I love," John replied.

———

"Why were you so rude to Mayor Martin?" David whispered as he caught up to his mother.

"Do you forget that she's the main person on that committee that framed your father? She's the forensic accountant that came up with all the evidence."

93

David looked over his shoulder at the retreating figures of Maggie and John. "You don't know that, Mom. We don't know what they had for evidence. And now that Dad's gone, we'll never know," he said with a catch in his throat.

"I know all right," she spat back.

"Dr. Allen has always been really nice to me and Dodger."

"Dr. Allen is a good man. I don't know what he sees in that woman."

"So are you going to look at his place tomorrow? I know you'll like it. It's way better than anything we've seen so far."

She nodded. "If we can help out Dr. Allen by renting his house and taking care of it for him, I think we should."

David lowered his face to hide his smile. If his mother wanted to think they were doing Dr. Allen a favor that was fine with him. He just wanted to leave the memories at their current home behind and start over, with Dodger at his side.

Chapter 21

Maggie Martin rocked back on her heels on the Wheeler's front porch and tried to discreetly peer through a crack in the blinds covering the window adjacent to the door. She'd rung the doorbell but hadn't heard any sound and wondered if it was still in working order. She stepped to the door and knocked firmly. This time, she heard footsteps approach. The door opened a crack. Maggie could see one eye of a disheveled-looking Jackie Wheeler, staring back at her.

"Mrs. Wheeler?" Maggie began.

"Why the hell are you here?"

"May I come in? I have something important to discuss with you. We need help in the fraud investigation."

"Why do you think I'd have the slightest interest in that? I've lost my husband to it and now my house. Get off my property," she said as she slammed the door shut in Maggie's face.

Maggie took a deep breath and raised her hand to knock again, but thought better of it. She slowly retraced her steps to her car. If she had turned around, she would have seen David Wheeler peering at her through a small opening in the blinds of the window next to the door.

Maggie retrieved her cell phone and placed a call to Alex as she pulled into the street.

"No go," she said the moment he answered.

"I take it Mrs. Wheeler respectfully declined our request for cooperation?"

"Something like that, yes," Maggie replied, stopping quickly to avoid a child chasing a ball into the street. She was abreast of a sedan with darkly tinted windows, parked in deep shade on the other side of the street, two houses down from the Wheeler residence. She took no notice of the man sitting, motionless, watching her behind the steering wheel.

"I'll start the process of getting a search warrant," Alex said. "We'll serve it on the new owners right after the sale. I think the Wheeler family has been through enough."

"I agree with you on that score," Maggie said, turning her car in the direction of Town Hall.

"You finally got somethin' for me?" Delgado snarled into the phone in his office above the liquor store. Since his release on bail, he'd been following his high-priced lawyer's advice and laying low. Mostly. He'd assigned a few of his guys to watch Martin, Scanlon, and Smith. That hardly counted as doing anything wrong.

"I do, sir. On Martin."

"Well?" Delgado barked.

"She just paid a visit to the grieving widow Wheeler. Or tried to."

"How's that?"

"The missus wouldn't let her in. Looks like she never took the chain off the door. Didn't give our esteemed mayor a chance to say much before she slammed the door in her face."

Delgado smiled. How he would have loved to have seen that.

"Martin looked like she wanted to try again, but had second thoughts. Finally put her tail between her legs and got back in her car and drove away."

"Did she see you?"

"No way. She got on the phone and was deep in conversation when she drove past me."

"You don't say," Delgado said. "Martin's an odd broad, but it's even odder that she went to see Jackie. Keep an even closer eye on her from here on out, okay? I'm talkin' 24/7. Somethin's goin' on."

"You got it, boss. If they're up to anything, we'll find out what it is."

Chapter 22

Frank Haynes pulled into his customary observation spot along the road below Rosemont. He'd just returned from New York City, and he needed to see Rosemont, now that he was secure in the knowledge that he could establish his claim to the house he'd coveted for a lifetime.

He looked up at the rear facade, the setting sun reflecting pinks and purples in its rows of windows. Perhaps he and his border collie, Sally, would be living there by Christmas. And their newlywed mayor wouldn't be hosting any grand celebrations at Rosemont this holiday season.

Haynes tried to force a smile onto his lips. Somehow, the thoughts that had always cheered him before, failed him this time. He imagined Sally roaming around in the large house all day, on her own. And himself eating his take-out dinner—alone—in the dining room. He'd get another dog, he decided. He was always finding another at Forever Friends that he wanted to bring home. He'd get a companion for Sally. That should do it, he told himself.

Haynes stretched his arms out in front of him. It was time to stop in at Haynes Enterprises, then call it a night.

Frank Haynes turned into Haynes Enterprises as the dim light of early evening cast long shadows across the deserted parking lot. As he approached the entrance, he could see that the door to Haynes Enterprises was unlocked. He sprinted up the steps and cautiously opened the door, expecting to find that the office had been broken into.

Loretta's computer was on, and the day's bank deposit lay strewn about her desk. Haynes slammed the door shut behind him and crossed to her desk in three strides. "What the hell?" he growled. He knew he shouldn't have trusted her while he was away. She was just like all of the other lowlife bookkeepers he'd employed over the years. Glad to cash a paycheck but not willing to go the extra mile. When would he ever learn? The only person he could count on was himself.

Haynes yanked her chair back and sat down, gathering the stacks of bills that made up the daily deposit from his fast-food restaurants. He was searching for a large rubber band in a drawer of the credenza behind him when the door opened, and Loretta Nash rushed in.

"Mr. Haynes," she began as he wheeled on her.

The words "get out; you're fired" froze on his lips. He'd never seen her look worse. It wasn't so much a matter of her hair or makeup—though both were disheveled—but more of the pain and fear in her eyes. He swallowed the angry words he was about to utter.

"I'm so sorry," she said. "I was just coming back to do that."

Haynes nodded and got up from her chair. She pushed past him and sat.

He moved to stand in front of her desk and regarded her silently.

"I was going to make this deposit first thing in the morning," she said, not looking at him.

"You know they're to be made at the end of every day. Why were you waiting until tomorrow?"

Loretta ignored his question and continued, head down, gathering up the deposit.

"The door was unlocked, Loretta, at eight o'clock at night. You left all of this cash lying on top of your desk, out in the open for anyone to take. I'm amazed that it was still here when I walked in," he snapped. "I should fire you right now."

Loretta began to cry, softly at first and then crescendoing into great, heaving sobs.

Haynes stood rooted to the spot. He wanted to stride into his office and slam the door, waiting for her to clear out her things and leave before he emerged. Somehow, his feet wouldn't move. He reached out a hand and placed it lightly on her shoulder.

Loretta looked up at him. "I'm soooory," she choked. "I came back because I was afraid I forgot to lock up." She drew a deep breath and tried to calm herself before continuing. Haynes nodded encouragingly.

"I know the deposits get made every day—I've been doing them for months. I also know we've got enough in the bank to cover all our checks without this deposit," she assured him.

"Why did you leave in such a hurry?" he asked, knowing the answer as he asked the question.

"Nicole," she whispered.

"What's happened now? I thought she was better."

"She was, and then she got sick again. It's been on and off all week. I had to take her to the doctor. She was dehydrated, so they gave her fluids. They think that should do it," Loretta said, dissolving again into fresh waves of tears. "It's all my fault, Frank. I wasn't giving her enough medication. She was doing so well, and the plan all along was to wean her from it, so I was waiting to refill her prescription. The medicine is so expensive," she said, turning her face to his.

How in the world can she look so appealing with red-rimmed eyes and a runny nose? "I'm sure it's not your fault," he said feebly. "What did the doctors say?"

"They put her back on the full dose and she was doing better, but then the babysitter called this afternoon to say that she was much worse."

"So why are you here?" he asked.

"I came back to lock up. Then I found you in here—at my desk—doing my job and clearly mad as hell. And rightly so," she added.

"How is she now?"

"She's better."

"No more dialysis?"

Loretta shook her head. "Thankfully, no." She leaned back in her chair and sighed. "I overreacted to the whole thing, Frank. When the sitter called, I just lost it. I'm always waiting for the other shoe to drop. I tore out of here like a bat out of hell, leaving the day's deposit on my desk. When I thought I might not have locked the door, I really freaked out. Then I found you here, and I knew you would fire me. You trusted me, and I let you down." She choked on the words.

Haynes held up his hands. "You don't need to worry about that, Loretta. I'm not going to fire you. I understand how hard this is on you."

Loretta brushed a long blond lock from her face and attempted to smile at him.

"If the money had been stolen, we'd have survived." He was amazed to hear himself say it. "And if you need money for medicine, you can come to me. I'm not going to let Nicole go without anything she needs."

"Thank you, Frank." She then uttered words he'd never heard directed at himself. "You're very kind."

Haynes cleared his throat and spun on his heel. "We're both tired. I'll drop that deposit in the night box at the bank. Let's get out of here."

Loretta handed him the bank bag and preceded him out the door.

"I'll lock up, and see you in the morning."

She headed to her car. "It's good to have you back," she called over her shoulder.

Chapter 23

Maggie had just started up the long staircase that swept along the front wall when she heard the knock on the door. John had left for a late-night emergency at the animal hospital, and she wanted nothing more than to get to bed early. She could use a few extra hours of sleep before facing the busy week ahead.

"Now who could that be at this hour?" she asked Eve, who had already raced to the top of the stairs. "Come on, girl, let's go see," she called as she peered out the window on the second-floor landing. She was surprised that she didn't see a car on the driveway. It would be unusual for anyone to make the long trek uphill on foot.

Maggie retraced her steps and found Roman waiting patiently by the front door. Although she knew that John's faithful golden retriever would greet any intruder with a wagging tail and profuse doggy kisses, she felt comforted that he was there. "Who is it?" she called through the massive mahogany door.

"It's David. David Wheeler."

"David," Maggie said, opening the door. "I thought that you were moving this weekend."

"We did, ma'am," he said.

"Is there something wrong at John's house?" she asked, expecting that the water heater didn't work or they couldn't find the remote control for the garage door. "John just left on an emergency call, but we can reach him on his cell."

"It's nothing like that. The house is great. I rode my bike over here to tell you that I overheard you talking to my mom the other day."

Maggie motioned for him to come inside, but he shook his head. He paused and drew a deep breath. "I want to search for more papers my dad may have hidden. I may not like what we learn about him if we find them, but I have to know."

Maggie nodded. "I understand. I'd want to know, too."

"I started ripping out baseboards right away, but my mom got real upset. So I decided to wait to let her cool down." He looked over his shoulder at the sloping front lawn. "Except now I'm out of time. It's now or never."

Maggie waited silently for him to continue. "So I'm going to do it now. After we left there with the last load, my mom said she'll never set foot in that place again."

"That's understandable," Maggie said.

"Mom made me leave Dodger at our old house last night, so we could get settled without him getting into stuff. I plan to find anything that's hidden there before I bring Dodger home with me tonight."

"Would you like me to send someone to help you? I'm sure Alex …" She stopped short as he vehemently shook his head. "Sam, then? Or Dr. Allen?"

David continued to shake his head. "Just you. You already know about the other numbers, so you're the one to come with me."

"Let me get my keys," she said over her shoulder. "We can put your bike in the back of my SUV." She snatched her purse from the kitchen counter, and they set off.

———

Maggie turned into the driveway of the Wheeler home at nine fifteen on the sleepy, late summer Sunday night. She pulled as far into the shadows as possible, wondering why in the world she was trying to be so secretive. She turned to David and smiled encouragingly. "I'll be right in. I just want to text John to tell him where I am, in case he gets home before I do."

David nodded and approached the house. Dodger let loose with a set of plaintive barks that were one part fear and two parts loneliness. Maggie watched as David fumbled with the key before it found purchase and the door swung open.

She plunged her hand into the cavern that was her purse and began churning the contents like a cement mixer, feeling for her cell phone.

She sighed impatiently and turned on the overhead lamp in her car, holding her purse directly under the weak circle of light. After a careful but fruitless examination, she abandoned her search and got out of the car. She must have left her phone at home. A chill ran down her spine. She knew she was being silly. Nothing was going to happen to them, and John would almost certainly be gone for hours. She and the dogs would be sound asleep by the time he got home.

Despite her resolve to be rational, Maggie hurried up the walkway and across the threshold. The kitchen and hallway were illuminated by overhead lights, but the remaining rooms were in deep shadow now that all lamps had been removed. Dodger greeted Maggie with a friendly wag of his tail, but he didn't leave David's side.

"You've made a good start," Maggie said, looking at the six-foot piece of molding that David had already dislodged.

"I've done this with Mr. Torres," David said. "It's easy. He gave me some of his old tools. Said every handyman starts with used tools. That way the tools know what they're doing even if the handyman doesn't."

Maggie smiled. "That sounds like something Sam would say. My aunts used to say that about pie tins, too. If the cook didn't know how to bake a pie, the tin did. Sort of a comforting superstition, don't you think?"

David didn't answer, concentrating on his work.

"Do you have another pry bar? Can you show me how to use it?" Maggie asked.

The sedan with the darkly tinted windows sat at the curb two doors down from the Wheeler house, on the other side of the street.

"They've been at it for almost two hours, sir."

"What the hell are they doing in there? You think our newly married mayor is gettin' it on with the young stud?"

The man shook his head. "I can't see what they're doing. Maybe cleaning? Wheeler moved out today."

"Cleaning before their house is foreclosed? Not likely, you moron."

The man remained silent.

"Get outta that car and take a look. Don't get seen, okay? Call me right back." The man reached for the handle of his car door. "And if our mayor is doing that kid, get pictures." Delgado cackled as the phone went dead.

———

Spying on Mayor Martin and David Wheeler proved difficult. All of the blinds and curtains were drawn tightly shut. He found a window in the laundry room that wasn't obstructed, and when he leaned to the far left, he could view down the hallway and into the living room. The room was vacant and he could make out David Wheeler, removing baseboards. Satisfied that he wouldn't be able to see anything else, he returned to his car.

"Sorry to disappoint you, sir, but it appears that all they're doing in there is removing baseboards." He waited for the anticipated explosion from the other end of the line.

"Sir?" he said and was interrupted by Delgado's throaty chuckle.

"There's something hidden in that house." Delgado paused, formulating his plan. "Got something to write with? I'm gonna buy myself a house tomorrow. I'm gonna tell you what you need to write down for me from the foreclosure notice that's posted by the front door."

The man clicked his pen, then cursed. "Hang on. I'm out of ink. Let me get a new pen out of my glove box." He leaned over to retrieve the pen and missed Maggie, David, and Dodger leaving the house.

———

Maggie opened her trunk and David removed his bicycle. "Can't I drive the two of you home?" she asked softly.

"No. That'll make Mom mad. Dodger will like running with my bike. We do it all the time. And it's not far."

Maggie nodded and put her hand on his shoulder. "You've been very brave and very helpful, David. More than you know."

David shrugged and bent down to stroke Dodger.

"I'm sorry about how hard this has been on both you and your mother," Maggie said. "I know what it feels like to have a family member do things they shouldn't."

David turned away and mounted his bike.

"Call me or John if you need anything, David. Day or night."

He waved and set off pedaling in the opposite direction of the sedan. Maggie got into her car, double-checked for the hundredth time that the sheaf of papers they'd uncovered behind the baseboard in the back of David's closet was safely stashed in her purse, and started her ignition. She wanted nothing more than to climb the stairs to bed.

Chapter 24

Maggie Martin crossed the street in front of the sedan with darkly tinted windows and entered the offices of Stetson & Graham. In addition to offering the town the services of Forest Smith to assist in the fraud investigation, the firm also allowed the town to use its conference rooms. Maggie preferred to meet with Special Counsel Alex Scanlon and Forest Smith outside of the prying eyes at Town Hall. The simple fact that she was meeting with the two men in charge of the prosecution of the case would appear on the front page of the next days' *Westbury Gazette*, accompanied by the usual editorial lambasting the investigation's lack of progress. It was better this way.

She nodded to the receptionist, who pointed her in the direction of their usual conference room. She was a few minutes early and was surprised to see that Chief Thomas was already seated at one end of the large marble table.

"Good afternoon, Chief," Maggie said, taking a seat across from him.

"I understand you uncovered some evidence on your own," he said with an unmistakable note of reproach. "You're doing my job, now, too."

"Nothing of the kind. You know I have a relationship with David. He's done odd jobs for me at Rosemont. You can also understand why he refused to come to you," she said, staring at him over the top of her glasses. "We were on a very tight time schedule," she continued, picking up steam. "The house is going into foreclosure today, and it was 'now or never' if we were going to go through that house without a warrant."

The door to the conference room opened, and Alex Scanlon and Forest Smith stepped into the room.

"You didn't follow proper channels," the chief retorted.

Maggie turned to the new arrivals. "The chief is upset about how we obtained this latest spreadsheet."

Alex nodded. "I understand. It was unorthodox. I approved of it—Maggie didn't act on her own."

"What if it hadn't worked?" the chief asked. "What then?"

"I have a search warrant ready to serve on whoever buys it at the foreclosure sale."

The chief nodded stiffly and turned to Maggie. "What did you find?"

Maggie handed each of them a copy of the spreadsheet that they'd uncovered in the Wheeler home. "These are the accounts that the offshore banks wired the stolen money into. They all belong to a Delaware limited liability company."

Alex raised an eyebrow. "The Delaware LLC we already know about from the records produced in response to our subpoena?"

"The same one," Maggie said.

"The LLC where William Wheeler is—or rather was—the sole member?" Forest Smith asked.

"I'm afraid so. These two spreadsheets corroborate the evidence we already have. We can prove that the money went from the town general fund and the pension fund into the offshore banks. It was transferred by a whole series of wire transfers," she said, pointing to the spreadsheet in front of them, "to accounts of this limited liability company that were owned by William Wheeler."

"There are no new account numbers on there that could belong to Delgado? Or anybody else?" Alex asked.

Maggie slowly shook her head. Alex sagged back into his chair.

"This spreadsheet, and the other papers that David found and gave us, were made in chronological order. They're all neatly done by hand. No erasures or whiteout anywhere. If I had to guess, I suspect Wheeler copied these from other worksheets and organized them into categories: money out of the town and pension fund; money out of the offshore banks into the limited liability company; and there should be another spreadsheet that shows the money going from the limited liability company to the accounts of the perpetrators of the fraud."

"You think there's another spreadsheet out there?" Smith asked.

Maggie nodded. "I feel sure of it. What I've seen was methodically prepared and very accurate. Everything matches the limited records we already have. Wheeler did this for a reason. He didn't trust these guys and thought he was protecting himself. In fact, now that I think about it, this reminds me of something that Tonya Holmes told me."

The three men leaned forward.

"Tonya was trying to get the other council members to investigate the shortage in the town's bank account. She suspected that there was something seriously wrong with the town's finances and was trying to get her hands on the bank statements. She was at Town Hall early one morning and overheard an argument in Wheeler's office, when he was mayor. She heard Wheeler say 'I'm out' and Delgado reply that he was out when they said he was out. Something like that. Wheeler stormed out of his office and collided into Tonya." She tapped her index finger on the table. "I'll bet he prepared these spreadsheets after that meeting."

The chief picked up his copy and flicked it with his finger. "All of this implicates Wheeler and only Wheeler. Why would he keep this around?"

"I'll bet he had no idea that they'd set him up as the sole owner of the limited liability company," Maggie replied.

"I have to agree," Alex said. "Wheeler was just a good ol' boy without much business acumen."

"He was smart enough to make these detailed spreadsheets," Smith supplied. He turned to Maggie. "I agree with you. There's got to be another spreadsheet."

"If there is," Alex said, "it's probably still somewhere in that house. Did you look everywhere?"

"We removed every baseboard, yes. These spreadsheets were both found behind baseboards. But that doesn't mean he couldn't have hidden the final one somewhere else."

"We need to get back into that house," Alex declared. "Do we know who bought it at the foreclosure sale? Did it go back to the bank?"

"Tim Knudsen will find out for us," Maggie said. "I'll call him when we're finished here and let you know."

Chapter 25

Maggie Martin stood back and admired the painting now hanging above the carved stone mantel in Rosemont's living room. She'd tracked its journey across the Atlantic and had cleared her calendar of appointments so she could be at Rosemont to sign for it when it arrived. She and Sam Torres had uncrated it and placed it in its new home. Maggie clasped her hands under her chin. *Just wait until John sees this.*

Sam broke her reverie as he came down the stairs. "I leaned the old painting against the furniture stacked up by the window in the attic."

"Thanks, Sam. The appraiser is coming back to look at all of that. Who knows—maybe that old painting is valuable. I didn't see a signature on it, though."

"This one's a mighty pretty picture," he said, pointing to the mantel. "I can tell what it is. I'm not a fan of shapes and lines that don't look like anything."

Maggie smiled at him as she snatched Blossom from the back of one of the wing chairs flanking the fireplace. "You don't belong up there," she scolded as she set the cat on the floor. "John's with you on that. We both fell in love with this one. It's not signed—in fact it's not completely finished—but it may be the work of a famous artist."

"Pretty countryside. The people look old-fashioned."

"It was probably done in the early 1900s. That's exactly the way Cornwall looks today. You and Joan should plan on going there," she said and instantly regretted it. Sam and Joan Torres had worked hard all their lives, putting money into the pension fund so that they could travel when they retired. The pension fund was now in serious financial trouble, thanks to the fraud and embezzlement at Town Hall. The way things were, the Torreses would be lucky if they got to retire in the next ten years, let alone travel.

Sam cleared his throat. "If you want it raised or lowered, just take it down and adjust the wire on the back. John can do that. I'll gather up this packing material and get it out of your way. I was headed to another job when I got your call, so I'd better go."

"Thank you for dropping everything to help me," Maggie said. "I hope the other people won't be upset."

"It's fine. David's there now, and we won't be finished for another week. This didn't make any difference."

Maggie scooped up a piece of Styrofoam that escaped his grasp and walked him to his truck.

"We're going to get these guys, Sam," she held his gaze. "I can't tell you anything about the investigation, but I promise you we won't let them get away with it."

Sam nodded. "I understand that you're doing everything you can, Maggie. I don't think about it much. I never figured I'd retire, anyway. But Joan's had a hard time with it all."

"Tell her to hang on," Maggie said, wondering if they would, indeed, be able to successfully prosecute anyone for the crimes. She stood and watched as Sam's taillights disappeared from sight down the driveway. She turned to mount the stone steps to Rosemont's front door when she saw the mail carrier coming up the driveway. She retraced her steps to meet him.

"Afternoon, Mayor Martin," he called. "Glad you're home." He riffled through his bag of mail. "I've got a certified letter for you. You need to sign for it."

Maggie took the letter and pen he offered and signed her name to the green card attached to the letter.

"I hope it's good news. Maybe a big, fat check," he said as he released the brake and pulled away.

Maggie turned the heavy envelope over in her hands. The return address showed Hirim & Wilkens, Attorneys at Law, with an address in Manhattan. Why in the world were they sending her a certified letter? She didn't think the letter carrier was right. This couldn't be good news.

Maggie shut the front door and felt—just like she did the very first time she entered the house and the door closed behind her—that she was home. She leaned against the closed door, supported by its strength, and pulled in a deep breath. Whatever was in this letter, she needed to know.

Maggie stepped into the library and picked up a letter opener from her desk by the window overlooking the back garden. She carefully slit the envelope and extracted its contents, smoothed the thick stack of papers on the desktop, and began to read. Before she got to the end of the first page, she pulled out the desk chair and sat.

The letter was from an attorney named Simon Wilkens, who represented Frank Haynes. He then recited a litany of facts that he said proved her late husband, Paul Martin, had tampered with evidence and willfully concealed the fact that Frank Haynes was a legitimate heir of Hector Martin and that Haynes was, legally, owner of a half-interest in Rosemont.

Maggie slammed the papers into her lap and moaned. Was this even possible? Surely Paul would not have done such a thing. She knew, however, that Paul was capable of everything the attorney had accused him of and more. After all, hadn't Paul embezzled money from Windsor College, while he was president of the college, for years? Hadn't he secretly maintained a second family—with Loretta Nash—in Scottsdale while they were married? Stealing recorded documents seemed mild in comparison.

Maggie lifted the papers and re-read them. Frank Haynes was asserting his half-interest in Rosemont.

She examined the attachments to the letter: a copy of a birth certificate and the affidavit of a recently deceased attorney who had aided Paul in carrying out his crime. These attachments would have to be authenticated, but she knew instinctively that they were valid.

Maggie carefully folded the letter, replaced it in its envelope, and propped it against the lamp on the desk. Once more, that bastard Paul Martin was messing up her life. His evil grip reached out from the grave.

She pushed her chair back and rose purposely. She'd be damned if she'd turn Rosemont over to Frank Haynes. She retraced her steps to the living room and stood looking at the new painting ensconced over the fireplace. It was a symbol of her new beginning with John and of their commitment to create their own legacy at Rosemont. Paul had taken a lot of good things from her, but she wouldn't let him take this.

What was it the lawyer had suggested? That they have Rosemont appraised and either party would have sixty days after the appraisal to make a cash offer to buy out the other? If she knew Frank Haynes, he'd already researched the value of Rosemont and had a cash reserve set aside, ready to make his move. He was counting on the fact that Maggie and John wouldn't be able to lay their hands on the necessary cash to buy him out. And on the surface, he was right. Buying out a half-interest in Rosemont would require several million dollars.

What Frank Haynes didn't know was that Rosemont had presented Maggie with a fortune in silver from its attic. She'd planned to auction the vast majority of it off, anyway, including the staggeringly valuable tea set by renowned eighteenth-century silversmith Martin-Guillaume Biennais. She had the means to raise the money. She just needed the time to do so.

Maggie headed to her laundry room and the big calendar that hung on the wall. The attorney demanded her response to his letter in two weeks' time or he would be forced to file suit. Filing suit and serving her would eat up another month beyond that, maybe more. She'd have twenty days to file her answer and the process of litigating the matter could take years. The lawsuit, however, would be front-page news in Westbury—probably the entire state. She had to avoid the notoriety it would bring.

Maggie ran her finger along the calendar. An auction sale of the silver would need to be advertised for at least ninety days. If she acted quickly, she'd be able to liquidate the silver and have the proceeds in hand by the end of the year. She'd hire an attorney to respond to Wilkens and request an open extension of time to authenticate the documents.

Maggie prayed Wilkens would grant it. While her attorney investigated the facts laid out in Wilkens' letter, she'd get the silver auctioned off. If the auction could be completed in time, she might have enough money in hand to outbid Frank Haynes for Rosemont.

What was it that the appraiser Gordon Mortimer had told her? That he'd worked for Sotheby's and still had connections there? Maggie went into the kitchen and retrieved her cell phone. She scrolled through her contacts until she found him. It was time to take Mr. Mortimer up on his offer to help her liquidate the silver.

Gordon Mortimer cut his eyes to his cell phone in irritation. He should have set it to vibrate. The constant interruptions by telemarketers were driving him crazy. The "do not call" list was a joke. He looked at the number on his screen and there was something vaguely familiar about it. He hesitated, then answered the call.

"Mr. Mortimer, Maggie Martin here."

"Mayor Martin. I'm delighted to hear from you. Are you ready for me to come see the furniture?"

"I am, actually, but that's not why I'm calling. I'd like to liquidate the silver. In the next four months at the latest."

Gordon Mortimer gasped. "That can't be done, madam. Not if you want to realize its full value. It takes time to properly catalog the items and advertise the sale. Putting the silver in the right sale at the right time is supremely important."

"I understand, but something's come up, and I must have it sold within the next four months."

"Surely not the Martin-Guillaume Biennais? That simply can't be done."

"That too. All of it."

"You'll be sacrificing price for speed. I recommend a much longer time frame to allow the auction company to solicit interest."

"I understand that this isn't ideal. It can't be helped. Do I remember correctly that you have ties to Sotheby's? I was hoping you could pull some strings and get us into one of their upcoming auctions in New York."

Gordon Mortimer sensed she was not going to be dissuaded. Ordinarily, he distanced himself from reckless ventures such as this hurried sale, but something in the tone of her voice made him change his mind. "If you insist on going through with this—against my advice—I can help you get placement in an auction. And I'll notify my collector clients and dealer network as well. The presence of such a large number of Martin-Guillaume Biennais pieces in pristine condition should drive significant interest to the sale. The big auction houses will like that. Maybe we can even get *The New York Times* to do an article on Rosemont and how you found the silver. Give it extra provenance."

"No," Maggie cut in sharply. "No one can know where the silver came from. We must remain completely anonymous, and Rosemont can never be mentioned." If Haynes suspected Maggie might have money, he would have the resources—and she was certain he had the desire—to offer her double the appraised amount. She couldn't risk losing Rosemont by tipping her hand. "I'm sorry if I was short with you. I need to insist on total anonymity."

"As you wish, madam."

"I knew I could rely on you. And I'm sure you'll do everything in your power to maximize my proceeds. I believe you will also receive a commission on the sale?"

"I will. You can count on me. I'll ring my contacts immediately and get back to you within the week with the details of the sale. I can't promise you that we can make this happen so quickly, but I shall do my best."

Chapter 26

John Allen tossed the thick envelope bearing the return address of Hirim & Wilkens, Attorneys at Law, onto the coffee table and turned to stare at the new painting above the mantel.

"What do you think?" Maggie asked, stepping in front of the fireplace.

"It's absolutely perfect. I'm so glad we indulged ourselves and bought it."

"I mean about this letter—about Frank's owning half of Rosemont?"

"I trust your instincts. If you think Paul was capable of this, you're probably right."

"But what about my idea of selling the silver? We don't know how much we can get for it, but it's our only way to raise the money."

John put both his hands on her arms and looked into her eyes. "I don't think it's our silver to sell, sweetheart."

"What do you mean it's 'not ours'?"

"It's part of Rosemont, part of Hector Martin's estate. If Frank owns half of this house, he owns half of that silver, too."

A guttural moan escaped her lips, and she brought her forehead to his chest.

"I never thought of that. You're right, of course." Tears slid silently down her cheeks. "We can't sell the silver."

"We could take out a mortgage on the place," John suggested.

Maggie shook her head. "We can't afford the payments on an almost three million dollar mortgage. I've got to come to grips with this, John. There's no way out. We're going to lose Rosemont."

Maggie clipped the leashes on Eve and Roman early the next morning. She'd slept fitfully, if at all, but couldn't stand to stay in bed any longer. She'd re-read Simon Wilkens' letter a thousand times in her mind and rehashed their situation from a dozen different angles. All with the same result—they would lose Rosemont. She and John had to look for a new home, and she must force herself to be excited about the prospect. The dogs pranced and circled, excited over the unaccustomed early morning walk, tangling themselves and Maggie in their leashes.

"Settle down, you two," she said as she unwound them. "And don't get used to this on a workday. I've got a lot on my mind and need to stretch my legs before I head into the office." She looked at the unlikely pair sitting obediently at her feet, waiting for her command.

"Heel," she said. "We're going to go once around the square and then come home."

They set off at a brisk pace through the early morning sunshine. Maggie needed to think. Could she sell the silver and not tell Frank? *Would that be so wrong?*

Maggie paused to let Roman and Eve sniff a fire hydrant. She looked at the storefronts of the shops facing this side of the square. Maggie knew the owners of every single establishment in front of her. *What would they think of me if they found out where I got the silver and that I used the money from the sale to buy out Frank's share of Rosemont?* Wouldn't she be cheating him?

The door to Candy Alley opened and Charla stepped out, broom in hand. Maggie watched as she swept the sidewalk in front of her shop and the print store next door. She pinched the dead blossoms from the vivid pink petunias spilling out of the urn between their entrances. The shopkeeper took a rag out of her apron pocket and ran it over the plate glass windows of both entryways. She looked up and waved at Maggie. "Ellen's gone to help her niece with the new baby," she called. "I'm lookin' after things for her."

Maggie returned her greeting. Charla was looking out for her neighbor. That's what the people of Westbury did for each other. The people of Westbury would expect her to be honest. She advised her children and grandchildren to do the right thing and tell the truth. Maggie was ashamed of herself for even thinking about the alternative.

She tugged on the leashes and turned toward Rosemont. Frank Haynes owned half of that silver. She'd never have enough money to outbid him. Rosemont would, inevitably, go to him. She put her head down and concentrated on putting one foot in front of the other.

She was almost at the end of the block when she realized someone had been calling her name. She drew a deep breath to compose herself and turned in the direction the voice had come from.

"Maggie," Judy Young called, motioning to her from the open door of Celebrations.

"Morning, Judy," Maggie said, waving and attempting to continue on her way.

Judy approached her. "Do you have a minute?' she asked. "I've got something I want to show you. I did some research while you and John were away on your honeymoon."

Maggie sighed. She might as well get it over with. Judy was not a person to be denied. "Sure," she said, glancing at her watch. "I've got fifteen minutes."

"That's all we'll need," Judy said, studying Maggie closely. "You look like you've just lost your best friend. What's up?"

Maggie shook her head. "It's nothing."

"Everything okay between you and John?" Judy probed. "Sometimes getting remarried after many years on your own can make for a difficult adjustment."

"I guess you'd have to ask John about that, but from my perspective, everything's wonderful. What have you got to show me?" she asked, following Judy through the shop to her back room.

"I've been curious about your silver," Judy began. "It didn't make sense that all of that gorgeous stuff was in the attic when more ordinary pieces were carefully stored in the butler's pantry."

"Why would that concern you?" Maggie asked. "Maybe they put it up there for safekeeping."

"That's not how you would handle something precious you wanted to preserve, now is it? Put it in a drafty old attic to become tarnished from decades of nonuse while you used the more mundane items when you entertained? I don't think so," she stated firmly. "I kept thinking about it over and over again."

"And?" Maggie asked, anxious to be on her way.

"I dug a little deeper into the newspaper archives, looking for stories about the Donaldsons. Do you remember the rumors I told you about them?"

Maggie racked her brain. "I'm afraid I don't," she said.

"They were the Martins' best friends. They made their money in banking and lost everything in the Great Depression."

Maggie nodded slowly. "Now I remember. They committed suicide together by jumping off the roof of their home." She shuddered. "A pretty gruesome way to get away from your creditors."

"That's right," Judy said. "I confirmed that they jumped the night before they were to lose their home to foreclosure."

"You thought some of that silver must have been theirs, didn't you?" Maggie said, turning to stare at Judy.

"Yes. The flatware was engraved with their coat of arms. I feel certain that the rest of it in the attic was the Donaldsons', too. They'd concealed their silver from their creditors by hiding it at Rosemont. By the time they were to lose their house, they'd lost everything else and decided to kill themselves."

Judy leaned in to Maggie. "Have you searched that secretary in the attic where all of it was stored? You might find something that indicates it belonged to them. I'm guessing the Martins never used it—even after the Donaldsons died—because it didn't belong to them, and they didn't want anyone to know that they'd been hiding assets for the Donaldsons."

"Does it now belong to the heirs of the Donaldsons?" Maggie asked.

Judy shook her head. "That's what I was researching. They didn't have a will, so I was trying to find out if they had any heirs. They never had any children and neither of them had siblings. Their line died out on that horrible day when they jumped."

"So who does it belong to, do you think?" Maggie asked, trying to conceal the seed of hope that was taking root. "Would the Martins have inherited it?"

"Not unless the Donaldsons left it to them in a will," Judy stated. "According to what I found, it would legally be considered 'treasure trove.'"

"What does that mean?"

"It means," Judy squared her shoulders, "that the silver in that attic belongs to whoever found it. In this case, *you*," she stated.

Judy rattled on, missing the relief that washed over Maggie, leaving her weak in the knees. "Maybe it doesn't make any difference, but I thought you should know," she concluded proudly. "That silver is your treasure trove."

Maggie thanked Judy profusely and tore out of Celebrations, breaking into a jog on the way back to Rosemont. She unhooked the dogs' leashes and dropped them on the hall table. Retrieving the attic key and a flashlight from the desk on the landing, she raced down the hallway. Maggie took the attic stairs two at a time and wove her way through the piled-up furniture to the secretary that remained along the back wall.

Maggie supplemented the meager light from the bare overhead bulbs with her flashlight as she opened the now empty cabinets and drawers. Her efforts were rewarded when she reached the bottom drawer. A folded sheaf of four pieces of paper lay face down in the back corner of the drawer. She withdrew the papers, yellow and brittle with age, and carefully unfolded them.

In neat and precise flourished handwriting, reminiscent of the days when fine penmanship was considered a mark of good breeding, was a list of items of silver and flatware. Although she would later confirm her conclusion by comparing this list with the one prepared by Gordon Mortimer, Maggie knew that the papers in her hand detailed each item of silver that would soon be headed for auction. And each piece of paper bore a signature at the bottom: Mrs. Alfred Donaldson.

Maggie rocked back on her heels and clutched the papers to her chest. The silver was hers. Frank Haynes didn't have a right to any of it. If she had good luck at auction, she'd be able to raise the money to buy out Frank's interest in Rosemont. She scrambled down the stairs and headed for the phone. John would want to hear about this.

Chapter 27

Frank Haynes checked his watch. It was after nine and Loretta was late, again. He glanced at the financial statements lying neatly across the top of his desk. He'd had time to review them last night after dinner and wanted to compliment her on them. She'd reorganized their chart of accounts and the financials made much better sense. They eliminated his need to make marginal notes and handwritten calculations. He'd been meaning to do this for months—years, actually—and she'd done it without being asked. He was truly impressed and anxious to tell her so.

He walked to the coffee station in the reception area, opened the blinds, and peered out into the parking lot as he waited for his coffee to brew. Loretta's car was in its usual spot. He turned expectantly to the door and waited. When she didn't appear, he took his cup of coffee and walked out the door and down the steps. Loretta was nowhere to be seen. He was beginning to get alarmed when he heard her raised voice coming from around the side of the building.

He sidled closer. "I'm sorry that my insurance company isn't prompt in its payments," she said curtly. "But I'm making my payments to you on time."

He held his breath and waited while she listened to someone on the other end of the line.

"What? You can't do that," he heard her say. "My little girl needs dialysis now. She can't wait until the insurance company pays their portion for her treatments from earlier this year."

Again, silence.

"I can't pay my account in full right now. I'm doing exactly what we agreed on," she stated indignantly.

"What do you mean you can't help me? You've got to. My daughter will die without dialysis," she pleaded, her rising panic undeniable. "She can't wait."

122

Frank Haynes spurred himself into action, rounding the corner and reaching for the phone.

Loretta, startled, nodded and handed him her cell phone.

"Who am I speaking to?" Haynes commanded. He nodded. "Well, Miss Smith, we seem to be at an impasse here. Nicole needs lifesaving dialysis and you're worried about your accounts receivable. Is that correct?"

Haynes arched an eyebrow at Loretta while he listened to Miss Smith.

"Here's a solution to our dilemma," Haynes said. "Draw up a guaranty for any amounts that the insurance company doesn't pay, and I'll sign it. How would that be?"

Haynes listened again. "Of course you may. Frank Haynes," he said importantly. "I own Haynes Enterprises. You may know some of my restaurants." He was smiling now. "Get Nicole Nash scheduled for dialysis, and I'll sign your guaranty."

He handed the phone to Loretta who stared at him, open-mouthed. "You didn't have to do that, Frank," she said.

"You can fill me in about Nicole on the way to the hospital." He ignored her response. "I assume this needs to happen quickly?"

Loretta nodded.

"Go get your purse and lock up. I'll bring my car to the curb."

⸺

Loretta fastened her seat belt as Frank Haynes turned his Mercedes out of the parking lot.

"We need to stop for Nicole on the way," Loretta said quietly.

Frank Haynes nodded. "I figured. She's at the babysitter's, isn't she?"

"She is. Do you remember where the sitter lives?" Loretta asked.

"I do," he replied. "What's happened?"

"The doctor's office called me this morning. They want to start her on dialysis this afternoon, so she doesn't get as sick as before. I was walking in from the parking lot when the billing office called me on my cell phone." She swiveled in her seat to look at him. "I walked around the corner so you wouldn't overhear my conversation."

"Sorry," he said, glancing at her.

"Were you looking for me?"

"I was worried about you. I saw your car in the lot, but you were nowhere to be found. What was I to think? I wasn't spying on you."

"I'm sorry about all of this, Frank. I love my work and want to do a good job. I feel like I'm finally able to use some of what I learned in college."

"The new financials are perfect." He wanted to reach over and squeeze her hand but stopped himself. "I have them spread out on my desk. I was going to compliment you on them when you came in."

Loretta smiled.

"Your daughter comes first. Let's get Nicole taken care of. She'll be in good hands at Mercy Hospital. And if she needs to see specialists somewhere else—and I'm not saying that I think she will—" he hastened to add, "I'll guarantee those payments, too."

Loretta turned sharply toward her passenger side window. Where was the conniving, selfish man she'd come to work for all those months ago? Was this kind and generous man the real Frank Haynes? If she wasn't careful, she'd fall for this guy. And probably get her heart broken again.

—⁂—

For the first time in his adult life, Frank Haynes attended to the needs of others for an entire day. He'd sat in the colorless waiting room, alone, for more than two hours while Loretta checked Nicole in and met with doctors. Even though it was now well past lunchtime and he'd skipped breakfast, he was unwilling to leave his post.

Loretta passed the waiting room shortly before two and stopped short when she saw Frank hunched over a cup of cold coffee, his elbows resting on his knees. "Frank!" she exclaimed. "Have you been here the whole time?"

He got to his feet and nodded. "How's it going back there?"

"Dialysis is hard on her. It's not as bad as the first time, but I wish she didn't have to go through it," Loretta said. "I've been afraid to leave her. I was just heading to the ladies' room," she said, pointing to the hallway in front of her. "I thought you'd just drop me off and go back to work."

"I wasn't sure if you'd need anything," he stated quietly. "Can I bring you something to eat?"

Loretta sighed. "Honestly—I'm starved. I should say no, but I'd love it."

Haynes smiled. "If I remember correctly, you favor a chicken Caesar salad?"

"I'm impressed," she laughed. "That's what I ordered when you took me to lunch during my interview. That would be my first choice. But anything you bring me will be fine." She turned. "I really need to make a pit stop and get back in there. Thank you, Frank. Text me when you get back."

Haynes smiled. Finding a salad for Loretta Nash seemed like winning the lottery.

<hr>

Haynes returned to the waiting room thirty-five minutes later, a chicken Caesar salad and a turkey sandwich on rye in hand. He'd also bought chips, a fruit cup, hummus, and a carton of yogurt, in case she'd like any of those. He'd almost bought cookies but decided that would be overkill.

Loretta appeared in the waiting room almost immediately after he'd sent the text:

Mission accomplished.

"She's done with the treatment, and they're keeping her under observation for a while," Loretta said as she led him to a table along the wall and unpacked the brown paper sack containing their food. She glanced up at him. "What army were you planning to feed?"

Haynes shrugged. "I figured if you didn't like your salad, you might want some of this other stuff," he said. "I also didn't know when you'd be getting out of here."

Loretta eyed him curiously. "That was very thoughtful of you, Frank."

"We can just toss what you don't want," he said.

She shook her head. "We'll leave it for the nurses. They never have enough time to get something to eat."

"When will you be able to leave?"

"Within the hour, I should think," she said, digging into her salad.

"I'll wait and take you both home."

"I'll have to take her back to the sitter's." Loretta sighed. "Marissa and Sean are coming home from camp late this afternoon. I'll have to pick them up. Plus I need to get groceries."

"I can help with that," Haynes offered, realizing he hadn't been grocery shopping in years. He never ate at home. "Just give me your list." He checked his watch. "If Nicole is ready soon, I'll have time to drop you two off, get the groceries delivered to your door, and pick up Sean and Marissa."

"What about Haynes Enterprises?" Loretta sputtered. "What about today's deposit?"

"Leave that to me," he said. "You just worry about Nicole and yourself. I can't have the best bookkeeper—no, financial analyst—in town running herself ragged."

Chapter 28

Chuck Delgado stood in line at the reception desk of the foreclosure company, a cashier's check clutched in his sweaty palm. He hummed tunelessly. He'd gotten the Wheeler house for a song. Turns out the shady past of its newly deceased owner suppressed interest in the otherwise desirable home. Nothing he liked better than a bargain. Not that he wouldn't have outbid anyone there. He had a gut feeling there was something hidden in the house that he needed to find.

The receptionist handed an envelope to the person in front of him, and Delgado surged forward, brushing the man aside.

"Hey, doll," he said to the woman on the other side of the counter. She was young enough to be his daughter. "What's a good lookin' gal like you doin' cooped up in this dump?"

"May I help you, sir?" she replied in clipped tones.

"In many ways, my dear. Maybe we can talk about them over a drink?"

She stared at him and remained silent.

Delgado cleared his throat. If this dumb broad wasn't interested in having some fun with one of the richest men in town, to hell with her. "I'm here to pay my bid. I bought the Wheeler house—the former Wheeler house—at yesterday's foreclosure auction."

"Address?" she responded, turning to her computer screen.

"1842 West Sycamore," he said.

She scrolled and found the entry for that address. "Your identification, please," she said, turning to him.

"C'mon, doll. You have to know who I am. Chuck Delgado. Council Member Chuck Delgado."

"I'm afraid not, sir. I'll need to see your driver's license."

Delgado shoved his hand into his pants pocket and pulled out his wallet. He tossed it to her, and it skittered across the desk top and landed on the floor behind her. She threw him an icy glare as she rolled her chair around and reached down to retrieve it. She held up the license and made the comparison.

"Payment, please," she said.

Delgado handed her the check, now wrinkled and soggy. She unfolded it, touching it only by the corners. She verified the amount against her computer screen, flipped it over, and stamped the back before slipping it into a drawer.

"Where's my key?" Delgado demanded.

Ignoring him, she unlocked the cabinet behind her and sorted through a stack of envelopes until she found the one marked "1842 W Sycamore." She removed the key from the envelope, laid it on the counter, and turned her attention to the next person in line.

Delgado didn't step aside. "What about the deed? Where's my deed?"

"We'll mail it to you next week, ex-Councilmember Delgado. I believe you got thrown out of office when you got arrested?"

Delgado spun on his heel and marched out the door. *Dumb broad.* Some people didn't know who they were messin' with. He'd be back in his council seat before Christmas.

The following day, Delgado lurched to his feet and staggered to the exterior stairway leading from his office to the parking lot where his car was sloppily angled in its usual spot next to the dumpster. He teetered on the top landing and grabbed for the handrail. Maybe he was a little too far gone to be driving, he thought.

One cheeky broad shouldn't send him to the bottle. What had he been thinking? He wanted to poke around the Wheeler house himself—to see if that bastard Wheeler had left something behind that would sink them all. At the very least, he needed to make sure the place was locked up.

Delgado stepped onto the top step and came down heavily on his generous backside. He wouldn't be going anywhere tonight. He gathered himself and stumbled back into his office, slid into his desk chair, and dialed the familiar number.

"After you see the lights go out at Rosemont tonight, go by Wheeler's place on Sycamore. I bought it at the foreclosure yesterday. Just make sure it's all locked up. Don't go in or anything," Delgado suddenly sounded sober. "You can come by my office to get the key. I'm workin' late tonight and don't wanna be disturbed," he said, trying his best not to slur his words. "I'll leave it in an envelope at the top of the stairs."

Delgado smirked as he hung up the phone. It was nice to have reliable help.

The driver in the sedan waited until the light in the windows at Rosemont—the ones he assumed were in the master bedroom—had remained out for a least fifteen minutes. Time to attend to more interesting matters. He swung the sedan out of his regular spot in the clearing below Rosemont and proceeded to his boss's liquor store, where he retrieved the key as instructed.

He drove slowly down West Sycamore. It was almost midnight. The only light he saw from within the handsome residences lining the street was the pale blue flicker of a television set in the front room of a house four doors down from his destination. He angled his car into the shadow cast by a tree across from the Wheeler house and quietly got out of the car. His gut told him to lay low, and he always listened to his gut.

He crossed the lawn and went up the front steps in a matter of seconds. The door was locked. He hesitated, then went to the back of the house, fingering the key. The back door was firmly secured as well. He trampled the bushes in the flower bed below a window to the left of the back door and peered into the laundry room. He removed the flashlight from his pocket and shone it into the room. Other than dust bunnies and dried leaves, all he noted was the baseboards that he'd seen David Wheeler pulling away from the walls. He rocked back on his heels, thinking.

The man pulled out his cell phone. The call went to voice mail after the fifth ring. Delgado was most likely in a drunken stupor. "The house is all locked up," he left the message in Delgado's voice mail box. "It was locked when I got here."

He turned to leave and noted the small, detached garage at the back of the property. Judging by the disrepair of the driveway, he guessed it hadn't been used for its intended purpose in years. They probably stored junk in it that should have been thrown away in the first place. He hesitated, then wandered in its direction. Why had Delgado been so adamant that he not enter the house, anyway? Didn't he trust him?

He tried to lift the heavy wooden garage door but it was painted shut. He switched on his flashlight and trained it along the side of the building. Nestled in the wall was a windowless door. He picked his way to it along the narrow walkway. The knob turned and the door yielded to gentle pressure, swinging in to reveal a jumbled mess of old tires, Christmas lights, a broken-down jungle gym, and stacks of newspapers. Even in the dim light, he could see the undisturbed blanket of dust covering every surface.

He trained his flashlight across the room. His boss owned all of this junk now. Delgado's next call would probably be for him to clean up this mess. The man bristled. That idiot didn't deserve him.

He was about to retrace his steps and exit the garage when his flashlight settled on an unusual feature in the abandoned, decrepit structure. Someone had taken the time to install baseboards. Clean and unblemished, they must have been added recently. Puzzled, he bent down for a closer look. The work had been shoddy, with a three-eighths-inch gap bowing out from the wall in the middle of the longest run.

He trained his light into the gap and thought he saw a piece of paper. He took his car key, shoved it into the gap, and pried the baseboard from its moorings. Three sheets of paper clung to the wall. He quickly plucked them from their hiding place and spread them on the floor. All three sheets were covered with neatly written lists of numbers.

The man turned the papers over, looking for a key to explain them. He came up empty-handed.

Taking great pains to ease the door noiselessly into place behind him, he locked the garage and returned to his car. He picked up his phone to call Delgado, then stopped. He had no idea what these numbers meant, but his gut told him that these papers were what Delgado was hoping to find. They were the reason he'd bought this house at foreclosure in the first place.

The man smiled. Maybe—just maybe—he'd stumbled upon something valuable. He could always give the papers to Delgado later, and he'd be none the wiser. He'd hang onto them for now to see what developed. It was good to save something for a rainy day, his mother always told him. He smiled; his mom would be proud.

Chapter 29

Maggie leaned into the microphone in front of her. "This meeting of the Westbury Town Council is adjourned." She pushed back her chair and turned to Tim Knudsen.

"How did you like your first meeting as a member of the council? You were certainly well prepared. You asked great questions."

Tim Knudsen smiled and waved Tonya Holmes over to join them. "Tonya and I got together for coffee earlier this week, and she went over things with me. Showed me the ropes."

"I'd expect nothing less of her." Maggie smiled at Tonya. "She's the hardest working public representative I've ever seen. Always does her homework, and votes for her constituents, every time."

Tonya flushed. "I try."

"Russ," Maggie called, trying to catch Council Member Russell Isaac before he exited at the far end of the council chamber. He turned, gestured to his watch in an exaggerated fashion, and continued out the door.

"He hasn't spoken to me in months," Tonya said. "The less I see of him, the better. I'll bet he's connected to Delgado in this whole thing. Haynes, too. Where is Frank today, by the way? It's not like him to miss a council meeting."

"He left me a voice mail that he'd be out of town on business," Maggie replied. "He's been gone a lot, lately."

"I didn't know he had business interests outside of Westbury," Tim said. "Maybe he's expanding his empire."

"With the town's money, if you ask me," Tonya said.

"We don't have any evidence of that," Maggie reprimanded gently. "We don't want to speculate. That's how rumors get started."

"I know, I know," Tonya said. "But I'm entitled to my opinion."

Maggie turned to Tim. "I need some information from you. I understand that the Wheeler house was sold at a foreclosure auction. Can you find out who bought it? I'm assuming that the bank ended up taking it back."

Tim spun around to look at her. "Didn't you hear?" he asked, looking from Maggie to Tonya and back again. "It went to a third party—not the bank. The house was sold to the only bidder at the sale."

"Who was the bidder?" Maggie asked.

"Chuck Delgado," Tim replied.

Maggie's head snapped up. They needed to serve their search warrant and get into that house before the day was done. She thanked Tim, again, for agreeing to step into Chuck Delgado's newly vacated council seat and promised Tonya she'd have lunch with her the following week.

"I haven't heard about your honeymoon, yet," Tonya reminded her.

"Next week, for sure," Maggie called over her shoulder as she made a beeline for her office.

"I've got these letters ready for your signature," her assistant called as Maggie sailed past.

"I'll be right out," Maggie said brightly. "I've got a call to make."

Maggie dove into her purse for her cell phone. She tapped her foot impatiently while Alex's number rang and rang, finally going to voice mail. This news couldn't wait. She buzzed her assistant. "Can you get me Forest Smith on the phone?"

Maggie waited for what seemed like an eternity until Smith was on the line. "Is Alex with you?" she asked, dismissing the usual formalities.

"He's right here, ma'am," Smith said. "Do you want to speak to him?"

"Put me on speaker. You both need to hear this," she replied.

Smith complied. "We're here," Alex said. "What's up?"

"Chuck Delgado bought the Wheeler house at the sale," she blurted out.

"Damn it!" Alex exploded. "Are you sure?"

"I heard it from Tim Knudsen."

"He would know," Alex said. "We need to get that search warrant served this afternoon. For all we know, he's been through the place and found what we're after."

"Maybe he bought it as an investment," Smith said. "He owns other rental properties in town. Maybe the fact that it had been Wheeler's home held some sort of macabre fascination for him."

"Forest's got a point," Maggie said. "I hadn't thought about that. This may not be as bad as it seems."

"From your lips to God's ears," Alex said. "In the meantime, we need to search that house."

———

Chuck Delgado turned onto West Sycamore Street. It was obvious that something big was happening halfway down the street. He proceeded cautiously in the direction of his newly acquired property and pulled to the curb three doors down from the house. The driveway and both sides of the street in front of the house were filled with police cars.

He hurried toward the commotion, stepping around a group of uniformed officers in his path. One of them held out his arm to block Delgado's progress.

"You'll have to cross on the other side of the street, sir," the officer said.

"Who the hell do you think you're talking to?"

The officer bristled but remained calm. "It doesn't matter who you are, sir. This is a police action, and you can't go through here."

"This is my house. I got a right to know what's going on."

The officer nodded. "In that case, you need to see Chief Thomas." He took Delgado's arm and escorted him up the sidewalk to the front door.

"Look who came strolling by, Chief," the officer said.

Chief Thomas nodded and handed Delgado the search warrant that Special Counsel Scanlon had delivered to the chief not more than thirty minutes earlier.

"What the hell ..." Delgado muttered.

Chief Thomas pointed to the key that Delgado was clutching in his left hand.

"May I?" he asked with a touch of sarcasm.

Delgado shoved the key into the lock. "Help yourselves, boys," he replied as he moved to step over the threshold.

Chief Thomas barred his progress. "You'll need to wait outside." He turned to the officer. "Escort Mr. Delgado back to the curb and make sure he stays there."

"This is my house," Delgado protested.

"And we'll let you know when we're done." The chief nodded to the officer who took Delgado by the elbow.

Delgado shook him off. "I don't need no escort." He stormed down the steps and took up a spot along the opposite curb among the growing crowd of neighbors and curious onlookers.

He watched as ten uniformed officers entered by the front door and maintained his vigil while the crowd around him thinned as people grew bored. The search lasted more than three hours, with officers coming and going. In the last hour, Delgado counted four large black plastic bags—containing who knew what—being taken down the front steps and placed in a waiting police van. Three final bags were carried from the garage and the back doors of the van were closed. Two officers got in and rolled slowly past Delgado.

Delgado crossed the street as Chief Thomas locked the front door. "Find what you were lookin' for?" Delgado sneered.

Chief Thomas turned and held the key out to Delgado.

"You'd better not have done any damage in there," Delgado said. "If you have, there'll be a lawsuit on your desk before you get back to the precinct."

"Everything is exactly as we found it," the chief replied calmly. "We've got before and after pictures to prove it." He stepped past Delgado.

"You took a lot of shit out of here," Delgado turned after him.

The chief kept on walking.

Chief Thomas knocked lightly and proceeded to enter the mayor's office. Maggie searched his face as she ushered him to the conference table in the corner.

"Alex told me he got you the warrant. Are you here to report on the results of the search?"

The chief nodded and opened his mouth to speak. Maggie held up her hand to stop him. "Let's get Alex on the speaker phone, first," she said as she dialed Alex's number.

"I've got the chief here with me," Maggie said. "He's served the warrant."

"Are you done?" Alex asked.

"Yes. I had ten officers with me and we spent a little over three hours. With Chuck Delgado watching from across the street. He showed up almost immediately after we arrived."

"How convenient," Alex said. "Wonder how he knew."

"Are you insinuating that there's a leak in my department?" the chief snapped.

"How else—" Alex began but Maggie cut him off.

"This is not the time," Maggie said sternly. "What did you find?"

"Nothing," the chief said. "Absolutely nothing. "The baseboards were removed in every room. We took off any crown molding, too. Nothing there or behind any of the cupboards. We even removed the medicine cabinets from the bathrooms. All of the floorboards were solid. We checked the house and the garage," he concluded. "No third report."

Maggie's inhaled suddenly. "Wait a minute. The garage?' She held her breath.

"Yes—the garage," the chief replied.

"We didn't check the garage. David and I didn't think to check the garage." She cradled her head in her hands. "What did it look like in there?"

"Same as the house, except it was full of junk. The Wheelers didn't clean it out. The baseboards were all pulled away from the wall."

Maggie moaned. "I'll bet that's where the third spreadsheet was hidden. I'm telling you—there has to be a third spreadsheet."

The line remained silent as they allowed the implications of this discovery to sink in. "Then Delgado must have it," Alex finally broke the silence.

Chief Thomas shook his head slowly. "Maybe, but I don't think so. We made a big show of taking black plastic bags out of the house and garage and loading them into a police van. Since Delgado was watching us from the opposite curb, we wanted to give him something to think about."

"That was smart," Maggie said.

"When I gave him back his key, he asked what we found. He seemed anxious about it. If he'd already been through the place and had his hands on that spreadsheet, he wouldn't have been."

"He doesn't have a reputation for having a poker face," Alex said. "I'll give you that." He sighed heavily. "Who has that third spreadsheet?"

Chapter 30

Maggie was putting away leftovers later that week while John was washing the skillet they'd used to make dinner when Gordon Mortimer called.

"Mayor Martin, I've arranged the sale, and I think you'll be pleased," he announced.

Maggie remained silent, waiting for him to continue.

"Sotheby's will auction your items and recommends that we place all of them, except the Martin-Guillaume Biennais, in a London auction to be held October twenty-fourth."

Maggie released the breath she had been holding. The timing would work. She'd read on the auctioneer's website that payments were made for sold items thirty-five days after the sale, provided that the bidder actually paid for the item. If everything sold, she'd have the money she needed in time.

"Why won't the Martin-Guillaume Biennais be part of the London sale?" she asked.

"The experts at Sotheby's—and they are truly experts, Mayor Martin; no one knows more about the value of silver and how to sell it than the team at Sotheby's—feel that the Martin-Guillaume Biennais will bring three times as much at a Paris sale in March."

Maggie swallowed hard. If she were going to sell it, she wanted to get as much as possible for it. "What do they think I'll get without selling the Martin-Guillaume Biennais?" she asked.

"On the low end, after commissions, five hundred thousand in U.S. dollars. On the best day, you might see one million five hundred. After commissions are paid."

"And with the Martin-Guillaume Biennais at the London auction?"

Gordon Mortimer paused, as if he couldn't bear to contemplate that she might insist on liquidating the most valuable items in her collection in a less than optimal way. "They feel certain that it will bring at least eight hundred thousand in London. In Paris, after they've had more time to promote it, they feel confident it will bring three times that amount."

Maggie coughed.

"You don't have to give me an answer tonight. I'm assuming you want to go through with the London auction for the bulk of it?"

"Yes. That's certain."

"Good. I'll email you the contracts tonight. Look them over carefully, and call me with any questions. I'll be up late tonight and early tomorrow morning. We'll need to move quickly. I'm planning a trip to Westbury early next week. I'll oversee the packing and shipment to London. That's part of the service I provide."

"I'm very grateful to you for that, Mr. Mortimer. I wouldn't know how to insure and send things this valuable."

"Why don't you think about the Martin-Guillaume Biennais overnight? Talk to your husband or your children about it. I know I've said this before, but I reiterate: my advice is to wait and sell it in Paris."

Maggie respected his opinion, but he didn't have all the facts. "I'll discuss this with my husband. You'll have my answer in the morning."

John was drying the final pan when she placed her phone on the counter and turned to him.

"The distinguished appraiser, I take it?"

Maggie nodded. Bubbles jumped onto the countertop, and Maggie drew the cat to her chest, drawing comfort from the familiar rumble that followed as Maggie stroked her side.

"By the look on your face, I'm guessing he didn't have good news?"

"It's not that. He's got the silver placed in an auction in London on October twenty-fourth."

"That's good." John knew the timeline Maggie had constructed as well as she did. Her lawyer had responded to Simon Wilkens' demand letter and begun the process of authenticating the facts and documents presented by Wilkens. He'd reported last week that his investigation had verified everything. He could only forestall a lawsuit until the end of the year. He advised Maggie to have her money together by early December if she wanted to avoid being sued. "Why the long face, then?"

"Mortimer recommended selling all but the Martin-Guillaume Biennais at the London auction. He thinks we should wait to sell it in Paris in March. It'll bring three times the price in Paris. He said that we should expect to receive between five hundred thousand dollars and a million and a half for the stuff he recommends we sell in London."

Maggie faced John and tears rimmed her eyes. "So even on its best day, it won't be enough. We'll need at least two million three to buy out Frank."

"Surely the Martin-Guillaume Biennais would bring enough in London to give us the two million three?"

Maggie nodded. "Yes, but isn't that just being foolish? How can we afford to throw away that much money—possibly millions—just to hang onto Rosemont? Come on, John. You have to think that's crazy."

John took her in his arms. "I think it would be crazy not to do everything we can to hang onto this place. You love it, and you know it. The house is happy with us living here, too."

Maggie nodded against his shoulder.

"Don't pretend that you don't think this house has feelings. I know you too well, Mrs. Allen. I've heard you come in from one of your thrift store excursions, whispering to Rosemont that you've bought it a present."

Maggie laughed. "And you don't think I'm kooky?"

"I think you're kooky, all right, but it's part of your charm. Can you imagine how horrified Rosemont would be if Frank Haynes were living here? There'd be no more Easter carnivals or Christmas high teas; impromptu pizza parties or Thanksgiving dinners with friends. You can't possibly think of letting that happen to Rosemont."

"I knew you'd help me see reason," she said.

"We're not counting on the Martin-Guillaume Biennais for our retirement. We didn't even know we had it or what it was until recently. May as well use it for something we really want, and that's Rosemont."

Maggie stood on tiptoes and kissed him.

"Now go call that man and set him straight. We're selling the Martin-Guillaume Biennais in London on October twenty-fourth."

Chapter 31

Loretta Nash flipped through a magazine while Nicole dozed in her hospital bed after her latest dialysis treatment. She tossed the magazine onto a stack on the table in the recovery area and stood to stretch her legs. If she sat watching her child's discomfort for one more minute she would scream. She headed toward the water fountain when she saw a familiar couple at the end of the hallway. David Wheeler and Dodger turned in her direction as she was raising her hand to wave to them.

"David," Loretta called. She motioned him toward her. "I'm Loretta Nash. I met you when you came to Haynes Enterprises. I'm Mr. Haynes' assistant."

David nodded in recognition.

"You and Dodger have met my daughter Nicole in this hospital before. She loves Dodger." Loretta bent to pet the dog standing obediently at his master's side. "And she's here now. Right over there, in that room," she said, pointing. "She's not feeling too well. I think a visit from Dodger might be just what she needs. Would you have time to go see her?"

David was about to tell her that they were done for the day and on their way home, but the anxiety in her eyes made him pause. "Sure," he said. "We'd love to—wouldn't we, boy?"

Loretta's smile was all the confirmation he needed. David and Dodger followed Loretta as she retraced her steps to Nicole's bedside.

"Look who's here," Loretta said, slipping her arm under Nicole's shoulders and propping her into a sitting position.

Nicole's eyelids fluttered, and she rubbed her eyes with her fists.

David positioned Dodger next to Nicole's bed. "Do you remember Dodger?" he asked the little girl. "He had a good time with you before."

She turned her head in David's direction and looked at the dog.

"Would you like to pet him?" David asked.

Nicole stared at Dodger, then slowly shook her head no.

"Sure you would," Loretta said. She took Nicole's hand in hers and reached for Dodger.

David shifted from one foot to the other. "We can come back another time," he said as a nurse approached.

"The doctors would like to see you, Ms. Nash," the nurse said.

"Now?" Loretta asked.

The nurse nodded. "I'll take you to them and come back to check on Nicole."

"Mommy will be right back." Loretta gently placed Nicole's hand under the blanket.

"Would you like Dodger to stay with you?" the nurse asked.

Again, Nicole shook her head no.

"We'd better go. We'll see you when you're feeling better," David pulled on Dodger's leash and led him away.

"Thank you for trying." Loretta called after them. She turned to the nurse. "Why do they want to meet with me?" Her voice sounded shrill, even to her own ears.

"Try not to worry, Ms. Nash. You've got the best team of doctors in the state. If my child were sick, these are the doctors I would choose." The nurse led her to a room at the end of a long hallway. She opened the door and motioned Loretta to step inside. Nicole's doctor and two others she didn't recognize were seated at a round conference table. Nicole's doctor rose.

"Come in, Ms. Nash," he said and extended his arm toward the chair next to him. Loretta clutched her purse to her body and tripped on the leg of a chair as she moved it aside to sit down. She turned to him, her fear palpable.

"I don't want you to be alarmed," he said kindly. "Nothing has drastically changed with Nicole's condition." Loretta released the breath she had been holding. "I've been concerned that she hasn't responded to the medicines we've prescribed and her kidneys aren't working well enough to allow her to go untreated. At this point, she'll need to be on weekly dialysis." He looked to his colleagues seated with him at the table and they nodded their agreement.

"I asked the other doctors in the department to review Nicole's records and give me their recommendations. We all came to the same conclusion." He faced Loretta. "We think you should place Nicole on the transplant list."

Loretta gasped and flattened herself against the back of her chair. "Transplant," she whispered, shaking her head. "Surely it's not that bad? Can't we keep trying medication and dialysis?"

"Yes, of course we can," the doctor replied. "But transplants are frequently a better option for children. They allow the child to live a more normal life. Weekly dialysis is a big disruption in a child's schedule. And the outcome for a transplant patient—particularly a child—is better the earlier it's done."

Loretta gulped air. "Aren't transplants risky? Don't most people die within a few years?"

"Kidney transplants have been done for more than sixty years and are highly successful. We expect Nicole to make a full recovery. You'd have to keep a close eye on her after the surgery, and she'd be on immunosuppressants for the rest of her life to prevent her body from rejecting the transplanted kidney. She'd have to be careful not to damage it playing sports. But many people live long and healthy lives after a transplant."

Loretta rested her elbows on the table and placed her head in her hands. "This is a lot to take in."

The doctor to her right leaned toward her. "You don't need to decide today. We want you to start considering this."

She turned to him. "When would this happen?"

"We wouldn't do the transplant here. You'd have to go to a transplant hospital to be evaluated. If they agree that Nicole is a good candidate, they would place her on the national list for a kidney donation."

"So we'd have time?"

"Yes. This can be a lengthy process. That's why we thought you should get started now."

"Won't her body destroy the new kidney?"

"Not in her case. A birth defect is causing them to fail. That won't happen with the transplanted kidney."

"Is there a transplant hospital near here?"

"One of the best for pediatric patients is at Indiana University," her doctor replied. "We can refer you to the doctors there."

Loretta nodded slowly, forcing herself to think. "All right, if that's what you want me to do."

"We think it's in Nicole's best interest," he replied.

"How long does it take to get a kidney once she's on the list?" Loretta asked.

"That can vary. There are two types of transplant donors," one of the other doctors answered. "Living and nonliving. Kidneys are unusual because a person can live with only one. Success rates are better with living donations."

Loretta faced him. "Who can be a live donor? Since she's a child, does it have to be a child?"

"That's a good question," he said. "Anyone can be a donor if they're healthy and have the same blood type and other compatible tissue characteristics. The best matches come from close relatives."

"So the kidney can come from an adult? Won't it be too big?"

"Adults can donate to children. The kidney is bigger, but we make room."

"I don't have the same blood type as Nicole," she said sadly.

"There's always the national donor list," the doctor reminded her. "What about her father?"

"He's dead," she stated matter-of-factly.

"It's too bad that her siblings aren't older," her doctor observed.

Loretta stared past him. Maybe now was the time to learn the answer to the question that had plagued her for years: Was Paul Martin really

Nicole's father? More importantly, were Susan and Mike Martin related to Nicole?

"Would you like us to make the referral to the transplant center at Indiana University?"

She drew a deep breath and exhaled slowly before nodding in agreement. "Yes. I think we should get started."

———

Loretta crawled into bed shortly before ten that night, praying that her exhaustion would allow her to fall asleep. She looked at her bedside clock at midnight and swung her feet to the floor in frustration. She padded to her closet and pulled the old calendar down from its hiding place on the back of the top shelf.

She didn't turn on her bedside lamp but brought it to her bedroom window and drew back the curtain. The light from the street lamp illuminated the page that she knew from memory. The large red X on the page marked the date when she felt certain Nicole had been conceived.

She sagged against the windowsill and leaned her forehead against the glass. Nicole had to be Paul's child. That other guy had been a drunken, vengeful fling she'd had when she'd quarreled with Paul over his promise to divorce Maggie and marry her. She stifled a sob. She didn't even remember his name. Why had she been so careless? The odds were heavily in Paul's favor, but she couldn't be certain he was Nicole's father. Until Nicole had needed a kidney transplant, she had been content to let the issue die with Paul. Now that Nicole needed a family member to donate a kidney, she had to know.

Loretta wasn't a match. She had to find some way to reach Susan and Mike. She had to convince them to get tested to see if they could be kidney donors for Nicole—and to donate a kidney if they were. This would be so much easier if Paul were still alive.

Loretta turned her face upward. Please, God, give me the words. Show me the way. Do this for Nicole.

Loretta returned the calendar to its hiding place and climbed back into bed. Her fatigue led her into a dreamless sleep.

———

Loretta Nash stood in the doorway of Frank Haynes' office and cleared her throat. He looked at her over the top of his reading glasses.

"May I come in? I have something I need to talk to you about."

"Of course," he said, motioning her to one of the chairs on the other side of his desk. He looked into her eyes and smiled.

Loretta lowered her gaze to her hands clasped in her lap. She cleared her throat and began. "I'm going to need some time off of work, Mr. Haynes …"

"It's Frank, for heaven's sake," he interrupted.

She glanced at him and a smile brushed her lips. "Frank. The doctors think that Nicole needs a transplant. It will be better for her in the long run, and she should have it done sooner rather than later. They want us to go to a hospital in Indianapolis that does a lot of pediatric kidney transplants. Nicole needs to be evaluated before she can even get on a transplant list."

He nodded encouragingly.

"So I'm going to need to be gone from work for the initial consultation. And when she has the transplant, I'll need a bunch of time off." Loretta's voice caught in her throat. "I'm not sure how much. And you've let me take off a lot already." She looked into his eyes, and her tone was pleading. "I've got to keep my job, Frank. I need the health insurance and the income. I don't know how, but I'll make it up to you. You don't have to give me a raise for the rest of my life."

"I'm not going to fire you, Loretta," he heard himself reassure her. "And I've already told you, I'll help with your medical expenses. That goes for this transplant center, too. Don't worry about being gone. I did all the work around here for years. I can pick up the slack again," he said, not feeling sure that he could.

"I've thought about that," Loretta said. "Could we hire a part-time assistant? A high school student on work study or an intern from the college? They could do the simple data entry, and I could work on the reports and financials remotely, on a laptop. I could take it with me. I'll be spending a lot of time in waiting rooms. I could easily work there. Or while Nicole's asleep."

"We'll see," Frank said.

"I know you don't like a lot of people poking their noses into your business," she said. "I understand that. But we're almost at the point where the two of us can't keep up anymore. I was going to suggest this even before Nicole got sick again." She paused. "Think about it."

He nodded slowly, knowing he'd never agree to bring anyone else on board. "What about Sean and Marissa?" he asked, changing the subject. "Will they go with you?"

"No. They'll be in school. My babysitter has agreed to take them."

"She's a very nice woman."

"You have no idea. She's agreed to keep them for free to help me out. I can't believe it, because it's not like she doesn't need the money."

Haynes made a mental note to make sure that the babysitter won the drawing for this month's Visa gift card from Haynes Enterprises—regardless of whether she had ever set foot in one of his restaurants and entered to win or not.

"When will you go?"

"I'm not sure yet but probably by next month. Her doctor is setting it up." She began absentmindedly twisting a strand of her hair around her finger, a nervous habit she'd picked up as a child that had grown more prevalent since her move to Westbury. "I'm so sorry that I can't give you much notice."

Haynes waved his hand in dismissal. "That doesn't matter. Why don't we buy you a laptop this afternoon? Then you'll be all set."

"Thank you, Frank." She began to rise, but he put out his hand to stop her.

"What have they told you about the transplant donor? Who would make a good candidate?" If Nicole were Paul's child, as he suspected, Maggie Martin's kids could be ideal donors.

"Anyone with the right blood type and tissue match can be a donor, but close family members are best. Nicole and I are different blood types, so I'm not a candidate, unfortunately."

"What about Nicole's father?" Frank asked. "Or other close relatives?"

Loretta shook her head. "I was adopted, so I'm not a blood relative to my sister."

Frank remained silent. *Surely she knows that Paul Martin's other children could be donors,* he thought. He wouldn't broach the subject with her just yet; he'd let her keep her secrets a bit longer.

Chapter 32

Susan Martin stared at the text message on her phone:

Can't go Westbury with you on 1st. Can't b away that long. You go. I'll come on 3rd. Explain later.

He could explain it right now. She punched his number into her phone and waited. Dr. Aaron Scanlon answered just before the call would have gone to voice mail. "I'm in the middle of something," he said in hushed tones. "I'll call you when I'm done."

"No. You promised me you'd make this trip. You've taken your boards and your vacation was approved. And it's your brother's surprise birthday party. You have no excuse."

"I know, sweetheart," he said. "I'll make it for the party. I've been offered the opportunity to assist a surgeon who's visiting here from Johns Hopkins. He's demonstrating some cutting-edge techniques that I'm very anxious to learn. This will be my only chance because nobody on the West Coast does this procedure."

"There's always going to be something like this, isn't there? Every time we plan something, I'm not going to be able to count on you."

"That's not fair, Susan. I'm only asking for a few days. You can go to Westbury as planned and spend time with your mother. It's not like I'm abandoning you where you don't know anybody. Why are you making such a big deal out of this?"

"Because I haven't spent any quality time with you for weeks." She struggled to hold back tears. "I was counting on this time to reconnect with you."

"I'll be out on the third, and we'll have three days together. I'll get the first flight out in the morning. How would that be?"

Susan remained silent.

"I've accepted this invitation, and it would look very bad if I now declined," Aaron said.

"All right. I guess it doesn't matter what I say. Next time, please consider my feelings and ask me."

"I'll do that. I'm sorry that I've upset you. And I'll be there on the third in time to take you to lunch, I promise you that. I want to be at Alex's party, but I'm more excited to spend time with you."

———

"The girls, too?" Maggie asked. "Aren't they just about to start school?"

"School begins the week after we get back." Susan sighed heavily.

"What's wrong, honey?"

"I'm bringing the girls with me on the spur of the moment because Aaron signed up for some surgical thing and isn't coming out until the third. Since you and John will be working and the girls have been nagging Mike and Amy to get back to Westbury to see their friend Marissa Nash, I decided to bring them with me. Mike had airlines miles, so he booked their tickets."

"That was nice of you. And I'm thrilled that I'll get to see them. So why do you sound so down?"

"I'm disappointed about Aaron. I gave him lots of leeway while he was studying for boards and I was so excited about this trip together. Then he accepted an offer to assist this prominent surgeon from Johns Hopkins with a surgical demonstration. He'd rather do that than spend time with me," she concluded glumly.

"I understand how you feel, believe me, I do. I spent years feeling let down because something I was looking forward to got canceled because of your father's schedule. But to be fair to Aaron, this sounds like a big deal for him."

"It is, I guess."

"And he's still coming, just two days later. I think your idea to bring the twins to Westbury is brilliant. We'll have fun. After all, when was the last time you spent two full days with them?"

"If you look at it that way, you're right. And he promised he'd be here by lunch on the third, so everything should work out fine. You always make me feel better, Mom."

Chapter 33

Maggie Martin and Gordon Mortimer stepped out of the back exit of the Ferndale bank shortly after two o'clock. The armored car that would be transporting Maggie's treasure trove of silver to New York for redeployment to London had just pulled out of the parking lot.

"I should be getting back to Westbury," Maggie said. "I didn't think it would take so long to pack and load this. I thought that Sotheby's would take their own photos for the sale catalog."

"They will, madam," Mortimer said. "I always take my own for insurance purposes. One can't be too careful, you know." He arched his brow as he looked at her. "We just loaded well over a million dollars' worth of silver onto that truck."

"You're right. Thank you, Gordon," she said, realizing she'd ruffled his feathers. "Do you want to get started tonight on the silver that's still at Rosemont?"

He shook his head. "I'd like to begin first thing in the morning. The light will be better for photographs. It's hard to use a flash with silver. I think I can be done by noon. I'll take the silver to the post office to ship to New York in the afternoon."

"Is it safe to send that way?"

Gordon Mortimer bristled. "Of course it is, madam, or I wouldn't be doing it. The silver that you kept at Rosemont wasn't nearly as valuable as the items here in the bank's vaults. Everything will be fully insured. And I'll have my photos, of course."

Maggie nodded. "Will you look at the furniture in the attic while you're there? We've added a painting to the lot, too."

"I'll have to do it another time. I'm planning to leave as soon as I deposit the silver at the post office."

"That'll be fine," Maggie said in a conciliatory tone as she slid into the driver's seat of her car. "Whenever you get a chance." She rolled down her window and called to him as he headed to his car. "Are you staying in Westbury tonight?"

Gordon Mortimer nodded.

"Then come have dinner with my husband and me at Rosemont. We'd love to have you," she heard herself say cheerily.

"I'd be delighted, madam," he replied.

"Seven o'clock," Maggie called, wondering what in the world she had in her refrigerator to feed him, and why she'd invited a dinner guest the night before Susan and the twins were to arrive. She needed to learn to keep her mouth shut.

Gordon Mortimer rang the doorbell of Rosemont precisely at seven o'clock. John Allen opened the door and welcomed him inside. Truth be told, he'd had a hard day at the animal hospital and wanted nothing more than to take his wife out for a bite to eat and fall asleep in his chair in front of the television. But this was important to her, so he'd be a good sport and make the best of it.

Gordon Mortimer handed John a very nice bottle of cabernet. Where in the world had the man found a bottle like this in Westbury? John wondered.

As if reading his mind, Mortimer said, "The Mill has quite a nice collection of wines. That's one of my personal favorites. I was very pleased that they had a bottle on hand."

"I'll open it now to let it breathe before dinner," John said. "Are you staying at The Mill?"

"I am. I discovered it on my first visit to Westbury and find it quite acceptable."

John nodded. He was sure that The Mill's owners would hate that it was being described as "quite acceptable."

Maggie emerged from the kitchen with a tray of cheeses, grapes, olives, and crackers. She placed it on the coffee table in front of the living-room fireplace and greeted their guest in the library.

"I'm so glad you could join us," Maggie said, extending her hand. "I see you need something to drink."

"Look at the wine he brought us," John said, pointing to the bottle. "We'll have it with dinner. In the meantime, I've opened a pinot. Would you like some?" he asked their guest.

"Yes, thank you," he replied as John poured three glasses.

"Let's go into the living room to enjoy this," Maggie said, leading the way. "I've got some nibbles in there." She ushered Mortimer to a chair opposite the fireplace and pointed to the tray on the coffee table.

He was almost seated when he jumped to his feet as a small gray-and-white cat that Maggie recognized as Buttercup screeched in protest and darted off the chair and up the stairs. "Good heavens!" he said, clutching his chest. "Is that the cat that created such a ruckus when I was here last time? I think she's got it in for me. Cats don't like me, and I'm not fond of them."

Maggie suppressed a laugh and avoided looking at John, who was also politely holding back. "It was Bubbles, last time," she said.

"How many cats do you have?"

"Three cats and two dogs," John interjected. "We're animal lovers. I'm a veterinarian, after all."

"Ahhh …" Mortimer cleared his throat and turned to the tray on the coffee table. He placed a slice of white cheddar on a cracker and had it halfway to his mouth when he noticed the painting over the mantel. "Is that new?" he asked, returning the cracker to the napkin on his lap.

"Yes," John replied. "We just hung it a few days ago. We got it on our honeymoon in Cornwall."

Mortimer nodded. "Yes. I would have guessed that it was Cornwall. It looks very much like it belongs to the Newlyn School." He sat, absorbed in the painting. "Do you mind if I have a closer look?"

"By all means," Maggie said, arching her eyebrows at John.

Gordon Mortimer set his wineglass on the coffee table and approached the painting, scrutinizing it in silence.

Maggie finally broke into his thoughts. "What do you think of it? We're not art collectors or anything. We just loved it and wanted to bring it home to remind us of our honeymoon."

Mortimer chose his words carefully. "You have very fine eyes," he said to them both. "It's unfinished, of course. I assume you knew that?" he asked. "Good," he said when they nodded. "That's why it's unsigned. But it's lovely."

"Are you familiar with the Newlyn School?" Maggie asked.

"I am, madam. Painting done at the turn of the twentieth century in both the United States and the United Kingdom are a real interest of mine. I've collected both professionally and personally."

Maggie screwed up her courage and asked, "Do you have any idea whose work this is?"

He paused, contemplating the painting, then turned to her. "I feel certain it was done by either Elizabeth Forbes or Dame Laura Knight. If this were finished and signed, it would be worth a very tidy sum."

"That's what the dealer we bought it from thought, too."

"I'm assuming you've insured this?" Mortimer asked, slipping back into his official capacity.

"Yes. For what we paid for it," Maggie replied, supplying the amount.

Mortimer raised an eyebrow. "Might I suggest you double the insurance?"

"He's a very interesting guy," John said as they were getting ready for bed.

"It was a fun evening, wasn't it?" Maggie asked. "I was afraid you'd want to kill me when I left the message that I'd invited him to dinner. I know you work so hard during the day and you need your evenings to relax and decompress. Did you enjoy him?"

"I did. I wasn't looking forward to being 'on' tonight, but it was fun. Plus the dinner you cooked was wonderful."

"Pricey steaks and twice baked potatoes are always a hit. The wine he brought was fabulous. We should get some to have on hand."

"Not if you knew the price. That's at least one fifty a bottle."

"No kidding? That was nice of him."

John pulled back the covers, and they slid into bed. Maggie wriggled into this arms. "Nice to hear him confirm what that dealer told us about our painting. And I'm thrilled he's giving us an appraisal for double what we paid for it. We're savvy art collectors and we didn't even know it."

"Don't get too carried away with yourself, Mrs. Allen. We just got lucky. Honeymoon luck." He began to trace her jaw line with kisses. "How about we relive some of that honeymoon now?"

"Don't you have to be up at the crack of dawn?"

John slid his hands to her waist. "No surgery tomorrow morning. I get to sleep in until at least six thirty. Mortimer won't be here until eight to pack up the remaining silver. So we've got plenty of time; the night is still young."

"In that case, Dr. Allen," Maggie breathed in his ear, "you're on."

Chapter 34

"Gramma!" Sophie cried as Susan ushered her nieces into the mayor's office. Maggie came around the side of her desk and scooped the girls into a hug.

"Look how much you've grown!" she cried. "You'll be taller than me, soon." She held them close. "You're early. I didn't expect you for another half hour." She looked up at Susan. "Good flight?"

"A bit bumpy, with tailwinds. But those winds pushed us here, and we landed ahead of schedule. The rental car was ready and waiting, and there was almost no traffic." Susan leaned in and hugged her mother.

"Is this where you work, Gramma?" Sarah asked, surveying the large office awash in sunshine from the large windows on either side. "Why do you have a dining room table?"

Maggie smiled. "That's a conference table. I have meetings in here sometimes and I need a table that's big enough for a group."

"You must be important," Sophie said, turning in a circle to look at the room.

"Your grandmother is very important," Susan interjected. "She's the mayor of Westbury. That means she runs this town. Do you know what an election is?"

Both girls nodded in unison.

"Gramma was elected mayor by the people of Westbury."

The twins turned solemn eyes to their grandmother. "Wow," Sarah whispered.

Susan beamed at her mother. "You two need to know how special she is."

Maggie flushed. "That's enough of that. I've got a job and I do it, just like everybody else. Which reminds me," she said, looking at her watch, "I've got a meeting upstairs in five minutes. Why don't you go to

Rosemont and get settled in? This won't be a long meeting. I should be home in an hour and a half. Roman and Eve are waiting for you."

"What about the cats?" Sarah asked.

"Blossom, Bubbles, and Buttercup will hide at first. Don't chase them—let them come to you." Maggie turned to Susan. "John arranged his schedule so he'll be done early today. He'll pick up a pizza on his way home." She kissed them each, then escorted them to the elevator. "See you soon."

"They're a handful, aren't they?" Maggie said later that night as the three adults sat on the veranda after the girls finally went to bed. Eve and Roman lay passed out at John's feet and the cats were nowhere to be seen.

John chuckled. "By the looks of these two," he said, gesturing to the dogs, "I'd say they got quite a workout today."

"The twins chased them up and down this back lawn all afternoon," Susan said. "After being cooped up on an airplane all day, I thought the exercise would be good for them. Was it too much for these two?" She pointed to the furry creatures at his feet.

He shook his head. "They're fine. I'm sure they loved it."

"What do you have planned for the next few days until Aaron comes? I've scheduled a vacation day on the fifth to spend with the girls. I'll take them to the mall to get new outfits for the first day of school."

"I loved how you always did that with me." Susan smiled at her mother. "It's supposed to rain tomorrow, so we'll go to a pottery painting place. We've invited Marissa Nash to join us."

Maggie's head came up sharply, but she remained silent.

"I talked to Loretta last night. Apparently things are touch and go with that sweet little Nicole. If she's well enough, we'll take her with us. I invited Sean, but he's not into that 'girly stuff.'"

John glanced at Maggie. "That's nice of you, Susan."

"Loretta's invited the girls to spend the night of the surprise party at her apartment. So we don't have to take them with us," Susan continued. Maggie opened her mouth to protest. "I know you had crafts planned to take with us to keep them occupied, Mom, but they'll be happier with Marissa. And we won't have to keep track of them."

"You're right," John jumped in. "The twins will love that."

"It's all set, then," Maggie said, rising stiffly. "I've got an early meeting, so I'm heading to bed."

"I'm beat, too," Susan said. "Coming with you."

Mother and daughter climbed the stairs in companionable silence. "Let's check on the girls," they said in unison at the top of the stairs.

They quietly opened the door to the guest room that Sarah and Sophie referred to as "our room." The girls were huddled together in the king-sized bed, bracketed by the trio of cats. All were in a deep sleep. Maggie gently closed the door and hugged her daughter tight before they set off for their own beds.

———

Loretta Nash took a deep breath to calm her nerves.

"Come on, Mom, they're here!" Marissa cried.

Loretta opened the door to her apartment. Marissa brushed past her mother to greet her friends and pulled them into the apartment. "Let me show you my room."

Loretta stood in the doorway, looking at Susan. It was uncanny how like her father she was in the set of her jaw and her expansive smile, even though her remarkable eyes were definitely Maggie's.

Susan smiled. "How are you, Loretta?"

Loretta quickly stepped aside. "Come in, please. I'm fine. How was your trip?"

"Uneventful. The girls are so excited to spend time with Marissa. How's Nicole? Will she be joining us?"

"I want to talk to you about that. She's feeling better today, and she'd like to go."

"Great. Then it's all set."

Loretta hesitated. "That's not all of it. Her condition is delicate. Nicole is back on dialysis and may need a transplant."

"I'm so sorry, Loretta," Susan said, reaching out to squeeze her hand.

"She needs to be tested before she can be placed on the waiting list, and then we wait for a donor. In the meantime, we'll continue to monitor Nicole very carefully. She can't get overly tired, and she can't be exposed to anyone who is sick. So I'm very hesitant to take her out in public."

"I understand completely," Susan said. "I'll keep a very close eye on her and call you the minute she doesn't feel well. The pottery place shouldn't be busy during the week, and if anyone there is sick, we'll leave immediately. I won't take any risks. And you can call me to check on her." She looked into Loretta's eyes. "This must be so hard on you."

Loretta turned aside and nodded. "I think she needs some fun in her life, too. She's borne so much pain without complaint. And she's so excited to go with you."

"Then it's all set. We'll be on our way, and I'll drop them off here when you get home from work."

Susan commandeered a table for two by the large plate-glass window of the pottery shop and set up the paints and supplies that she and Nicole Nash selected for their projects. Susan was working on a jewelry tray that she thought would go perfectly in her mother's bedroom, and Nicole selected a ceramic teddy bear. "For my Susan," she said.

Susan gave her a quizzical glance. "Who is your Susan?"

Nicole pointed to her beloved doll, propped onto a chair at the end of their work table. "Her name is Susan. Like you."

"Ahhh … that's nice. I didn't know we had the same name."

"Nicole named her after you," Sarah supplied from the next table over, where the three girls were hard at work on their projects.

Susan swallowed the lump in her throat. "I'm sure your Susan will love this teddy bear. If you need any help, you let me know."

Nicole tackled her project with patience and restraint rarely seen in a four-year-old. While the three older girls chattered away at the next table, Susan and Nicole worked in companionable silence. When it came time to fill in the eyes and nose on the bear, she held out her paintbrush to Susan. "You do," she commanded.

"That looks tricky," Susan agreed. "You've done a perfect job," she said as she supplied the requested details. They both leaned back to admire the completed bear. "We'll leave him here to be fired. That'll make him shiny and the colors won't rub off. They'll call my mom when they're ready to be picked up, and she'll bring them to you. Would that be okay?"

Nicole nodded.

Susan ruffled the little girl's hair. If she'd had a sister, she'd want her to be just like this little girl.

Chapter 35

Susan Martin rolled over in bed and reached for her cell phone on the nightstand. The ping was probably a text message from Aaron, telling her he'd boarded his flight to Westbury. She stretched. It was nice to linger in bed instead of racing to the shower and then off to her office or the courthouse. Susan opened one eye and clicked on the message.

Slight snafu. Driver's license expired and couldn't get thru TSA. Will get it renewed today. Booked on late morning flight tomorrow. Will be there before party. So sorry. Didn't want to wake you. Love u!

"Didn't want to wake me, my foot!" Susan fumed. "He doesn't want to tell me over the phone. *Coward.*" She sank back into the pillows and began typing her response. Before she could hit the Send button, her phone rang.

"Hi, Mom. What's up?"

"I was just calling to check on everybody. You were all sound asleep when I left for Town Hall. Who stole your sunshine?" Maggie asked. "You sound terrible."

Susan filled Maggie in on Aaron's predicament. "I was just typing my reply when your call interrupted me."

"I hope it's a sympathetic reply," Maggie said. "Remember when that happened to me right after your father died? It can happen to the best of us."

Susan remained silent for a beat. "I'd forgotten about that. I guess you're right."

"I'm sure he's incredibly irritated with himself. I know I was. You don't need to rub salt in the wound. He'll be here tomorrow in time for the party, and it'll be fine."

"Okay, okay. You're right."

"So what will you and the girls do today?"

"I'm feeling pretty lazy. Any ideas?"

"Why don't you get out the spare sheets and let the girls make forts with them in the library? You can have a tea party in there with the cats."

Susan laughed. "That'll be quite the affair. Sarah and Sophie will love it. Not sure about Blossom, Bubbles, and Buttercup, though."

"They can take care of themselves. See you tonight. And cheer up. In the grand scheme of things, this disappointment is inconsequential."

Susan scrambled through an opening in the sheets and headed in the direction of her ringing cell phone. Bubbles, wearing a lacy baby bonnet and one tatted bootie, saw her chance to escape and streaked after Susan.

"You let her out!" Sarah protested as Sophie dived for the opening in time to prevent Blossom from joining her sister. Only Buttercup seemed content curled up in Sarah's lap, a crocheted shawl strewn over her back, while Sarah brought an empty cup to Buttercup's mouth and pretended to serve tea to the purring cat.

Sophie motioned for her twin sister to remain quiet. They both leaned toward the hallway, where Susan now stood talking to her boyfriend. The girls exchanged a knowing glance and eavesdropped as best they could.

"These things happen to everyone, Aaron. Don't worry about it. At least you've gotten it renewed and have a flight tomorrow." Susan was silent for what seemed like an eternity. Her tone was warm and mellow when she spoke again. "Me, too. I can't wait until you get here, and we can concentrate on each other for a few days. I love you, too."

Sarah hugged Buttercup and grinned at Sophie, who nodded in return. Their aunt Susan was in love and that's exactly how things should be.

Susan inserted her key into the back door of Rosemont the following day. She'd dropped the twins off at Loretta Nash's apartment and had twenty-five minutes before she had to leave to pick up Aaron at the airport. He'd texted her when he'd boarded his flight and told her they expected to be on time.

The morning had been sunny but late afternoon clouds were rolling in and thunderstorms were predicted. She hoped they wouldn't spoil the fireworks Marc had arranged for later that evening.

She eyed her watch. She'd touch up her makeup and be on her way.

Susan's phone rang as she was merging onto the freeway. She attempted to retrieve it from her purse sitting on the passenger seat but knocked the purse onto the floor, sending its contents scattering. "Darn it," she mumbled, casting a quick glance at the items rolling around the rental car. She'd either have to pull off the highway or wait until she got to the airport to find her phone. Since Aaron would still be in the air, she reasoned, it couldn't be him. Anyone else would have to wait. She'd be parked at the airport in under an hour.

Susan pulled into a spot in the short-term parking lot and lunged over the passenger seat to retrieve the contents of her purse. Her pulse quickened when she saw that the missed call had been from Aaron. They must have arrived early, aided by strong tailwinds from the storm that was rolling in. She punched the playback button as she hurried to the terminal.

She was pushing through the heavy glass door when she stopped abruptly. Aaron's flight had been delayed on the tarmac for almost five hours before they'd been told that it had been canceled for mechanical issues. He was waiting in line at the ticket counter to book himself on another flight. Susan slumped against the large trash barrel outside the door.

"Are you all right, miss?" asked an older gentleman in an expensive-looking business suit. He peered at her over the top of his half-moon glasses.

"Yes, thank you." She straightened. "Fine. I've just had some disappointing news."

He nodded and moved on. Susan retraced her steps to her car and placed a call to Aaron.

"I'm so sorry, sweetheart," he said. "I can't believe the damned airline let us sit on that blasted plane all afternoon. If they would have returned to the gate and let us off, I'm sure I would have been able to get on another flight. As it is, I've been waiting in line at the ticket counter for almost an hour and there are still at least fifty people in front of me. Some customer service!"

Susan drew a deep breath. "Even if you leave within the hour, you won't make it to the party. And we're all scheduled to come back day after tomorrow. There's no point in your raising heaven and hell to get here now. Don't bother."

"This is all my fault. If I hadn't let my license expire, I'd be in Westbury right now. I hate not being there for Alex's party, but I mainly regret not having the time with you. I know I've been busy, but don't think for a moment that I haven't missed you. That's the worst part of all of it," he concluded miserably.

"Don't beat yourself up over this," Susan said. "You're not responsible for the flight cancellation, and I know you wanted to surprise Alex and spend time with me. You've worked yourself to the bone, and you deserved this break." She drew a deep breath. Now was the time to swallow her disappointment and comfort him. "Here's what you do. Get out of that stupid line and go straight to the nearest steakhouse. Order the biggest steak on the menu, then go home and watch the Padres on that enormous television of yours. I'll text you at the right moment, and you can call in your toast to Alex."

Aaron paused. "That sounds awfully tempting. Are you sure?"

"Positive. You need to do something fun for you. Since what we'd planned can't work out, you need to go to plan B."

"I'm exhausted. Sitting on the tarmac all day was horrendous. I'd love to get something to eat and take a long, hot shower. I'll be ready for your call. I have things I'd like to say to my big brother."

"And you will say them. You go eat, and I'll turn around and head back to Rosemont before the storm hits. I'll talk to you tonight."

"You're wonderful. You know that, don't you? One in a million. I'm the luckiest guy on Earth."

———

Alex Scanlon tossed his keys onto the kitchen counter and headed for the stairs. He was exhausted from the months of long days working on the fraud case as special counsel to Westbury. Marc was right—it was his birthday, and he was entitled to leave the office at a normal hour. All he wanted was to take a shower and park himself in front of the television. The Padres were playing, and it would be a real treat to watch his favorite team on the tube.

He was starting his assent of the stairs when his partner, Marc, called out to him. "Happy birthday!" He approached the stairway. "Where are you headed?"

"To the shower and then the couch. With no stops in between." He surveyed Marc. "Looks like you're going somewhere."

"I left the cord for my amp at The Mill last night. You know how hard it was to find a replacement last time I did that. I should have bought two, like you suggested. Anyway," he said, motioning to Alex. "Why don't you ride out there with me? It's a gorgeous drive. We can have dinner and come straight home." Alex began to shake his head. "It's your birthday," Marc pressed. "You deserve a decent meal. And they have that new chef. Everyone was raving about him last night. We'll be back in a couple of hours. I've got the game set to record."

Alex turned and retraced his steps down the stairs. "Sounds good. I'd rather watch the game when I can speed through the commercials. A good meal and a quiet evening are just what I want for my birthday."

———

Alex took two quick steps back and grasped the hostess stand to steady himself when fifty of his best friends yelled "Surprise!" as he entered the rear dining room at The Mill. He clutched his chest with one hand while turning to his partner.

Marc beamed. "Happy birthday, buddy."

Alex made his way around the room, shaking hands and accepting hugs. Waiters circulated with trays of appetizers

"You knew, didn't you?" Susan whispered in his ear as she drew him close.

"I'll neither confirm nor deny," he replied softly. He leaned back and looked at her. "Was it obvious?"

Susan shook her head. "Not really. You're a good actor. I was standing by the door and saw the look on your face as you approached. You were anticipating your next move—or so I thought."

"I wasn't sure. No one said anything. But I caught wind of the fact that you were in town, and Maggie didn't mention it to me. That was odd. And Marc has been secretive about something lately. I put two and two together."

"Glad you didn't spoil his surprise," Susan said, patting his arm. "Aaron planned to be here, too, but a comedy of errors got in the way."

"I'd have bet he wouldn't take time away from work. That seems to be a common failing of the Scanlon brothers."

"That's part of it. He can fill you in on the rest." Susan arched her brows at him. "The two of you need to learn how to lighten up."

"True enough. I'll talk to him. He doesn't want to become a workaholic and lose the best thing that's ever happened to him." Alex smiled at Susan.

"See that you do. Now, go mingle with your other guests."

The dinner of lobster bisque, an heirloom tomato salad, filet mignon, and tri-color potatoes au gratin was flawless. The new chef clearly intended to impress the crowd. The head waiter wheeled in a two-tiered cake dressed in fondant that replicated a stack of law books. Forty candles blazed on top. Servers circulated with glasses of champagne.

Alex inhaled deeply and blew out the candles in one long, sputtering breath. He closed his eyes, presumably making his wish, and the room erupted in applause when he opened them.

Susan walked over to him, cell phone and wireless speaker in hand, and motioned for the crowd to be quiet. "Alex's brother planned to be here today to mark this momentous occasion," she gestured to Alex and the cake, "but airline maintenance got in the way. I've got Aaron on the phone with me now, and he'd like to deliver a toast to his brother.

"I'm so sorry that I'm not with you all tonight to celebrate in person." The speaker projected the voice into the room. "Here's to a man that exemplifies courage, tenacity, and integrity. From working your way through college and law school to recovering from your horrific injuries in that crash—without a moment's complaint or self-pity—to your tireless efforts to bring the perpetrators of fraud to justice, you are a role model and tireless public servant. I also want to say, personally, that you have been a kind, supportive, and generous big brother. TO ALEX SCANLON!"

The room erupted in a chorus of "Hear, hear!" as Alex's friends raised their glasses and drank.

With the toast completed, Marc leaned in. "The weather's cleared enough to allow the fireworks to go forward. Grab your cake, and let's head out to the back lawn."

"You two go find a spot. I'll bring us all a piece of cake," John said to Maggie and Susan.

Mother and daughter linked arms and wove their way to the edge of the crowd. Susan sighed heavily and leaned against her mother.

"You miss him, don't you?" Maggie asked.

Susan nodded. "I just hope I don't have to spend my whole life missing him during every big occasion or event. I don't want that kind of life."

"I understand that, sweetie, but I think you may be jumping to conclusions. I know that this isn't what you want to hear—no one really likes to hear this—but my advice? Give it some time. Quit reading too much into this. Aaron's failure to get here doesn't mean he doesn't love you. The airlines got in the way here. Stuff happens. Don't condemn him for that."

Susan brushed the hair off her face. "You really think so?"

"I know so." Maggie smiled as John approached, juggling three plates loaded with thick slices of birthday cake. The first fireworks exploded over the crowd. "Let's enjoy this night and leave tomorrow's worries until tomorrow."

Maggie Martin settled their shopping bags on the bench of the booth at the ice cream parlor and handed Sophie and Sarah laminated menus featuring photos of burgers and fries, sodas and sundaes. They looked identical to the menus in use when she was their age; it was nice that some things didn't change. She looked at the shining faces of her granddaughters, seated opposite her. "You've both picked out wonderful outfits for the first day of school," she praised. "You've become quite the savvy shoppers, and you know what you like. And the outfits are both very different from each other."

Sarah nodded. "We each have our own style now, Gramma. We're too old to dress alike."

"I still like to, sometimes," Sophie cast her sister a reproachful glance. "But I'm okay with not doing it at school."

"I know," Sarah said. "We talked about this. I still like our matching jammies. That's at home. We can do it there and not get teased."

They're growing up, Maggie thought. How much longer will they want to come visit their grandmother? "Did you have fun this visit?"

Both girls nodded vigorously.

"What was the best part?"

"I liked the pottery place," Sophie replied.

"That was fun," Sarah agreed, "but I liked horseback riding the best. I'm going to ask Mom and Dad if I can take lessons when we get home."

"Did you have fun at Marissa's?"

Sarah shrugged. "It was fine. We made pizza and her mom taught us how to upside-down braid our hair. But her little sister is really sick. So it was kinda sad."

Maggie felt her chest tighten. "The last I heard, her medication was working," she said, a touch of chill in her voice.

Sophie shook her head sadly. "Not anymore. She had to go to the hospital again to get her blood cleaned. Like when we went to the hospital to see her last time we were here. Didn't Aunt Susan tell you?"

"She didn't mention it."

"Marissa is really scared for her," Sarah said. "So are we. We're praying for her, Gramma. Every night. Is there anything else we can do?"

"Praying is exactly what you should be doing for her," Maggie replied. *But there might be something else I can do,* she thought.

Chapter 36

Loretta Nash checked her watch. It was almost time for them to board their flight home. It had been an exhausting ten days at the transplant center. All the doctors agreed with the recommendation, and Nicole was now on the national transplant list. Loretta took Nicole's hand and approached the boarding agent. "We're here for early boarding of families with children," she said.

The agent took in Loretta's weary countenance and noted the hospital brochure protruding from her carry-on. "Let's move you two lovely ladies to the front of the line, shall we?" She reached for their tickets "You can go right on through. Why don't you sit up front, so we can help you be the first to get off the plane?" She watched Loretta lead the listless child down the Jetway to the plane.

Nicole, exhausted from her hospital evaluation, snuggled into her mother as soon as they sat down, and fell asleep. Loretta's mind was swirling with all she'd learned during their visit and sleep eluded her yet again.

One thing was certain: her deep, dark secret would come out. Nicole was almost certainly Paul Martin's daughter. In Scottsdale, that truth would not have been a big deal. But in Westbury, where Paul's wife was the owner of Rosemont and mayor of the town, that truth would be another matter. She would be the subject of gossip and the butt of crude jokes at every turn. She might deserve that treatment, but her children did not. Her innocent kids would be tarred and feathered with the same brush. Sean and Marissa were old enough to understand any cruel rumors they heard. Loretta's cheeks burned. For the thousandth time, she wished she could undo her past.

She considered again the possibility of leaving Westbury behind and returning to Scottsdale or moving somewhere new. As she thought about it, she knew it wasn't possible. She couldn't switch insurance plans now, and who would hire her and put up with her absenteeism? She was stuck. And as she thought this, she knew there was another reason she wanted to stay. Frank Haynes. Her feelings for him were complicated, and she didn't have the energy to think about them.

Loretta shifted carefully in her seat, taking care not to wake her sleeping daughter. She needed to convince Susan or Mike to be the donor if they proved to be a match for Nicole. But how was she going to do that?

Should she approach Maggie Martin? Loretta shuddered as she remembered their tense meeting last winter. She had tried to give Maggie the jump drive, which she'd felt certain contained incriminating evidence related to the fraud and embezzlement from the town.

Maggie hadn't given her the time of day. She had known that Loretta was Paul's mistress. But how? Had Paul told his wife about them, like he'd promised Loretta he would? Maggie was angry with her and didn't want anything to do with her, telling her to take whatever evidence she thought she had to the police and escorting her to the door. Loretta doubted that Maggie would be more receptive this time.

What if Susan and Mike wanted proof of Nicole's relationship to Paul? She didn't know if she could get Paul's body exhumed for DNA testing. Could she turn to Frank Haynes for help? Whatever good opinion of her he might have would surely be ruined by revelation of her affair with Paul Martin. Aside from her growing feelings for Frank, it was imperative that she retain her job at Haynes Enterprises. She had to tell Frank the truth and deal with the consequences.

She closed her eyes and smiled at the memory of Nicole's brief meeting with Susan in the hospital right before Maggie's wedding. Loretta had been astonished that Nicole had insisted Susan hold her doll while Nicole got dressed. She guarded her doll with the ferocity of a mama bear. And she'd renamed her doll Susan. There was an undeniable connection between those two. She'd seen it in that moment.

Loretta relaxed back into her seat. If she could just get to Susan, she felt certain that this kind and generous woman would agree to be a kidney donor for her half-sister. Loretta sent up a silent prayer. *Let her be a match.*

Frank Haynes hovered in front of Loretta Nash's desk shortly before two o'clock. "Let me know when you have the deposit ready. I'll run it to the bank, and you can go home. You've worked hard to get your desk caught up. I'm sure you want to spend time with Marissa and Sean after being away with Nicole."

Loretta Nash studied her mercurial boss carefully. Today was definitely one of his good days. He'd had a lot of those lately. Maybe now was the time. She knew she had to have this conversation with him and the sooner, the better. For Nicole's sake. "The deposit is ready now," she said, pointing to the bag on the corner of her desk.

"Then you're free to go—" he began before she cut him off.

"Actually, I'd like to talk to you about something," she said, twisting a strand of hair around her fingertip.

He nodded and waited.

"Can we go into your office?" she asked.

"Of course." He led the way and sat in the client chair next to her rather than on the other side of his massive desk. "What's troubling you? It isn't the cost of the transplant, is it? You know I've guaranteed anything that insurance won't cover."

"Yes, Frank, and I'm incredibly grateful for that. I can't tell you how much," she said, her voice cracking.

Frank Haynes waited patiently.

"I have something to tell you that you're not going to like. Something I'm not proud of, either." Loretta drew a deep breath and said in a rush. "I think Paul Martin is Nicole's father."

She paused, waiting for his reaction. Frank Haynes remained motionless in his chair.

Loretta continued. "I met Paul when I was in college, and we had an affair. I was so naive and stupid. He used every cliché in the book—how bad his marriage was and that he was waiting for the right time to leave

173

his wife and marry me. I bought it all, hook, line, and sinker." Loretta dropped her gaze. "I know now that they were all lies."

Frank Haynes absorbed this information. "You say you *think* he's Nicole's father. You aren't sure?"

Loretta glanced at him quickly, then looked away. "I got mad at him toward the end—right before he died—because he hadn't filed for divorce. I had a fling—out of revenge—to hurt Paul and bring him around. Instead, Paul died and I ended up pregnant. And now my daughter desperately needs a kidney transplant. A donation from a close relative would be the best solution. It could mean the difference between life and death." With this, Loretta began to cry. "I've made a mess of my life, and now my child has to pay for it."

Frank Haynes leaned forward and took both of her hands into his.

"I knew about your relationship with Paul and wondered if he was Nicole's father," he said softly.

Loretta raised her eyes to meet his. "How did you know about us?"

"I had a background check done when I hired you."

"So you're not shocked? You're not disappointed in me?"

Frank Haynes shook his head.

Loretta hung her head. Frank Haynes held her hands and let her cry. When her sobs began to subside, he handed her his handkerchief. "What can I do to help?" he asked.

"I have to talk to Susan and Mike. Except I'm not sure how I'm going to do it. I feel it would be best if I talked to Maggie first. She should be the first to know. This news will be devastating to their family. I feel terrible about it. That's why I kept the secret for so long. I didn't see any point in creating so much pain, especially since I wasn't sure." She began to cry again.

"So go tell Maggie," he said gently.

"She hates me," Loretta replied.

"She doesn't even know you."

"I was her late husband's mistress." Loretta wouldn't tell him about the night when she'd gone to Rosemont to give Maggie the copy of the jump drive.

Haynes lifted her chin so that he could look into her eyes. "I have my differences with Maggie Martin. Everyone knows that. There's not much we see eye to eye on. But she's a kind and fair person. She's not going to penalize Nicole for any grudge she may hold against you."

"I was hoping you might talk to her for me," Loretta pleaded. "Broach the subject?"

He shook his head. "You should be the one to ask her, Loretta. If she says no, I may have a trick or two up my sleeve." Would he really be willing to abandon his claim to Rosemont if it were necessary to help Loretta and Nicole? The thought set his stomach acids churning. He didn't even want to consider the idea. "Let me know how it goes. We'll take it from there."

Chapter 37

Susan Martin shoved her cell phone into her purse and made one final pass through her kitchen, making sure she'd turned off the oven and put all the food into the refrigerator. She'd taken the afternoon off to prepare a celebratory meal to congratulate Aaron on passing his medical boards. When he'd called two hours ago to tell her he couldn't make it, she'd been up to her elbows in preparations. This would be their first opportunity to spend a long evening together since she'd returned from her trip to Westbury—the trip that he had planned to take with her.

Aaron had met her return flight with flowers and a heartfelt apology. She knew he was terribly sorry for missing his brother's surprise party, but now this? She had to wonder if he really wanted to be with her. He was breaking another promise. All for his blasted career. She'd been longing to have him all to herself.

She'd bitten her tongue and agreed to meet him for a quick cup of coffee instead. It was time for a serious talk. She didn't want to spoil his special day, but she needed to find out where she stood and where they were headed. She couldn't allow things to continue as they were. She'd been second fiddle before, and she didn't want another relationship like that. If she had to break it off with him and start over in her search for Mr. Right, so be it. Susan checked her reflection in the mirror that hung by her back door before setting the alarm and heading out. She hoped she wouldn't lose her nerve.

They made plans to meet at a little dive around the corner from the hospital. He'd told her he could take a break and meet her there to celebrate.

Susan drove past the diner twice, looking for a parking spot. A stretch limousine idled in front, taking up the space of at least three parking meters. Annoyed, she finally pulled to the curb two blocks down the street. As she hurried to the diner, the chauffer got out and called her by name. She turned as he opened the rear passenger door. Aaron was waiting for her inside the limousine.

"What in the world?" she asked.

"I wanted to celebrate tonight, too. But I didn't want you to have to cook. I've been looking forward to taking you out."

"Wow," she said as she got in beside him. The chauffer pulled away from the curb, and Aaron opened a bottle of champagne and poured them each a glass. "To us."

Susan smiled. "To you, Dr. Scanlon."

As they sipped their champagne, all of her earlier arguments dissolved. She relaxed into Aaron's outstretched arm. "I've never been in a limo before. Pretty fancy. Look at all these cool lights. What do these buttons do?" she asked, pointing.

"Open the moonroof, I think. Want to try it?"

Susan nodded and Aaron opened the roof.

"So where are you taking me?"

"You'll see in about ten minutes," Aaron said. "I'm told it's one of the best restaurants in California. It sits on a cliff, overlooking the Pacific. The sunset should be spectacular."

"Did you rob a bank?" Susan asked.

"This is a special night, and I'm splurging on the most beautiful woman I know."

The restaurant was housed in a Spanish-style bungalow, retrofitted with floor-to-ceiling windows facing the Pacific. The interior was done in quiet taupe Venetian plaster and the tables were dressed in thickly starched linen. Low arrangements of burgundy roses graced every table. The maître d' whisked them to a secluded table in the corner by the windows.

They watched the clouds over the ocean turn from crimson to magenta as the sun sank below the horizon. They made their way through appetizers and entrees, relying on suggestions from their waiter and sampling everything brought to their table. They both remembered that the food was fabulous, but neither of them could later recall what they ate.

"I hope you've saved room for dessert," Aaron said.

"Honestly? I'm stuffed," Susan said.

"They have your favorite—bananas Foster."

"That takes forever to prepare. You won't want to wait."

"Actually, I ordered it when I made the reservation."

"Really? Aren't you wonderful? You've thought of everything."

Aaron signaled their waiter. The man brought the cart to their table and prepared the dessert with great showmanship. As he finished, the sommelier arrived and uncorked a bottle of champagne. Both men left the table together and Susan swore one of them nodded at Aaron in encouragement. She felt herself flush and raised her eyes to his. Could this be the moment she'd longed for since she was a teenager?

He smiled fleetingly and made a show of pouring them each a glass of champagne. Susan steadied her hand as she picked up her fork and quickly put it back down as Aaron pushed back his chair and dropped to one knee. He took her hands in his and spoke from his heart. "I adore you, Susan Martin. You're the woman I want to share all of life's joys and traverse all of life's hardships with. You are the kindest, most loving person I've ever known. Will you do me the great honor of marrying me?"

Susan cupped his face with her hands and kissed him. "Of course I will. You've been the one for me since the day we met. I love you completely." She broke off, crying.

Aaron handed her his handkerchief. He glanced into the restaurant and noted that all eyes were on their table. He smiled and made a thumbs up gesture, and the restaurant burst into applause.

"When I called you earlier to tell you I couldn't make it for dinner, I was afraid that you'd be really mad at me for interrupting your plans at the last minute. You hadn't started dinner yet or anything, had you?"

Susan snorted. "I most certainly had started dinner. I made your favorite cheesecake after work last night, and I'd taken the afternoon off to cook. Everything was well underway."

"I had no idea. I'm so sorry." He squeezed her hand. "I've got a lot to learn about domestic life. No wonder you paused for so long before responding. You were probably getting ready to let me have it."

"You have no idea," Susan replied. "If we'd met for a cup of coffee, like you led me to believe, we'd be having a much different conversation."

Aaron raised his eyebrows at her quizzically. "Tell me."

Susan leaned over and kissed him. "It doesn't matter now. Let's just concentrate on our future."

Maggie's phone rang as she was about to step into the shower. She glanced at the screen to see who was calling at this early hour and was alarmed to see that it was Susan. It would be three in the morning in California. Maggie answered the call on the second ring.

"What's wrong, honey?" she said, pulling her robe around her.

"Nothing's wrong, Mom. Everything's right." Susan paused and continued excitedly. "Aaron proposed!"

"That's wonderful! When?"

"Last night. I'm too excited to fall asleep. I've been waiting for it to be late enough to call you."

Maggie smiled. "You could have woken us up for this news." She was about to tell her daughter to give her all the details, but Susan launched into her tale without further invitation.

"Ohhhh ... so romantic. Did you suspect this was coming?"

"No. Not even during dinner. But my hopes got really high when our sommelier opened the champagne. He knew what Aaron was planning, and both he and Aaron looked like kids who got their hands caught in the candy jar. We were at a table in the corner and when the sommelier left us alone, Aaron dropped to one knee and proposed."

"Did you cry?"

"Of course I did. You know I did. I also got bananas Foster all over my dress."

Maggie laughed. "Congratulations to both of you. John's already left for morning surgery. I can't wait to tell him. He'll be so pleased. Do you have a ring?"

"Not yet. He decided to take a leaf out of John's book and let me pick it out. But he warned me that I shouldn't expect a four-carat diamond like yours. He can't afford that yet."

"Do you have any idea what you'd like?"

"An oval solitaire in platinum. Simple and elegant."

"That'll suit you to a tee," Maggie agreed. "Did you set the date?"

"Next summer. At Rosemont, of course," Susan said. "But way smaller than your wedding. I want to walk down those stairs and get married in front of the fireplace in the living room."

"That'll be the perfect setting. We can garland the banister and bank the mantel with flowers."

"And have a DJ on the terrace. I want to dance until the wee hours."

"Have you told your brother?"

"Not yet. It's too early to call him. I wanted to tell you first, anyway."

"I haven't talked to Mike since the miscarriage," Maggie said. "Is everything okay with them? Every time I call, I get their voice mail."

"Amy's doing better now; she's just gone back to work. And they've been busy with the beginning of the school year. I can't wait to tell the twins. They'll be so excited to be in another wedding. They had the time of their lives in yours." Susan yawned. "I've got to go to work today, so I suppose I should try to get some sleep. We'll talk more this weekend."

Chapter 38

Maggie forced herself through her morning routine to get ready for work. The email from Susan that she'd read while eating breakfast had shaken her. Nicole Nash needed a kidney transplant. She was now on the national donor list. Her granddaughters and their friend in Westbury—Nicole's older sister, Marissa—were scared and upset. Maggie felt certain that Marissa Nash and her brother weren't Nicole's only siblings; Mike and Susan were her half-brother and half-sister. Maggie didn't know much about transplants, but she knew that relatives were preferred donors. The decision she had been dreading was now upon her. She needed time to think things through, but right now she had work to do at Town Hall.

She got into her SUV and turned left out of her driveway. The blaring horn of a car in the oncoming lane jolted Maggie out of her reverie. She looked in the direction of the sound and headlights blinded her. Panicked, she stepped on the gas and the oncoming driver swerved, narrowly avoiding a collision.

Where did he come from? Still shaking, she turned onto a side street and pulled to the curb. Maggie lifted her tablet out of her briefcase and opened the picture she'd looked at dozens of times in the last few months. She turned the tablet first right, then left—examining the photo from every angle. There could be no mistake. Nicole Nash might not bear every feature of her late father, but the likeness was undeniable. She didn't need a DNA test to confirm that Nicole was Paul's daughter.

Maggie replaced the tablet and leaned back against her seat. If Nicole was really in need of a kidney transplant, she had to tell Susan and Mike. If they could save their half-sister's life, she wouldn't interfere with that.

Maggie breathed deeply. Revealing the truth about Nicole would open the whole can of worms about their father, and the timing couldn't be worse. Susan was so excited about her engagement to Aaron Scanlon. Would this news throw a pall on her happiness?

Maggie rested her head on the steering wheel. Donating a kidney— like all surgery—was risky. What if one of her kids were a donor and ended up damaging their remaining kidney in an accident later in life, leaving *them* on dialysis or in need of a transplant? Maggie didn't want to think about that possibility.

She turned her face upward. The warm morning sunshine streamed through her windshield. Her kids were grown, and in the end, it was their choice, not hers. If the little girl was really in need of a transplant, she would fly to California and tell her children.

Maggie started her car and headed toward Town Hall. She would verify Nicole's situation and book round-trip tickets to California for her and John.

———

"Frank," Maggie said, stepping into his office at Town Hall. "I'm wondering if you can confirm something."

"I'll try," he said.

"Loretta Nash works for you, right?"

"Yes. She's my financial analyst. Why?"

"Do you know if her daughter Nicole is on the transplant list for a kidney?"

Haynes let out a deep breath. News traveled fast in Westbury. "Nicole just got back from a transplant hospital in Indianapolis. She's on the list."

Maggie hesitated. "Will you do me a favor, Frank? Keep me posted on her condition?"

"I will," he replied. "They don't know how long it will take to find a donor."

"I don't think it'll be long."

Haynes thought he detected sadness behind her eyes.

"I'm counting on you, Frank. We've had our differences in the past, and now there's the question of the ownership of Rosemont." She held up her hand to silence him. "I know we agreed to keep that issue out of Town Hall, to let the lawyers handle it. I want to make sure that we set all of our other issues aside where this is concerned."

He nodded slowly. "Of course, Maggie. Why is this so important to you?" he probed.

"It just is. And I'd like you to keep our conversation private. Will you do that, Frank?"

Part of Frank Haynes wanted to run to Loretta with this information, but he instinctively knew better. "I will, Maggie. I'll let you know as soon as Loretta tells me anything."

"Will she confide in you?"

"She'll have to. I'm giving her the time off," he replied without adding that he was paying the bulk of the expenses for the transplant.

"Thank you, Frank. We can fight over the running of this town, but we shouldn't fight over this child."

Alex Scanlon reached for his cell phone and was about to tap the button that would send the incoming call to his voice mail when he noticed that the call was from Maggie. He hesitated, then swiped the screen and answered.

"Maggie, I'm in the middle of drafting a very difficult motion. Can I call you back in a bit?"

"Sorry to interrupt you, Alex, but I'll be on a plane shortly. John and I are about to board."

"I didn't know you were going anywhere."

"That's why I'm calling. This trip just came up, and I wanted you to know."

"Where are you headed?"

"California."

"To see your family?" Alex asked. "That's wonderful. Give my best to that brother of mine when you see him."

"I most certainly will," Maggie said.

"Have a good time. Call me when you get home. I must get back—" Alex began.

"That's not all," Maggie interrupted. "This isn't just a social visit." She drew a deep breath. "I'm telling you this in strict confidence, Alex, because your brother is engaged to Susan. I'm making the trip to tell Susan and Mike that their father had a long-standing affair with Loretta Nash before he died and that I believe Loretta's youngest child is Paul's daughter, their half-sister." She waited while he assimilated this information.

"That'll be a shock," he replied.

"There's more. The little girl—her name is Nicole—is extremely ill and needs a kidney transplant. The ideal donor would be a sibling—Susan or Mike—if either of them is a match."

"If I know Susan, she won't hesitate to agree to be a donor."

"That's what I think," Maggie said. "I'm sure she'll discuss it with Aaron. You're the only person I've told, other than John. I wanted you to know because you are both Aaron's brother and my dear friend. But I'd like you to keep this to yourself until after I've told my kids. I want them to hear it from me."

"You have my word on it, Maggie. Let me know when you've told them. And good luck. I know this won't be easy."

"Thank you, Alex. I'm going to need all the luck I can get."

Chapter 39

John lifted the arm rest and drew Maggie against him, his arm around her shoulders. He kissed the top of her head. "Thanks for coming with me," she murmured. "This is a long trip for just a weekend."

"No problem. I wasn't going to let you do this alone."

Maggie nodded. "It'll be good to see Sophie and Sarah, too. They're so excited to show me their new bedrooms. Mike painted them over the summer, and Amy bought new bedspreads that the girls picked out. And they remodeled the kitchen, too."

"Keeping busy after Amy miscarried. Probably a good idea."

"I feel bad that I didn't give Mike or Susan any hint of why we're coming. They think we miss them and are squeezing in a visit."

"We do miss them," John reminded her.

"I know. I just hope they won't feel too blindsided when I tell them about their father and their half-sister."

"You're still going to tell them everything?"

"I am. Once I start, I'm not holding back. Where does one deceit stop and another begin? I've been exhausted trying to figure that out. Keeping it from them was a mistake. I should have told them when I found out."

"You did what you thought was right at the time. Don't second-guess yourself now."

"I'm anxious to get this over with. By the time we go to bed tonight, everything will have been revealed."

"You could have stayed with one of us, you know." Mike gestured to his sister. "We both have room. You didn't need to book a hotel room," he said as they left the restaurant.

"We thought it would be better this way," Maggie replied. "We can't wait to see the girls and Amy and Aaron, but tonight we have something very serious to discuss and I wanted to have the two of you to myself.

I'd like you to come up to our room. John is going to park himself downstairs in the bar."

"For heaven's sake, Mom," Susan said, "John can stay. We don't mind him hearing anything you have to say, do we, Mike?"

Mike nodded his agreement. They rode the elevator to the eleventh floor and walked down the long hallway in anxious silence. Maggie switched on the harsh halogen lamps that cast a cold pallor over the room. Maggie turned the air conditioner off, and Mike took the desk chair while Susan perched on the end of the bed. They turned expectant eyes to Maggie. John leaned against the wall behind her.

"I've got some distressing things to tell you about your father. I discovered them shortly after he died and wrestled with the idea of telling you then. I thought I was doing the right thing—protecting you—but something's come up that requires me to tell you now."

"Come on, Mom," Susan began, but Maggie held up a hand to silence her.

"All I ask is that you hear me out, without interruption. There will be plenty of time for questions when I'm done. This will be hard on all of us, and if you're mad at me, I won't blame you. I've been mad at myself for a long time." She looked between the serious faces of her children. *Their world is about to be blown apart,* she thought, *and I hate being the one to light the fuse.*

"Paul was a wonderful father to both of you. He loved you unconditionally and none of what I'm about to tell you changes any of that." She took a deep breath and continued. "But he had a darker side as well. A secret life." She launched into the long, sordid tale.

Both children sat motionless, frozen by Maggie's account of their father's misdeeds and hidden world.

"Why in the hell didn't you tell us this at the time, Mom? You should have explained when you inherited Rosemont. We're not children, you know," Mike said, shoving himself to his feet.

Maggie tried to catch his eye, but he turned away. "I'm sorry. I should have. I see that now."

"Mike's right," Susan said, choking back tears. "It would have explained a lot. We would have understood your desire to move away and start over. As it was, we thought you were being impulsive, and we worried about you constantly."

"I'm not convinced of any of this," Mike said. "I don't know what to think. I've got to get some air." He strode to the door, and Maggie rose to go after him.

John reached out and grabbed her elbow. "Let him go, sweetheart. He'll be back."

"I've made a mess of this," Maggie said quietly.

"This is all so hard to understand, Mom. I wouldn't believe any of it, except for my gut feelings about Nicole. There's always been a powerful bond between us. I felt it when I first met her in the hospital last year, and it was even stronger when we spent the afternoon together at the pottery place. We have a special connection. And now I know why. She's my half-sister."

Maggie sat on the bed and put her arm around her daughter's shoulders. Susan swiveled to look into her mother's eyes. "This has been hell for you, hasn't it? I'm sorry that you had to bear all of this alone. You should have told us."

Maggie gestured to John. "I haven't borne it alone. And based upon Mike's reaction, I'm not sure I should have told you now."

"I'm going to get some ice," John said, picking up the ice bucket. "Give you two some time." He slipped quietly into the hallway.

"Did you have any clue before he died that Dad had another family?"

"No. I've gone over and over those last few years with your father. As my consultancy business as a forensic accountant took off, we grew more and more apart. We both traveled a lot and sometimes didn't see each other for a week or ten days. I always knew your dad resented the time I spent away from home. I grew weary of his criticism and was relieved that I didn't see much of him. I just wasn't paying attention. Thinking back, there were warning signs."

"Mike and I both knew that you and Dad weren't getting along at the end," she said. "We chalked it up to empty nest syndrome and thought you would work it out. To be truthful, though, neither of us liked how Dad spoke to you. He was so impatient and condescending. It didn't seem to bother you, so we let it go. And then Dad died." She stifled a sob.

The two women turned as John re-entered the room with a bucket of ice. Mike was on his heels.

Maggie began to rise, but he motioned her to remain seated.

"I'm sorry about that," Mike said. "I had to clear my head." He swung the desk chair to face his mother and sister and sat. "I hate to believe any of it, but in my gut, I know it's true. Dad kept up his calm, controlled exterior in front of us, but I overheard him on the phone once when I was in college. I'd come home unannounced. He thought he was alone in the house. He was arguing with someone about money. He was livid—almost in a rage. I'd never seen him like that. It scared me, so I went back to my dorm. I asked him about it later and caught him completely off guard. He was embarrassed and unnerved. Made up some crazy story about the bank messing up his account. I knew it was a lie, but I didn't want to challenge him." He turned to Maggie. "I should have told you, Mom. I'm sorry I didn't."

"It wouldn't have made any difference," Maggie said.

"If he embezzled two million from the college, why didn't they come after dad's estate?" Mike asked.

"I settled with the college for the proceeds of his employee life insurance. The trustees weren't anxious for this scandal to be made public. I think they were afraid they'd be criticized for their poor oversight."

"Rightly so," Mike said, cupping his head in his hands. "This is so hard to get my mind around."

"I know," Maggie nodded. "That's why I hired a private investigator. I wanted to find out what he'd done with the money he'd taken from the college. That's also why I flew out to Westbury when I learned about

Rosemont. I was searching for answers. I needed to understand who your father really was."

"Did you get any answers at Rosemont?" Susan asked.

Maggie shook her head.

"How did you find out about the other woman?" Mike asked.

"The private investigator," Maggie replied. "He found Loretta Nash in Scottsdale."

"And now she works for Frank Haynes?" Susan asked. "That's weird, isn't it?"

"I'm suspicious of Frank's motives in hiring her," Maggie agreed. "He was probably trying to dig up dirt on your father and use it against me. He hasn't, so far."

"So what prompted you to tell us now?" Mike asked.

Maggie cleared her throat, but Susan jumped in. "It's because Nicole is so sick, isn't it?" Susan raked her fingers through her thick blond hair. She turned to her brother. "Nicole is the daughter of dad's mistress. She's our half-sister, Mike." He stared back at her. "And our little sister needs a new kidney."

Susan stood up suddenly. "One of us could be the perfect donor." She spun on her heel to look at her mother. "That's why you two flew out here to tell us all this, isn't it? That little girl is desperately ill and needs a transplant. You thought one of us might want to be a donor. That's why you suddenly broke your silence." Susan turned away, letting the realization wash over her.

"It's a huge decision," Maggie said. "It's generally very safe to be a donor, but no medical procedure is risk-free. And it leaves you with only one kidney for the rest of your life."

"You only need one kidney," Mike supplied.

"I know, but if you donate one, you won't have a spare," Maggie said.

Susan walked to the window, pulling the drapery aside to stare at the busy California street below.

"I'm going to have to think about this, Mom," Mike said. "I'm not convinced that Nicole is our sister. I'll have to see the test results and talk to Amy about it. She needs to be part of this decision," He turned to John. "What do you think?"

"You need to sleep on this. It's a lot to take in. While there's some urgency to Nicole's situation, nothing needs to be decided overnight."

Susan let the drape fall back into place. "I know what I have to do. I have to get tested to see if I'm a match. That child is my sister." She drew a deep breath. "I'm going to be a perfect match. I know it in my bones. And I'm going to donate a kidney to Nicole."

Chapter 40

"Thanks for meeting me," Susan said as Dr. Aaron Scanlon slid into the booth next to her and wrapped his arms around her. She leaned in to kiss him.

"What's up?" he asked. "You sounded very mysterious on the phone. What could you be giving away that could change our lives?"

"A kidney," she replied and watched his face carefully.

He immediately grew serious.

"That could change our lives," he finally replied. "Are you on a donor list? Did you get contacted?"

Susan shook her head. "I need to tell you the rest of the story. The real reason my mom and John are here."

The waitress stopped by their table. Aaron ordered them each the daily special without bothering to look at the menu and sent her on her way. He turned back to Susan. She took a deep breath and told him about her father's secret life, ending with the revelation that Nicole Nash was a very sick little girl. She leaned back into the booth. "She's my little sister, Aaron."

"I'm sure you think that, but you can't be sure. You just got this news and you're emotional—"

"I know it, Aaron. I look at her photo, and I know it's true. So does my mom."

"And if she is your sister?"

"Then I need to get tested to see if I can be a donor. I've done the research, but I don't have to tell you. You're a doctor. Kidney transplants are done all the time, and they save lives. You can live a long life with only one kidney."

Aaron nodded. "That's true, if nothing goes wrong. But if you ever injure your kidney, you'd be in trouble."

"Seems like an unlikely 'what if,'" Susan retorted. "And very wrong to hang onto an extra kidney that could save Nicole's life, just so I have a 'spare' on hand."

"That's if you're even a match," Aaron said. "And there's always the possibility of infection after the surgery. You're allergic to penicillin and other antibiotics. As a doctor, I'd advise you to be very hesitant to undergo unnecessary surgery."

"It isn't like this is cosmetic surgery. This is lifesaving for Nicole." She touched his cheek. "I think you're scared."

He looked long into her eyes, then nodded.

"I'm scared, too," Susan said. "I'm the biggest wimp there is when it comes to medical things. I don't even get a flu shot," she said and immediately regretted it. "I know I told you I'd gotten one, but I chickened out at the last minute."

"This will be a whole lot harder than a flu shot," he pointed out.

"I know that. But if I'm a match—if I could donate a kidney and save my sister's life—I have to do it. I'd like your blessing and to have you by my side."

The waitress placed plates of steaming chicken and biscuits in front of them. Susan ate silently, watching Aaron in profile as he picked at his food.

"I understand," he finally said. "If the situation were reversed, I would do the same thing."

"Then you'll support my decision to get tested and move forward as a kidney donor if I'm a match?"

Aaron nodded.

"Can you take off work to be with me during the transplant?" she asked. "Nicole will be having it done at Indiana University's transplant center."

"I wouldn't let you undergo anything like this unless I were right there with you. I'll see if I can get privileges to observe during surgery."

"Thank you, sweetheart. I'll be a lot less nervous with you there. I'm sure Mom will be, too."

"Do you have any idea when this might take place?" he asked.

"I'm getting tested this week," she said. "That's why I had to see you today. I didn't want to start down this road if you didn't know about it."

"I appreciate that," he said. "I don't think I could have talked you out of it."

"No. You couldn't have." She cleared her throat and picked up her fork. "If I donate a kidney, what happens to her?"

"This isn't my field, but I think they'll keep her in the hospital until they're confident the new kidney is working and the surgical site hasn't gotten infected. They'll send her home on immunosuppressants, with instructions to avoid anyone that might be ill."

"That doesn't sound too bad," Susan said. "Can she live the rest of her life with my kidney?"

"She can," he said. "Her childhood should be largely unaffected."

"What about my recovery?"

"Yours should be easy. A day or two in the hospital, at most. They'll do some testing to make sure the remaining kidney is doing its job. If you don't contract an infection, you'll be fine."

"You hear a lot about hospital infections these days, and it's scary," Susan said.

"It's a factor, for sure. I'll give you special soap to use when you shower and shampoo during the last few days before the surgery. We've had good luck with it in our practice."

Susan looked into his eyes. "Thank you for supporting me in this. It means the world to me. Nothing is going to go wrong. We're going to have a big splashy wedding at Rosemont, and I'm going to be your wife. We'll have a passel of kids and live happily ever after."

Chapter 41

Loretta Nash waited along the side of the road across from Rosemont and watched as Dr. Allen's Suburban exited the driveway and turned in the direction of Westbury Animal Hospital. She looked at the clock on the dashboard of her car. It was shortly before seven in the morning. She'd dropped her kids off with the babysitter in the hope of catching Maggie Martin at home before she headed to the office. Loretta didn't want to ring the doorbell before seven. In fact, she didn't want to ring the doorbell at all. But she knew she had to do this, for Nicole.

Loretta waited for the traffic to clear, then pulled her car onto the driveway and slowly proceeded through the trees to come to a stop in the large clearing in front of the house. She gripped the steering wheel as she scanned Rosemont's stone facade, looking for movement at any window and seeing none.

Loretta opened her car door and forced herself to climb the stone steps to Rosemont's massive mahogany door. She took a deep breath and said a silent prayer. *Please, Lord, guide my words and open Maggie's heart.* Loretta lifted her hand and grasped the iron door knocker, letting it fall loudly into place.

Loretta stood, rooted to the spot, shifting her weight from foot to foot. After what seemed like an eternity, Maggie opened the door. The two women stood, staring at each other. "Mayor Martin," Loretta began, "I'm sorry to disturb you so early."

"You'd better come in," Maggie said. "I've been expecting you." She motioned Loretta to follow her through the house to the large farmhouse table in the breakfast room and pulled a chair out for Loretta. "Can I get you a cup of coffee?"

Loretta shook her head. Maggie sat opposite her and waited.

Loretta twisted a lock of her hair. "I know you hate me, Mayor Martin," she began.

Maggie shifted in her chair. "I don't—"

"Please. Let me get through this," Loretta interrupted and placed her palms solidly on the table. "Before I lose my nerve."

Maggie nodded.

"I wouldn't blame you. I've done a lot of things in my life that I'd like to undo. My relationship with Paul is one of them," she looked down at her hands. "I'm very sorry that I hurt you. And now I have something even harder to tell you." Loretta's voice cracked. "I believe that Paul is my daughter Nicole's father." She paused and cast a quick glance at Maggie, who remained motionless. "Nicole is very sick. She has a congenital birth defect that has caused her kidneys to fail and she needs a transplant." Her voice was barely audible as she said, "Your children are the best possible donors for Nicole. They might be the only ones who could save her life." Loretta choked back a sob. "I'm going to contact them, and I wanted to tell you myself."

Maggie looked at the terrified young mother in front of her. She leaned across the table and brought both of her hands to rest on Loretta's. "I know," she said softly.

Loretta gulped and turned her face to Maggie's. "What do you know?"

"All of it," Maggie said. "Susan sent me a photo of you and your children, taken in the hospital. I knew the moment I laid eyes on Nicole that she was Paul's. I tried to talk myself out of it." Maggie sat back in her chair. "But I knew. Susan heard about Nicole's condition through my granddaughters. I thought that she was getting better. But then she took a turn for the worse."

"I was so hopeful earlier this summer." Loretta glanced out the window. "But here we are."

"I'm so sorry," Maggie said.

Loretta turned back to her. "This will come as quite a shock to your children, but I've got to call them. Nicole has no time to lose. I was hoping you wouldn't turn them against me," she concluded in a rush. "For Nicole's sake."

Maggie held Loretta's gaze. "I've already spoken to them," she said. "When?"

"John and I flew out to California last weekend. I needed to tell them about their father in person," she said. "Just like you're doing now."

"And?" Loretta felt like she couldn't breathe.

"They've both agreed to be tested. Whichever one is the best match will donate a kidney." Maggie watched as relief washed over Loretta Nash.

"They said yes?"

Maggie nodded. Loretta sat, trying to take it all in. She turned to Maggie. "You both went all the way out there because you knew Nicole needed a kidney from one of them?"

Maggie nodded again.

"That was a very kind thing, Mayor Martin."

"For heaven's sake, call me Maggie. I'd be lying if I told you that this hasn't been difficult for me, but when I thought of your sweet little girl, I knew what I had to do." Maggie went to a drawer in her kitchen and pulled out a pen and piece of paper. She printed her children's phone numbers on it and handed it to Loretta. "They're expecting your call."

Loretta folded the paper carefully and put it into her purse. She rose from the table and faced Maggie. "You'll never know how grateful I am," she said.

Maggie walked with her to the door. "I did some research. I understand that kidney transplants in children are very successful."

Loretta tried to smile. "That's what they tell me."

"We pray for Nicole and your family every day, Loretta," Maggie said.

Loretta walked down the steps. She had been so scared of Maggie, but Maggie had been kind. This wasn't at all like the last time. She turned back to Maggie, who was silhouetted in the open door. Paul had lied about his wife all along. Maggie Martin wasn't a cold, calculating shrew.

"You were brave to come here, Loretta," Maggie called as Loretta got into her car. *I shouldn't have been so rude to her when she came to see me last winter,* Maggie thought as she watched her drive away. She'd been angry—even cruel—and turned Loretta out without giving her a chance speak. *I wonder what she wanted those months ago.*

Frank Haynes was already hard at work in his office when Loretta rushed through the door of Haynes Enterprises an hour later than usual that morning. He immediately got up and went to her desk.

"Is Nicole all right?" he asked.

Loretta nodded. "Yes, she's about the same."

"I was worried when you were late, without calling."

"I'm sorry." She looked up at him. "I went to see Maggie Martin this morning."

"How did that go?"

"You were right. She was nice."

He nodded, willing her to go on.

"Said she'd known about Nicole when she'd first seen her picture." Loretta hung her purse on the hook under her desk. "Did you know that she and her husband flew to California to tell her children about Nicole? About everything?"

"I didn't know that."

"It was kind of them to do that."

Frank Haynes tapped his pencil into his palm. "So what will you do next? Are you going to call her kids and ask them about getting tested to be donors?"

Loretta smiled. "I didn't have to. They'd already agreed after speaking with their mother. I spoke to both of them as soon as I left Maggie and put them in touch with the people at the transplant center. They said they'd get tested right away."

"That's wonderful news," he said, thinking that now he didn't have to offer up his interest in Rosemont in exchange for their cooperation.

"With any luck, she'll have her transplant by the end of the year," Loretta said. "Maybe a new kidney by Christmas."

Frank Haynes stopped and stared. If the transplant were this year, he'd have to tap into his Rosemont fund to pay for it. He wouldn't have the money to buy out Maggie. He shook his head, pushing the thought from his mind. *No point in thinking about that now. These things take more time than anyone expects.*

"Good news. I'll leave you to it," he said and retreated to his office.

Chapter 42

Frank Haynes sat on the concrete bench reading the *Westbury Gazette*, while he waited for the attendants to finish the Super Deluxe Car Wash that he got every week on his Mercedes sedan. A shadow fell on the page, and he turned to see what was blocking the light.

"Charles," he said, trying to conceal his annoyance.

"Knew I'd find you here, Frankie," Delgado replied. "You're as regular as clockwork with that car of yours."

"So how are you?" Haynes forced himself to make an effort. "You got out on bail right away."

Delgado snorted. "Of course I did."

"How's it going? What does your lawyer tell you?"

"That their evidence is almost nonexistent, and he doesn't expect to go to trial. Says he'll get it all dismissed on motions."

"There you go, then. It'll all turn out fine."

"Turn out fine?" Delgado raised his voice.

Haynes stood and began to move away. "Keep your voice down. We're not supposed to be seen together, remember?"

Delgado followed. "It doesn't matter to me if we're seen together. I've already been arrested."

"And you just said you'll get off."

"With my reputation tarnished, and stripped of my council seat."

"If your lawyer gets you off, they'll have to restore you to the council."

Delgado paused. "I guess you're right about that. And I still have enough clout to win an election against that idiot Knudsen, if he gets grandiose ideas and decides to run against me."

"You mean you have enough money to buy the election," Haynes observed.

Delgado smirked. "Same thing."

"Why are you here?" Haynes asked. "I've never known you to be particular about your car."

"I wanted a word with you, Frankie. Thought it would be good to run into you someplace. Make it look like a chance encounter."

Haynes waited.

"I'm following my attorney's advice—keeping my hands clean and leaving it to him. But I want you to know, Frankie, that I've got my boys out on the street, watching everything and everybody. I'm not going to get caught flat-footed again. If someone needs to be taken care of, I'm ready to do it." He leaned in close. "Including you, Frankie. Don't go gettin' no ideas of goin' to the authorities to save yourself. I'll know if you do, and I won't like it." He chuckled. "That Forest Smith kid should be shoppin' for a coffin. Our precious mayor and the Wheeler kid are in my crosshairs, too." Delgado glanced at Haynes, then turned and retraced his steps to the bench.

"You car's ready, Mr. Haynes," the attendant said, extending his palm for the customary tip. Frank Haynes' hand shook as he fumbled in his pocket for his wallet.

Chapter 43

John Allen got out of bed each weekday morning by four fifteen in order to be at Westbury Animal Hospital for morning surgery by five thirty. October twenty-fourth was a busy surgery day. He slid quietly out of bed, as was his custom, so he didn't disturb his sleeping wife, and padded noiselessly toward the bathroom.

"It'll be starting in an hour," Maggie said from the wing chair in their bedroom, not more than four feet from him.

John started and grabbed his chest.

"Sorry. Did I scare you?"

"Yes, you scared me!" John said, doubled over and breathing hard. "I didn't hear you get out of bed. When did you get up?"

"About an hour ago. I came over here and started reading emails on my phone. I didn't want to go downstairs. The minute you do that, Eve and Roman want to go out and those cats insist on being fed."

"Too nervous to sleep?"

Maggie nodded, even though he couldn't see her in the dark.

"Are you going back to bed, or can I turn on the light?"

"I'm up. I may as well get ready and go to work."

"Will you track the auction online?"

"No. That would drive me crazy. Besides, I have another transit committee meeting." She rolled her eyes at him in the mirror. "You know how riveting those are. But it'll force me to stay away from the Internet and focus on something besides this auction. And our future at Rosemont," she concluded glumly. "Gordon Mortimer is attending the auction, and he promised to call me as soon as it's done."

"I think we're going to get all the money we need. And if we fall a bit short, I've got some savings I can get to."

Maggie turned and smiled at him as he stepped into the shower. "You're as kind and generous as you are good-looking. If only the appraisal of Rosemont hadn't come in so high," she said, raising her voice to be heard over the running water of the shower. "We've got to come up with two million four hundred seventy thousand dollars in order to buy out Frank's share."

"The good news is," John yelled, "that this place is worth almost five million."

I hope we'll be able to continue to call it home, Maggie thought as she glanced at the clock on her vanity. We'll know soon enough.

Mayor Maggie Martin called the meeting of the transit committee to order promptly at nine o'clock and did her best to pay attention to every speaker. If later asked to summarize what was discussed, she would have been hard-pressed to supply any details. When the meeting finally adjourned shortly before eleven, she darted out of the room and back to her office before anyone could detain her.

She asked her assistant to hold her calls and shut the door to her office firmly behind her. She dug into her purse for her cell phone and was gratified to see a missed call from Gordon Mortimer. He hadn't left a message, and she punched in his number. He answered on the first ring.

"Mayor Martin," he said, sounding chipper. "The auction has been completed and all items sold."

Maggie remained silent, willing him to get to the point: How much money had they raised?

"You'll be wanting to know the winning bids. Do you have your bid sheet handy?"

"I don't need to know the amount for each item," she said, stopping herself from snapping. "You can email that to me. Right now, I'm most anxious for the total."

"Of course. The silver that I recommended you place in this auction did rather well," he said officiously. "Our joint efforts—Sotheby's and mine—produced a lot of interested bidders." He sounded pleased with himself.

Maggie wanted to scream at him. *Get to the point!*

"Taken together, your share is one million five hundred and sixty thousand dollars."

Maggie's pulse raced. "That's more than you predicted on its best day."

"It is indeed. We know how to place things for auction."

"So what did the Martin-Guillaume Biennais go for?"

"That, madam, was a disappointment. As we advised, waiting for the Paris auction—"

"What did it sell for, Mr. Mortimer?" she asked, cutting him off.

"Your share will be eight hundred seventy thousand dollars."

Maggie did a quick sum on a scratch pad and slumped into her desk chair. That left them forty thousand short. She knew she and John could scrape together the remaining money, but they wouldn't be able to offer more than the required minimum to buy out Frank Haynes. He would almost certainly offer two million six or seven, to assure that he ended up with Rosemont. She had wanted to beat him at his own game, but that was now impossible. She should have forced him to sue her so that she had time to wait for the Paris auction. Then she might have had the money she needed. But the die had been cast. Her ace in the hole—the Martin-Guillaume Biennais tea set—had sold for less than she needed.

"Mayor Martin? Are you still there?"

Maggie forced herself back to the present. "I'm here," she said, fighting back tears, "but I have to go. Please send me an email with all the details, and thank you for all you've done," she said before she ended the call.

Maggie rose and walked to the window of her office. She should be grateful for all that Rosemont had brought into her life. If it weren't for Rosemont, she wouldn't have found Eve in the snow outside her library doors that first fateful night in the house. Eve had led her to her wonderful new husband. She was mayor of Westbury because she had moved to Rosemont. Even with all of its headaches and challenges, being mayor was the most fulfilling job she could imagine. Not to mention that, if she had to sell her half of Rosemont to Frank Haynes, she'd suddenly have more than two million dollars in cash. *Why in the world do I feel like my heart is being ripped from my chest?*

Maggie returned to her desk, shut down her computer, and said goodnight to her assistant on her way out the door. Dr. John Allen would have to make time for an unscheduled visitor. The only thing she needed right now was to have his arms around her.

Chapter 44

Frank Haynes looked up from the spreadsheet he was studying on his computer. Loretta Nash had been on the phone all morning and from the snippets of conversation that he'd heard from his office, she was not attending to company business. Although her back was to him, something in the tone of her voice drew his attention. He rolled his chair closer to his door and leaned toward her, straining to hear the conversation she was making an effort to conceal.

"The transplant has been scheduled for the Tuesday after Thanksgiving," Loretta stated. "We've already found the donor, and everything's been scheduled. My daughter's half-sister is taking time off of work to donate her kidney. It's all arranged."

Loretta's back stiffened as she listened to the lengthy reply.

"What do you mean, my insurance won't authorize the transplant? How can they disapprove it? You're the ones that tell them it's necessary, aren't you?"

Again, Loretta listened, clicking her pen repeatedly.

"No, I don't understand at all. You told me Nicole needs a transplant. How can they say that it's premature—that she should stay on dialysis longer? Why can't you explain it to them?"

She stood and swayed from side to side as she listened.

"I don't agree that you've done all you could do! Where does this leave Nicole? She's not going to get a lifesaving transplant because some pencil pusher wants to save the insurance company money? Why would I give a damn about that?" she asked, her voice hard and shrill.

"No, I don't want to schedule Nicole for dialysis. We can do that here in Westbury. I want the transplant booked. I can pay for it myself—without insurance," she said, thinking of Frank's promise to help. Haynes strained even harder to hear. "How much will it all cost?"

Loretta listened. "That doesn't sound too bad." She sat down in her chair and picked up a pen to scribble numbers on a piece of paper. "That's just the acquisition cost?" she asked, writing furiously. "I didn't realize everything wasn't included."

Frank Haynes watched as she took down a long list of numbers.

"That's more than a million dollars!" Loretta shrieked. "No. I don't think my guarantor can pay all that." She stifled a sob. "So I'm supposed to put her back on dialysis and wait for her condition to get worse? Is that what you're telling me?" Loretta stabbed the pen into the paper.

"I'll be sure to do that," she was losing her grip on her self-control. "Have yourself a great day while my child suffers," she yelled into the phone before she slammed it down on its receiver.

Loretta spun around quickly and caught sight of Frank Haynes as he tried to wheel his chair back behind his desk. She threw her pen onto her desk and stalked into his office.

"Did you hear that?" she demanded.

He knew better than to deny it. He nodded.

"So my insurance company says she hasn't been on dialysis long enough. They want to see if she'll recover."

"I thought this was a birth defect and wasn't something she could recover from."

"That's exactly right. That's why the doctors recommended a transplant now."

"Can't they tell that to the insurance company and convince them to change their mind?"

"They said they tried. We now have to appeal the denial, which they've already started. But that will take months," she said as she crumpled into the chair across from his desk.

"The transplant is set for the end of November, isn't it?"

Loretta nodded.

"Surely they'll process the appeal by then. Is the transplant center giving them all the information they need?"

"They promised that they will."

"There you are. Everything is in the works," he said, amazed at himself for being the voice of optimism.

"Do you really think so, Frank?" she said in a small voice. "Susan has agreed to be the donor, and it's all set up. What if they postpone it and she changes her mind? Or Nicole gets really bad and dies before she can get the new kidney?" Tears began to course down her cheeks. "I'm so afraid, Frank."

He came around his desk and took her hands in his. "We won't let that happen, remember? You keep that November surgery date, and I'll pay for anything that isn't covered by insurance."

Loretta wiped at a tear that had fallen onto their joined hands. "That's a very sweet offer, Frank, but a kidney transplant costs way more than you know." She brought her face up to look at him. "It'll cost more than a million dollars, Frank."

Frank Haynes was proud of himself for not flinching.

"We'll cross that bridge when we come to it" was all he said.

Chapter 45

Frank Haynes looked up from his computer screen to see Nicole Nash staring at him silently from the door to his office. She was wearing the same long blue dress that he'd seen on a lot of little girls in his fast-food restaurants. She was holding a Styrofoam cup and spoon.

He cleared his throat. "Good morning, young lady."

Nicole held out the items in her hands.

"What have you got there?" he asked, getting out of his chair and coming to meet her.

"Soup," she said. "Like Mrs. Walters makes."

"Ah, I see," he said, looking into the cup containing two sizes of paper clips and a handful of rubber bands. "Chicken noodle?"

The little girl smiled and nodded vigorously.

"Thought so. With extra noodles," he said, pointing to the rubber bands. "Just the way I like it."

"It's for you," she replied.

Frank Haynes smiled and took the proffered cup and spoon. "If I finish this, will you make more?"

Nicole beamed.

"Thank you, Nicole," he said as Loretta Nash hung up the phone and called to Nicole.

"We can't bother Mr. Haynes," she scolded. "I told you, Nicole." She turned to her employer. "I'm so sorry about this, Frank. Mrs. Walters has a cold, and I can't risk having Nicole catch anything. Not this close to the surgery. She has to be healthy, or they won't do the transplant."

"I understand completely. She's been no trouble whatsoever." He looked down at the cup in his hands. "It's been a very long time since anyone's made me paper clip soup." Had anyone—ever—made him paper clip soup?

"I appreciate that, Frank."

Haynes waved away her thanks. He stood suddenly. "I've got to go out."

"Will you be back today?"

Frank Haynes looked at his watch and an unfamiliar warmth spread from his heart to his head. He had a plan. "I don't think so," he said. "You can lock up when you make the bank deposit and go home. I'll see you in the morning."

He whistled as he made his way to his car.

Frank Haynes pulled into the parking lot of the big-box toy store. He'd never been inside one of these places and almost beat a hasty retreat when he stepped through the automatic doors. He stood, rooted to the spot, and surveyed the rows of floor-to-ceiling racks filled with every toy imaginable. Haynes was glad that the parking lot was nearly empty. Fighting through a crowd in this place would be intolerable. He vowed he'd never come here on Black Friday or Christmas Eve.

A clerk at the customer service desk called, "Sir, may I help you find something?"

Haynes tore his eyes away from the scene in front of him and approached the young man.

"Mr. Haynes," the man said. "I worked for you all through high school and college."

Haynes nodded. He didn't recognize the man but knew he'd employed most of the town's teenagers at one time or another. "And now you're here," he stated the obvious.

"I'm the manager," the man stated proudly. "I got promoted last week. I learned a lot when I worked for you."

Haynes looked at him closely. Was he being sarcastic? He didn't think so. "I'm glad to hear it. Congratulations."

"Are you looking for something special?" the young man asked.

"I am. I want to buy toys for a little girl. She's four."

"What does she like?"

Haynes rubbed his hand over his chin. "She's got a doll—about this big," he said, indicating a two foot stretch with his hands. "That doll goes everywhere with her." He wracked his brain. "She likes to pretend to cook. And she wears that long blue dress the little girls love," he concluded, looking at the man hopefully.

"How much do you want to spend?"

Frank Haynes shrugged. "It doesn't matter. I'm not on a budget."

"I've got just the things," the delighted man replied. Today's sales would look good for his first week as a store manager.

After he and the store manager had somehow managed to wrangle all of his purchases into his Mercedes Sedan, Frank Haynes drove over to Pete's Bistro for a cup of coffee and a sandwich. Even the front passenger seat was loaded with toys. He had books, puzzles, art supplies, and doll clothes, but the pièce de résistance was the wooden kitchen set and play food. Haynes was certain Nicole would love that. The manager assured him the kitchen set's "some assembly required" would pose no problem; he'd easily be able to put it together in under an hour. The set came with all the hardware and tools he needed. Haynes hoped so.

He finished his sandwich, refilled his coffee, and got back into his car. Loretta and Nicole should have left by now. He'd bring in all of his purchases, set up a play area for Nicole, and be home in time to walk Sally.

Haynes pulled to the curb at the entrance to Haynes Enterprises and quickly unloaded his car. He eyed the waiting area and decided that there would be just enough room between the filing cabinet and the front wall to install the play kitchen. It would even add a "child friendly" air to his business. Why hadn't he thought of this before?

He unboxed the kitchen set and inventoried the parts and tools against the packing list. He cursed under his breath and checked his watch. He'd have just enough time for a trip to Westbury Hardware before it closed. He grabbed the parts list, circled the items he was missing, and set out. He was back, half an hour later, with eighty dollars' worth of nuts, bolts, and tools. The clerk smiled when Haynes had handed him his list; they were very familiar with this play set and had supplied missing parts and tools on numerous occasions in the past. "The last hour before closing on Christmas Eve? Busiest hour of the whole year, selling parts for bikes and toys."

Haynes secured the last bolt at ten o'clock. He cleared away the trash and began to move the toy kitchen into place. When he'd put the first two pieces into position, he knew he'd misjudged the space. There wasn't enough room. He stepped to the front door and surveyed the scene in front of him and shook his head slowly. He'd have to move the filing cabinet into his office.

It was fully loaded and weighed a ton. Haynes managed to remove the top drawer of the cabinet and was able to drag and push it into its new location in his office. He put the remainder of the kitchen set into place and mopped his brow with his handkerchief. He retraced his steps to the entrance to view his handiwork and nodded.

He checked his watch. Sally would be frantic without him; he needed to get home. He stacked the puzzles and art supplies on the coffee table and placed the stiff, plastic clam-shell packages of pots and pans, dishes and food on the floor next to the kitchen. *I should let Loretta deal with opening these,* he thought. He reached for his pocket knife and slit open the package of pots and pans. He placed the Dutch oven and a frying pan on the pretend burners and stowed the remaining pans in the drawer below the play oven. He picked up the next package and was soon arranging fake apples, bananas, and oranges in a bowl that he placed on top of the refrigerator. He'd need to stop by the toy store tomorrow and buy the toaster and mixer he'd seen. He gave the room one last glance and pushed through the front entrance, locking the door behind him.

It was almost midnight when he pulled into his garage. "Sorry, old girl," he said, greeting Sally who had been anxiously awaiting his return. She shot out the kitchen door and into her favorite corner of the yard to take care of her business. Haynes leaned against the door frame and rubbed the left side of his back. He'd be sore tomorrow, no question about it. Haynes smiled. He'd had the time of his life.

This must be what it feels like to be a father on Christmas Eve. Haynes sighed deeply, stepped into the yard, and whistled for Sally. "Come on, girl," he said as she raced to her master. "We've got to get to bed. I need to be there to see Nicole's face when she walks through the door tomorrow morning."

———

Haynes arrived at his office at six forty-five. His body was, indeed, rebelling from the unaccustomed activity of the day before. Despite his aches and pains and lack of sleep, Haynes was in a jubilant mood.

He spotted Loretta and Nicole as they got out of Loretta's car and made their way to the entrance of Haynes Enterprises. He positioned himself by the door to his office, pretending to look for something in the filing cabinet that he'd moved there less than twelve hours earlier. He held his breath as Loretta pushed through the door and held it open for Nicole.

"Mommy. Look!" she squealed, dropping her beloved doll and racing across the room to the play kitchen.

Loretta stood, speechless, and watched her daughter. She turned to Haynes' office and their eyes locked. He smiled and shrugged. Loretta burst out laughing.

"Is this what you hurried off to do yesterday?" she asked as they both approached the scene where Nicole was excitedly opening doors and drawers and pulling out their contents. He nodded. "Oh, Frank," she said, grasping his hand and squeezing it.

He squatted down and spoke to Nicole. "Since you're such a good cook, I decided you need a kitchen of your own."

Nicole spread her arms and flung them around his neck. He rocked back on his heels, bringing his arms up to hug the little girl nestled in his arms and drinking in the joy of holding a child. She reached up and took his hand, pointing to his thumbnail. 'Scratchy" was all she said.

Haynes nodded. "I gouged it when I was putting your kitchen together. Building things isn't my strong suit." He gave Loretta a sheepish smile.

Nicole brought it to her lips and gave the injured thumb a wet kiss. "Mommy says you don't have anyone at home. I'll kiss your boo-boo."

Haynes turned his face to the floor and coughed. "Will you make us lunch today?" he asked.

She nodded.

"And if you get tired of working in the kitchen, I've got some things for you over there." He pointed to the toys he'd stacked on the coffee table.

Loretta gasped. "Have you lost your mind? This must have cost a fortune."

Frank Haynes got slowly to his feet. "Can't remember when I've ever enjoyed spending my money more than I did on this."

Chapter 46

Frank Haynes sat in his Mercedes sedan in the familiar opening in the road that ran below Rosemont. He'd intended to drive to clear his head. But Rosemont asserted her pull on him, as she so frequently did, and here he was.

He leaned back in his seat and looked up at Rosemont's rear facade, the bright afternoon sun shimmering off her mullioned windows. The warm stone walls seemed to glow from within. He knew every detail of her sweeping roofline and elaborate chimneys, every corbel and elaborately carved stone ornament. How he loved her.

He'd wanted to live there his entire life. He'd been coming to this spot to look at her—lust after her—for decades. The desire to accumulate enough money to buy Rosemont was the principal reason he'd been so successful in his business. And now, after all of these years, he had the legal right to buy out Maggie Martin's share and own Rosemont himself. Not only that, but he had enough cash on hand to buy her out. He felt certain that his planned bid of two million eight hundred fifty thousand dollars would carry the day. He doubted that Maggie would be able to scrape together the cash to offer the minimum bid of two million four hundred seventy thousand.

Haynes got out of his car and began to pace. By Christmas he should be living in Rosemont. Maybe he'd put up a big tree and invite Loretta and her children—have lavish gifts for all of them. He smiled. He'd enjoyed buying the kitchen set for Nicole. He could imagine the fun he'd have buying gifts for Marissa and Sean. Especially Sean—he'd give the boy toys he'd dreamed about in his own childhood but never received.

He'd have a twelve-foot spruce brought in, and he'd hire a florist to decorate it. And he'd buy Loretta the nicest piece of jewelry she'd ever owned. Maybe a diamond-and-sapphire bracelet. He'd make her forget all about that creep Paul Martin. Maybe this year he wouldn't treat Christmas like a normal work day. He would celebrate.

He grabbed a dry thistle and ripped it from the ground. His fantasy of Christmas at Rosemont could only become a reality if he didn't dip into his "war chest." If he took out the million dollars necessary to pay for Nicole's surgery, he wouldn't have enough left to buy the thing he'd spent his whole life working toward. But without the little girl who had stolen his heart, owning Rosemont would be meaningless.

Haynes Enterprises was leveraged to the hilt and he had the balloon payment on Forever Friends coming due in January. He couldn't let the no-kill shelter that he founded be foreclosed on. Haynes wouldn't be able to replenish any of his Rosemont money before the end of the year. Every penny was needed to buy out Maggie.

The toe of his Italian leather shoe caught on a tangle of roots and Haynes stumbled, catching himself with his hands. He picked stones and twigs out of his palms, smiling as he remembered how Nicole had kissed his "boo-boo" when she'd seen the gash in his thumbnail.

He turned and studied Rosemont. It looked dark and cold, a large stone house baking in the hot sun. *What good will it be if I don't have someone with me who will kiss the boo-boos of my life?* He was an idiot. He was going to pay for that transplant—Rosemont be damned. How could he ever have his fantasy life with Loretta if he didn't do everything in his power to save her child? And he had the power to make that transplant happen in November. A later transplant might be fine, but he couldn't risk it.

He got into his car and headed back to Haynes Enterprises. He needed Loretta to know, now, that she could count on him. She and her children could count on him.

Chapter 47

Maggie Martin checked the clock on the hospital waiting room wall for the hundredth time. They'd expected the doctors to be out long before now with news about the transplant surgery. She closed her laptop and stowed it in the satchel she brought with her. She'd been well-prepared to use this time productively, but had been unable to concentrate. John put his hand on her back and rubbed her shoulders.

"This is torture," she said.

"Sitting in a hospital waiting room is like eight hours on the rock pile," he agreed. "These straight-backed chairs couldn't be any more uncomfortable if they tried."

Maggie stood. "I can't just sit here. I've got to move."

"Would you like me to come with you?"

Maggie shook her head. "They should be done by now. The doctor may be out any minute. I'm going to the ladies' room. Call me if he comes." Maggie nodded at Frank Haynes as he looked up from his newspaper when she passed by.

Maggie made her way down the busy hospital corridor and entered the cavernous restroom. She was washing her hands and checking her reflection in the mirror when she thought she heard someone crying. She turned off the water and listened. She was right—someone in the last stall was in distress.

"Are you all right?" Maggie said softly, approaching the stall. "Can I call someone for you?"

"No ... oo ... oo," came the halting reply. "I'm fine."

"Loretta? Have you had news?" she asked in alarm.

"No," Loretta quickly replied. The latch clicked as she slid it back and emerged. "Nothing like that. I'm still waiting for word."

"You scared me."

"I'm sorry. I guess the waiting is getting to me," she said, wiping at her eyes with a wad of toilet paper.

"Here," Maggie said, handing her a pack of tissues from her purse. "I'm on my last nerve, too."

Loretta nodded. "We're both waiting on news of our daughters. Only yours didn't have to be here. I'm still so grateful to Susan."

"There was never any doubt in her mind," Maggie said. "She wanted to do this." Maggie's cell phone chirped. She snatched it out of her purse and read the text message.

"Aaron's back." She put her arm around Loretta's shoulders as they made their way to the waiting room.

Maggie knew the moment she saw Aaron that the surgery had gone well. His back was to them, but his shoulders were relaxed. John pointed to the door, and Aaron turned to them as they approached. His tired smile told them all they needed to know.

"They're both doing great," he said. Loretta sagged against Maggie. "No complications. Everything went as planned. A textbook procedure."

Maggie felt tears prick the back of her eyes. "We were getting so worried. They told us the surgery would take four hours, and it's been six. We figured there must be complications."

"The only hitch was that the anesthesiologist was called away for a family emergency, and we had to wait for another doctor before we could get started. The surgery only took three and a half hours." He glanced between Maggie and Loretta. "I should have sent word to you. I'm sorry."

"As long as they're both all right, you're forgiven," Loretta said. "When can we see them?"

"Soon. They're getting them set up in recovery. You should be able to see them within the hour, I think."

Maggie and Loretta turned to each other. Maggie stepped toward Loretta and the two women embraced as fear was replaced by gratitude.

They parted and Loretta beamed at Frank. "She's going to be fine," she said as he approached.

"I'd better call the folks back in Westbury," Maggie said. "I'm sure Alex has been on pins and needles, and Joan Torres and Tonya Holmes will want to update the prayer chain."

"You've both had a lot of people pulling for you," Frank stated, wondering if anyone would care if he were in this situation.

"Nobody has been better to us than you have, Frank," Loretta said, taking his hand. "I can never repay you."

Maggie stepped away as she pulled her phone from her purse. If she didn't know better, she'd think those two were an item. *Ridiculous,* she thought. Or was it? She brought the phone to her ear as Alex answered.

Chapter 48

Susan was sitting up in bed, pushing scrambled eggs around on her breakfast tray, when John and Maggie entered her room the next morning.

Maggie kissed the top of her head. "How are you feeling, sweetheart?"

"I'm fine."

"Any pain?" John asked.

Susan nodded. "A bit. I asked for something last night, and I slept like a rock. If they came in during the night, I didn't wake up. I'm sore, but haven't needed anything this morning."

"Aren't you hungry?" Maggie asked, pointing to her tray.

"I am, but this is inedible."

"Why don't I go down to the hospital cafeteria and get something for all three of us?" John asked.

"Thank you," both women said in unison.

A half hour later, they were watching the morning news as they ate their breakfast when Aaron entered the room. He crossed to Susan and leaned down to kiss her.

"You must be over the anesthesia nausea," he said, looking at the empty Styrofoam container in front of her.

"Thankfully, yes," Susan said.

"Have they gotten you up yet?"

Susan shook her head.

"They'll take you for a walk this morning. The doctor will be in to check on you, but I caught him in the hall. As soon as they're sure that your remaining kidney is functioning properly and you're steady on your feet, you can go home. With any luck, that will be tomorrow."

"Awesome," Susan said. "I'll be much happier recovering at Rosemont. Do you know anything about Nicole?"

"The doctors are with her now. Apparently she had a good night."

"Can I see her?" Susan asked.

"She was asking the same thing," Aaron said. "One of the first things she said when she came around was 'Where's Susan?'"

Susan was waking from a well-earned nap after her second lap around the hospital ward when Aaron appeared in her doorway with a wheelchair. "I've been authorized to escort you to Miss Nicole Nash's room," he announced. "Your sister is demanding to see you and won't take no for an answer."

Susan smiled. "I can walk. We don't need that," she said, waving away the wheelchair.

"Why don't you ride down there, and if you feel well enough, you can walk back?" Maggie suggested. "You might be more tired than you think."

"You're not going unless I push you in this," Aaron said, ending any discussion.

Nicole was quietly watching television with her beloved doll tucked at her side when Aaron pushed Susan into the room and up to her bed. The sisters smiled at each other. "How's she doing?" Susan asked, pointing to the doll.

Nicole nodded. "She's feeling better."

"I hear that you're being a model patient," Susan said. "You're a very brave girl, Nicole. I'm proud of my sister."

Nicole beamed.

Loretta, who had been observing from the recliner in the corner, now spoke.

"You're looking great, Susan. How are you?"

"If my tests tomorrow morning look good, they'll release me. We'll all drive back to Rosemont."

"That's terrific news."

"How's Nicole?" Aaron asked.

"They're extremely pleased. They're monitoring everything very carefully, of course. They think her new kidney—your kidney, Susan—has already started to work."

Susan brought her hands to her heart. "That's the best news, ever. I was praying for it."

"When you get well enough, I'm going to hug you like you've never been hugged," Loretta said.

Susan smiled and turned back to Nicole. "So I'll see you again when you come home. You continue to get better, okay? Do everything that the doctors ask of you."

Nicole nodded solemnly.

"We hope to be discharged next week," Loretta said. "Frank was here for the surgery but returned to Westbury this morning. He said he'd come back to drive us home."

She followed Aaron as he wheeled Susan to the door of Nicole's room. "Please let me know how she's doing." Susan said.

"I will. Safe trip home, Susan. You saved your sister's life."

⸺

Susan stirred and opened her eyes slowly in the dimly lit room. Aaron glanced up from the medical journal he was reading and rose from the recliner to stand by the side of her bed. Susan reached up and pulled him in for a proper kiss on the lips.

"That's better," she said. "I needed that."

Aaron smiled at her. "Me, too."

"What time is it? I thought you were going back to the hotel with Mom and John."

Aaron checked his watch. "Ten. I'll leave in a few minutes. I wanted some alone time with my girl."

"I'm glad you're here. I've been lying here, thinking."

"About?"

"The wedding."

"Ahhh … I should have known. You've had lots of time to think of all the details."

"I know you feel I've been a bit overboard on it," Susan said. "And now that I'm in this place—with all these people facing life and death decisions—I'm rethinking it."

"Marrying me?"

"No, silly. I want to marry you with every fiber of my being. I mean I don't want to spend the money on a big fancy wedding. "

"You've wanted a big wedding all your life, and you know it."

"I don't want it any longer. And I know you've never been crazy about the idea."

Aaron shrugged. "It's never been my thing, but I want whatever will make you happy."

"Admit it—you'd be thrilled with a small, intimate affair. I think that's what we should do"

"I'd be fine with that. And the sooner you're my wife, the happier I'll be. But are you sure?"

"There are families here that have lost their homes because of the medical bills they face. Even with insurance, a transplant can bankrupt a patient. I understand Frank Haynes paid for Nicole's transplant. Without his help, Loretta would have had to wait for her insurance company, which wouldn't have paid until Nicole got sicker."

"Our wedding won't change that," he said.

Susan took his hands in hers. "What if we donated the money we would have spent on the wedding to the hospital? It's not a fortune, but it would be enough to help at least one family."

"That's very generous of you, but I think you'd regret it down the line. You've got a dozen Pinterest boards devoted to our wedding. Don't make any snap decisions. You've got time to think about this when we get back to California."

Susan shook her head. "That's the thing," she said. "I'd like to get married at Rosemont when we get back to Westbury."

Aaron sucked in his breath. "Are you sure?"

"I'm positive. Let's talk to Mom and John tomorrow. We can get a license and get married next week before you have to go back."

"What about Mike and Amy and the girls? Sophie and Sarah will be so disappointed if they can't come and be in our wedding."

"They got to be in Mom and John's wedding. They'll get over it."

"Sleep on it. I won't say anything to Maggie or John. If you still feel this way in the morning, I'd love nothing more than to marry you next week."

Chapter 49

"The doctor has released you," the nurse said brightly. "I've got your discharge instructions and prescriptions to go over with you, and then you're free to go."

Susan pushed herself onto her elbows and swung her feet gingerly over the side of the bed. Maggie eyed her daughter closely. "Are you feeling all right, honey?"

Susan nodded. "Of course I am, Mom. I'm just anxious to get out of here."

"It's a six-hour drive home. We can wait until tomorrow."

"No!" Susan snapped. "I want to go now."

Aaron turned to Maggie. "It's natural to feel worse two days after surgery. Don't worry, I'll keep my eye on her all the way home." He looked at John. "Why don't you bring the car around to the entrance? I'll listen to the nurse's instructions, and we can be on our way. We should be back at Rosemont by dinnertime."

Maggie nodded reluctantly. "You're the doctor. If you're sure she's okay to leave the hospital."

"I am. See you downstairs in fifteen minutes."

—

Aaron helped Susan into the backseat of John's Suburban, placing a pillow on her lap before securing her seat belt.

"You look exhausted," Maggie said, unable to conceal the alarm in her voice.

"We gave her a pain pill before we came downstairs," Aaron reassured Maggie. "She'll probably be out the whole way home."

Maggie lifted an eyebrow at John. "It'll be fine," he said. "Let's get to Rosemont before it wears off."

John drove the entire way, with only one quick stop for gas. Aaron and Susan slept in the backseat. They made good time on the clear, dry roads, and turned into the driveway to Rosemont shortly after four o'clock.

John pulled into the garage and shut off the engine. He and Maggie got quietly out of the car. "I'll help Aaron get Susan upstairs, then I'll go fill her prescriptions and pick up dinner."

Maggie nodded. "I'll go with you. I need to get groceries." She opened the back tailgate and reached for Susan's duffel bag.

Aaron stirred and looked around. "We're here?" he asked. "Did she sleep the whole way, too?"

"You were both out cold from the time we pulled out of the hospital parking lot," John said.

"Sorry about that," Aaron unfastened Susan's seat belt.

She opened her eyes and inhaled deeply. "Home," she said.

"Let's get you inside," Maggie said. "Would you like to sit up for a while in that big chair in the library? We can open the French doors and you can get some air. You've slept all day."

Susan leaned heavily on Aaron's arm as she got out of the car. They walked slowly through the house. When they reached the staircase, Susan turned to Maggie. "I'm still really tired. If you don't mind, I'd like to go up to bed. I'll sit in the library tomorrow."

"Whatever you want, honey."

"Why don't you and John go fill her prescriptions? I'll keep a close eye on her," Aaron said. Maggie studied his face. "Everything's fine. I just want to have her pain pills if she needs them."

John dropped Maggie at the supermarket while he headed to the pharmacy and then to Tomascino's for a pizza. Maggie was waiting for him with a cart full of groceries when he pulled to the entrance to pick her up. He helped her stow the bags in the back of his Suburban.

"Expecting to feed an army this week?" he asked.

"I want to be prepared. I've got the fixings for all her favorite dishes."

"You're a wonderful mother," he said as he shut her car door for her. He looked at her as he climbed behind the wheel.

"I'm worried," Maggie confessed.

"Remember what Aaron said? Patients are worse two days after surgery. It's the same with animals."

Maggie shook her head. "I can't put my finger on it, but it seems like she's getting worse, not better."

"If that's the case, we know what to do," John replied. "But I think you're making yourself miserable about nothing."

Maggie turned to look out her window and remained silent on the short drive home.

John brought the groceries into the house while Maggie hurried up the stairs to bring Susan's prescriptions to her. "Do you need something for pain, honey?"

Susan shook her head. "Is that pizza I smell?"

Maggie nodded. "Tomascino's. We got one loaded with veggies and a sausage and pepperoni. We also got macaroni and cheese. Can I bring them up here? We can all eat upstairs."

"No," Susan said. "I'd like to come down."

Maggie beamed. "I'll go put the groceries away. We'll be ready for you whenever you want to eat." She reached for the door handle, then turned back. "And I got Oreos, chocolate ice cream, and those big, crunchy pretzels you love, too."

Susan laughed. "You don't need to fatten me up, Mom. I'm going to be in a wedding dress, soon. Very soon." She looked at Aaron. "Let's tell them at dinner," she mouthed and he nodded, a smile spreading from ear to ear.

John rose to clear away the paper plates and pizza boxes when they were done eating.

"Can you leave that for a minute?" Susan asked. "Sit back down." She glanced at Aaron. "We have something we'd like to talk to you about."

John reclaimed his seat.

"This sounds serious," Maggie said.

"We've decided to change our mind about the wedding," Susan began.

"What?" Maggie gasped.

"We're still getting married," Susan hastened to assure her. "And we'd like to get married at Rosemont. We just don't want to spend the money on an expensive wedding. We'd like to donate it to the hospital, instead."

"But sweetheart …" Maggie began.

Susan held up her hand. "We've talked about it, and our minds are made up. I'm sorry if you'll be disappointed."

"It's not that, honey. Are you sure?"

"Positive. We'd like to get married here, next week, before we go back to California."

"That's really fast," Maggie replied. "What about Mike and Amy and the girls?"

"I'll call him tomorrow. Maybe they can come."

"I'm not sure we can get things together in a week."

"Of course we can," Susan replied. "It'll just be you and John, Marc and Alex, the Torreses, the Holmes family, and Mike's family, if they can make it. We can order flowers for the mantel, and we'll go to The Mill for dinner afterward. Marc will play the piano in the conservatory. I've even decided what I'm going to wear."

Maggie smiled at her uber-organized daughter. "What?"

"That cream tea-length lace cocktail dress with seed pearls that you bought on sale but have never worn."

"The one Amy convinced me to buy, telling me I'd need it one day?"

Susan nodded. "The very one. You haven't gotten rid of it, have you?"

"Nope. It's in my closet, with the tags still on it."

"Good." Susan clapped her hands. "I've got a gorgeous dress, and we've got a plan."

Maggie looked at John, who nodded. "If this is what you want, let's do it. I'll get the town clerk to come by here tomorrow to take your application for your license. It's one of the perks of being mayor—probably the only perk," she added.

"We'll get manis and pedis this weekend, and I'll go to that salon on the square to get my hair put up the day of the wedding."

"Are you sure you don't want to wait until you're fully recovered?" Maggie asked.

"I should be fine by next week," Susan stifled a yawn. "But I'm tired now. And I'm starting to feel a little bit queasy."

"That could be the medication," Aaron said. "You've had enough excitement for one day. Let's get you up to bed."

Susan nodded as he helped her to her feet. "We'll get the wedding all figured out tomorrow, Mom." She looked at her mother. "This really is what I want."

Maggie started a load of laundry and checked the time on the grandfather clock in the entryway. *John should be back any minute. Where had he gone at this hour, anyway?* He'd called "back in a few" to her as he headed out the door.

Maggie climbed the stairs and proceeded down the hall to Susan's room. She checked under the door. The light was out. She'd let her daughter sleep. Maggie unpacked the small suitcase she'd taken with her to the transplant hospital, removed her makeup, and washed her face. She had just turned off the water when she thought she heard the familiar jingling of collars racing up the stairs. She tossed her towel over the bar as Eve rounded the corner to the bathroom in search of her master. Roman followed at a polite distance.

Maggie dropped onto one knee and embraced her Jack Russell terrier mix as she showered Maggie with excited kisses. "I missed you, too," she cooed. She extended her arm to Roman. "Come here, boy," she said, ruffling his ears.

John stood in the doorway, looking at his wife.

"So that's where you went," Maggie said. "To get the animals out of captivity."

"One of the advantages of owning the kennel," John said. "I knew you'd sleep better if they were home."

"I sure will," Maggie said, nuzzling Eve. "And you will, too, John Allen. Don't try to tell me otherwise."

John shrugged. "I'll neither admit nor deny."

Maggie stood. "Where are the cats?"

"They scattered as soon as I opened the carrier. They'll make their presence known shortly, I should think."

Maggie turned at the soft meow of Bubbles as she strutted between the two dogs to her mistress. She scooped up the boldest of the three cats and had her purring within seconds. "I think Susan was better tonight, don't you? Maybe the drive really took it out of her?"

"I'm sure of it," John said. "What do you think about their getting married next week?"

"I'm relieved, actually. I'm afraid we won't be living here next year when she planned to get married."

"You don't know that Frank is going to outbid us. We've been able to sweeten our offer. Frank isn't known for overpaying for anything. He probably figures we can't come up with even half of the appraised value. He'll bid the half that is the required minimum and think he's got it in the bag."

Maggie bent to greet Blossom and Buttercup. "I hope you're right, but my gut tells me Frank Haynes will do anything to get his hands on Rosemont." She looked up at John. "I'm trying to come to terms with the idea that we'll be leaving this house. I'd love to have Susan's wedding here. If she gets married next week, we can be sure of it."

Chapter 50

Maggie folded her reading glasses into their case and closed her laptop. It was no use. She was too tired to focus on her emails; they would have to wait until the next morning. She leaned back in her chair. Susan had rallied when the clerk arrived to get their signatures on the application for their wedding license, but she'd been increasingly listless the rest of the day. Aaron was a doctor—if he said she was doing fine, she didn't need to worry. And she'd started her post-operative prescription of antibiotics. Maggie was doing what she always did—worrying needlessly about her children.

She collected John from the sofa, where he'd fallen asleep in front of the television, and they went up to bed. She'd finally fallen into a deep sleep when she was awakened by a firm knock on their bedroom door. She grabbed her robe from the foot of her bed.

Maggie opened the door to find Aaron, fully dressed, on the other side. "Susan's spiked a fever," he said calmly. "We need to take her to the hospital."

She took a step back. "Let me put some clothes on," she started, but Aaron interrupted her.

"No. Give me John's keys, and I'll take her now. I'll call you."

Maggie scooped up John's keys from their usual perch on his nightstand and handed them to Aaron. "You go and we'll follow. How high is it?" she asked as she hurried down the hall with him to Susan's room.

"One hundred four," he said.

Maggie gasped.

"I've given her ibuprofen and acetaminophen to bring it down, but I think she'll need intravenous antibiotics. The sooner they start them, the better."

"The incision is infected?" Maggie asked.

"Yes," Aaron said as he lifted Susan out of bed.

"Let me get John to help you take her downstairs."

"I'm right here," John said from the hallway. He and Aaron carried Susan down the stairs and into John's car.

"Honey," Maggie said to Susan. Her eyes fluttered open, then closed.

"We'll be ten minutes behind you," John told Aaron as he started the ignition.

Maggie turned to John. "She's going away from us, John. I felt it all day. She was getting sicker and sicker," her voice cracked.

John took Maggie by the shoulder and steered her into the house. "Get dressed, and we'll go to the hospital. Post-operative infections are not uncommon, and they know how to treat them," he said with as much confidence as he could muster.

"You really believe she'll be all right?" Maggie asked in a small voice.

"I do."

———

Maggie wrapped her arms around herself and rocked back and forth in her chair in the frigid emergency room waiting area of Mercy Hospital. John slipped his arm around her shoulders and rubbed her arm.

"Why do they always keep these places so cold?" she muttered.

"You've got a spare jacket in the car. I'll go get it for you," he said, starting to rise. She pulled him back into his seat.

"I don't want you to leave me alone," she said. "I want you here when the doctor comes out."

"She's going to be fine, sweetheart. Whatever's going on, she's in good hands."

Maggie leaned her head into his shoulder but didn't respond, keeping her eyes trained on the door that led from the waiting area to the exam rooms. They both tensed when the door opened and a man in surgical scrubs and a clipboard called to an elderly woman who had been sitting, alone, clutching her purse on her lap. The man smiled at the woman as she approached, and said, "He's doing just fine." The woman's relief, as she passed Maggie and John, was tangible.

"We've been here for almost two hours," Maggie said, "and no word. That can't be good."

John had been thinking the same thing. "No news is just that, sweetheart. No news. I'm sure someone will be out shortly." But no one came for them, and they sat, watching the door open and close three more times, as people who entered the waiting area, long after she and John had arrived, were called back to see their loved ones. Finally, it was their turn.

The nurse ushered them into a small private consultation room. "The doctor will be right in," he said.

"How's my daughter?" Maggie asked the young man.

"The doctor will be right in" was his only reply.

Maggie turned scared eyes to John. John put his arms around her and pulled her to him.

There was a soft knock on the door, and Alex leaned into the room. "Aaron called me about twenty minutes ago. Do you mind if I wait with you?"

John motioned him into the room. Maggie bowed her head and they waited in silence.

Aaron and an older man finally entered the room. "She's had a close call, but we think she'll be all right," Aaron said.

Maggie leaned forward. "What do you mean, 'close call'?" she asked shrilly.

The older man stepped toward her. "I'm Dr. Jacobson," he said, extending his hand. "Susan is stable and will be moved to a room in the ICU. Her surgical site is infected, and she's had a severe allergic reaction to the antibiotic she was taking. Her throat was almost completely swollen shut, and she was in anaphylactic shock. We had to intubate her to allow her to breathe. We've put her into a medically induced coma and are giving her a different intravenous antibiotic to fight the infection."

Maggie shook her head, trying to take it all in.

"How long do you plan to keep her under?" John asked.

"Hopefully, only a day or two. It's a very mild coma, and we'll bring her up each day to assess her situation."

"Is the new antibiotic going to work?" Maggie asked, seeking reassurance.

"We've had good luck with this one and have every confidence that it will," the doctor replied.

"Can I see her?"

"Normally, we don't allow visitors until the patient is moved to a room, but I think we can make an exception this time. I'll take you back. But you can only stay a few minutes."

Maggie nodded.

"One of you can be with her when she moves to the ICU," the doctor said.

Maggie turned to Aaron. "I hate the idea of leaving her, but since you're a doctor, I think you should be the one to stay."

"Thank you, Maggie," Aaron said. "I think so, too. I promise you, I'll call you the minute anything happens."

"Will she know me?" Maggie asked.

"We can't be certain," the doctor answered. "There's no scientific proof, but I believe she will."

The doctor held the door for Maggie, and they headed down the corridor toward a long room with curtained partitions lining each side.

When they had gone, John turned to Aaron. "I think it's time to call Mike. Should I tell him that he needs to come?"

The sadness in Aaron's eyes was unmistakable. He nodded slowly. "Yes. I think you'd better. These superbugs are unpredictable. We don't know if we'll be able to stop this infection."

Maggie steeled herself for what she was about to see as she followed the doctor to the last partition on the right side of the room. The doctor drew the curtain aside, and there was Susan—her Susan—caged in a hospital bed, dwarfed by monitors forming a semi-circle around her. A tube emerged from her mouth and a noisy breathing machine wheezed at her side. The doctor put his hand under Maggie's elbow. She drew a deep breath and stepped to the side of the bed opposite the breathing apparatus.

She took her daughter's hand, being careful not to dislodge the electronic probe attached to her finger, and leaned over to kiss a spot on the top of her head that she could reach without disturbing any tubes. "You're going to be fine," she whispered in her ear. "The new medicine is doing its job, and all of this is helping you while it works. You'll be home in no time, my love. And you're the best daughter any mother could ever hope to have. I'm so proud of you, and I love you so much."

The doctor motioned toward the door.

"Aaron will stay with you, and I'll be back tomorrow. You just rest and get better." Maggie couldn't be sure, but she thought Susan squeezed her hand before she stepped away from the bed.

Chapter 51

Frank Haynes knocked softly on the partially open door of Nicole Nash's hospital room, concealing something large and lumpy under his raincoat. Loretta looked up from a stack of papers she was studying and blinded him with her dazzling smile.

"Look who's here," she said to Nicole.

Nicole tore her eyes from *Sesame Street* on the television and stretched out her arms to him. Frank Haynes strode to her bedside and awkwardly leaned in to her as she circled his neck with her arms and hugged him.

"You look like you're feeling much better, young lady," he said. "What do you think I have here?" he asked, patting his raincoat.

Nicole's eyes widened and a smile crept across her lips. "For me?"

Haynes nodded as he opened his coat and pulled out a large stuffed dog with soft, curly fur and floppy ears. "They told me at the toy store that she needs someone very special to take care of her. I said I knew just the girl."

Nicole unwound her arms from Frank's neck and pounced on the dog, scooping it and her doll to her chest. She nodded vigorously.

"Your mother told me you've been wanting a dog."

"Real dog," Nicole said, turning to her mother.

"Maybe when you're all better," Loretta answered.

"When you're ready, you can come to Forever Friends to pick out any dog you like. Until then, you can have this one. Would that be all right with you?"

Nicole nodded again.

Loretta folded the paperwork and placed it carefully in her purse. "These are Nicole's discharge instructions. We're ready to go."

"Excellent," Haynes replied, rubbing his hands together. "Let's get out of here. I'll bring the car around."

Thirty minutes later, they were cruising along the interstate, Nicole asleep in the backseat with her doll and new stuffed dog at her side.

"This is awfully nice of you to pick us up, Frank," Loretta said, shifting in her seat to look at him. "Especially since it'll be twelve hours of driving for you today."

Frank Haynes shrugged. "I don't mind. I've always enjoyed driving. Sometimes I just get in and drive with no destination in mind. Whenever I need to clear my head or think."

Loretta nodded. "I wondered what you were doing all those afternoons when you'd leave the office without a word to me. I'll bet you were driving."

"Could be."

"Well—even though you love to drive—if you want me to take over for any part of the trip home, just say so."

"We'll see."

"So what's the news from Westbury? Has Susan gone home to California yet? I left her a couple of voice mails about Nicole, but I never heard back. Nicole and I would like to see her if she's still there. I want to thank her, again."

Haynes glanced at her. "She's still there." He put on his turn signal and got off the highway at the next exit. He pulled the car onto the shoulder of the road, put it in park, and turned to Loretta. "Susan is in the hospital."

"What?" Loretta gasped. "She was doing so well. They both were," she said, looking over the backseat at her sleeping child. "What happened?"

"Apparently her incision got infected, and she had a severe allergic reaction to the antibiotic they gave her."

"She's going to be okay, isn't she? She's getting better?"

"She's holding her own. The infection is one of these new superbugs, and they've had her on intravenous antibiotics to fight it. But it's a hard bug to treat." He laid his hand over hers. "They put her into a medically induced coma and hooked her up to a breathing machine. They did that to fight the allergic reaction."

"Is she still in a coma?" Loretta whispered in disbelief.

"The last I heard, yes. Maggie hasn't been at Town Hall, and I haven't talked to her. I found out through David Wheeler, because he was at the hospital with Dodger when he ran into John Allen."

"This is horrible," Loretta cried. "She's got to get better, Frank. God can't take one sibling to save the other."

"I'm not on the best terms with God," Frank said, "but I called my friend Glenn Vaughn to ask him to pray for Susan and Nicole. He said that they'd put them on the prayer chain at their church."

Frank Haynes never ceased to amaze her. "Thank you, Frank. How's Maggie doing?"

"I honestly don't know," Haynes said.

"I'd be out of my mind with fear. And I'd be furious that I'd let my child get into this situation in the first place. If I were Maggie, I'd hate Loretta and Nicole Nash."

Frank searched her face. "I don't think you would, Loretta. There's too much kindness in you, and there's too much kindness in Maggie." He shifted in his seat and started the car. "I wanted you to hear about this from me. I knew you'd be upset."

Loretta nodded.

"There's nothing you can do about it. Take care of Nicole so that she gets better, and let God and the doctors take care of Susan."

Chapter 52

Maggie lunged for her cell phone when it rang at four o'clock in the morning on the fifth day after Susan had been put into a coma. Mike had arrived three days earlier, and they'd spent long hours at the hospital. In the clumsiness of her half-awake state, she knocked her purse to the floor. She was dislodging Buttercup from her usual place in the curve of her knee when John threw back the covers and dashed around the side of the bed to retrieve the phone. Maggie answered it just before it would have gone to voice mail.

Her hand trembled as she waited for what she assumed would be bad news.

"Maggie," came Aaron's familiar voice. "She's coming out of it. Waking up. Her vital signs took a turn for the better in the middle of the night, and they've started to bring her out of her coma."

"We'll be right there," she said as she tossed the phone onto the bed and began throwing herself into the clothes that she kept on a nearby chair in case she needed to get to the hospital quickly.

"She's better," she called to John who was doing the same. "They're bringing her out of her coma. She's going to be all right."

Maggie grabbed her purse. "I'll go wake Mike. He'll want to come, too. What about the dogs?" she asked.

"They'll be fine," John replied. "Let's get to the hospital. I'll come back to feed them."

Maggie, John, and Mike pushed through the doors of Mercy Hospital twenty minutes later and took the stairs to the ICU. Susan's room was a hub of activity, with nurses going in and out and a team of doctors surrounding her bed. Aaron was holding Susan's hand. Maggie pushed herself into place at the foot of Susan's bed. Mike and John edged along the wall inside the doorway. A doctor was giving direction to a nurse, and they were both focused on one of the monitors flashing in the corner. Maggie stared at her daughter. They'd taken the breathing tube out, and she looked peaceful and natural. Maggie held her breath and prayed.

Susan's eyelids fluttered, then remained open. She stared at Maggie with the expression of someone trying to place a person they know they've seen before. A smile suddenly released the tension from her daughter's face. Susan mouthed the word "Mom."

Aaron squeezed her hand and brought it to his lips.

The doctor intervened and began talking to Susan, asking her questions, telling her to nod for yes and shake her head for no. Maggie ignored everything in the room except for her gorgeous, alert daughter. *Praise you, God,* she repeated over and over in her mind.

The doctor pulled a pen from his pocket and placed it on his clipboard. "You've been in a coma for the past five days," he told her. "You've had a breathing tube, and your throat may be sore from it. If there's anything you want, you can write us a note," he said, handing the clipboard to Susan. "Do you understand?"

Susan nodded and began to scribble. When she was done, she held the clipboard out to Aaron and smiled.

"We're supposed to be getting married day after tomorrow," Aaron told the group assembled in the room. "She wants to know if she missed the wedding." He turned to Susan. "You didn't miss it, but I think we'll have to postpone it."

The doctor quickly agreed. "You won't be walking down any aisles this week, I'm afraid. You're getting better and you're going to be fine, but these things take time. You won't be able to leave the hospital for at least another four or five days."

"Or we can get married here, if you want," Aaron said. "We could use the hospital chapel, couldn't we?"

The doctor paused and the nurse broke in. "I'm sure we could arrange it. We've had other weddings there. Mostly staff."

"Why the rush?" Maggie asked.

Susan tried to speak but couldn't make herself heard. She took the clipboard and wrote, "Life is short. Tired of waiting."

Susan looked at Aaron, who nodded his agreement. "Susan Martin, it will be my honor to marry you day after tomorrow in the Mercy Hospital Chapel."

"Aaron said you wanted to see me," Mike said, stepping into the hospital room the next morning. "I wasn't sure you even knew I was here."

Susan smiled and motioned him closer. "Still hard to speak," she whispered as he bent toward her. She pulled his cheek to her and gave him a kiss. "I saw you yesterday, over there"—she pointed to the wall—"with John. But I knew you were here with Mom before that."

Mike took her hand. "You gave us quite a scare," he said. "I wasn't ready to lose you."

"It was pretty serious, wasn't it? Did you come for the wedding—before I got so sick? Are Amy and the girls back at Rosemont?"

Mike shook his head. "They couldn't make it. I came out when John called to tell me you were in a coma. I thought …" he began, and his voice broke.

Susan squeezed his hand. "Good thing you're here now. Will you walk me down the aisle tomorrow?"

"Nothing I'd like better. We all thought this day might never come. Do you know how close you came to not making it?"

"I'm getting the picture. I had a sense of being away from you all, in my own peaceful place. But Aaron was always with me. He read to me and talked to me about the life we would lead. I kept trying to get back to him. That's why I wanted to keep our wedding date. No more delays or interruptions. And now you're here. I want you at my wedding."

"I wouldn't miss it."

"When do you go back?"

"I'll take the red-eye tomorrow night."

"Perfect. The wedding will be a simple affair, and you'll be done in plenty of time to get to the airport."

Mike ran his eyes over his sister. "You're my hero, you know. That was a very kind and brave thing you did—giving Nicole your kidney. I'll always admire you for doing that."

Susan flushed. "Okay, you. Go back home and let a girl get her beauty rest. I'll see you tomorrow, on my wedding day."

———

Glenn Vaughn hung up the receiver and turned to Gloria, his wife of a little over a year. They'd been the talk of Fairview Terraces when, at their advanced ages, they'd gotten married in a surprise wedding at the conclusion of the town's annual Thanksgiving Prayer Breakfast. "Looks like another unusual wedding is in the works," he told her. She raised an eyebrow at him over the top of the morning paper.

"That was David Wheeler. He and Dodger were at Mercy Hospital, and he heard that Maggie's daughter is out of her coma and is getting married in the chapel there tomorrow."

Gloria dropped the newspaper and clapped her hands. "Praise God," she said.

"Indeed."

"But why the rushed wedding? Isn't she expected to recover?"

"David thinks she's going to be fine. We didn't talk about why she's getting married so soon."

"Men," Gloria shook her head. "I'm going to call Debra."

Glenn raised his eyebrows. "Debra?"

"The gal that works at the hospital thrift shop. She knows everything that goes on around the hospital. I wonder if Maggie needs any help with anything."

"I don't think they'll want any of us meddling ..." he started to say, but she was already past him, on her way to get dressed and spring into action.

Chapter 53

Maggie arrived at the hospital on the day of her daughter's wedding with the cream-colored cocktail dress in its zippered garment bag. She didn't know if the doctors would allow Susan to be unhooked from her monitors and IVs long enough to get married in it, but they were going to try. When she rounded the corner of the hallway, the door to Susan's room was shut and there were three rolling suitcases and two large medical carts in the hallway outside the room. She quickened her pace. *Please, God—let there be nothing wrong today.*

Maggie knocked and pushed the door open without waiting for an answer. She took two steps into the room and stopped short. Susan was sitting on the edge of her hospital bed as Anita Archer made the final adjustments to a full length silk and organza wedding gown. Susan's makeup was done and flowers were woven through her long blond hair. She turned to her mother, and her smile could have lit the entire Eastern Seaboard.

"What in the world?" Maggie began.

Anita Archer looked up and removed the pins she was holding in her teeth. "The Martin women always get married in attire from Archer's," she said, winking at Susan. "Good thing Joan Torres called me. I don't know what you were thinking."

"This is the dress I saw last year that I told you about, Mom. The one I was going to order for my wedding next year. And now I get to wear it, anyway."

Maggie stood, dumbstruck. "You look remarkable" was all she could manage.

"Anita got a lady from the salon to come put my hair up. The nurse washed it last night. Everyone's being so kind."

"How did Joan know about the wedding?" Maggie managed to ask.

"Gloria Vaughn told her," Anita Archer chimed in.

Maggie threw up her hands. "I give up."

"There's one more thing," Susan said, eyeing Maggie's sensible navy blue suit. "You look like you're going to a council meeting in that thing. Slip into that dress you brought with you."

Maggie laughed. "I knew I needed this dress for a very special occasion. I can't think of anything more special than this."

Gloria Vaughn had, indeed, gotten the scoop from Debra and called Judy Young and Joan Torres. This might be a last-minute hospital wedding, but they'd make it an elegant, gracious affair or die trying. Word travels fast in a small town. Judy called Anita, who contacted the stylist. Gloria arranged for the flowers, and Joan spoke to Laura at the bakery. Laura began work on the wedding cake at the crack of dawn.

By the time Maggie was escorted to her pew by best man Alex Scanlon, everything was in place. The altar was adorned with a spray of white calla lilies. A two-tiered cake waited in the hospital boardroom, where the reception was to be held. Pete's Bistro was supplying the luncheon.

Maggie looked at the small group gathered in the chapel, and her breath caught in her chest. These people were always there for each other, without question and without exception. The Torreses and the Knudsens, Tonya and George Holmes, Anita Archer, Judy Young and her husband, Glenn and Gloria Vaughn, and Pete and Laura Fitzpatrick. She turned and rose as Marc Benson struck out the wedding march on the chapel piano. And here was her precious daughter, glowing and beautiful, coming down the aisle on the arm of her brother. Nothing about this moment could be more perfect. Absolutely nothing.

Susan walked slowly down the aisle, leaning heavily on her brother's arm but looking every bit the traditional bride. When she reached the altar, Aaron took her elbow and steered her into a chair that Sam Torres had procured from a nearby office. He knelt at her side. The hospital chaplain's sonorous voice led them through the familiar vows, each couple in attendance joining hands and reliving their own commitment. When he pronounced them husband and wife, Aaron leaned in to kiss his bride. Maggie dabbed at her eyes and noted that Alex was blinking rapidly. The other women in the pews were reaching into their purses for tissues.

Susan rose and, supported by her new husband, retreated down the aisle. When they got to the back of the chapel, Aaron insisted that Susan reclaim her seat in the wheelchair and turned to the small group of guests. "I promised to bring her back to her room as soon as we were done. When everything checks out, we'll join you in the boardroom at the end of the hall to cut the wedding cake."

The group made their way down the hall and accepted champagne from Pete, who was busily filling glasses and unwrapping trays of finger sandwiches. The doors opened, and Aaron ushered Susan into the room in her wheelchair. Everyone clapped.

Mike stepped forward. "I'd like to propose a toast to my sister and brother-in-law." He beamed in their direction. "Aaron—welcome to our family. I always liked and respected you, but my admiration and affection have deepened as I've watched you care for my sister. I know you are devoted to her and will be the kind, loving husband she deserves. And now, three pieces of advice for you as you embark on a lifetime with Susan: Buy the luggage with the sturdiest wheels—my sister does not know how to travel light; increase your gym membership because my sister is an incredible cook; and always be thankful that you've married the kindest, most generous person I've ever known." Mike raised his glass. "To Susan and Aaron."

"Hear, hear!" cried the group as they toasted the couple.

Susan cut the cake and continued to hop in and out of the wheelchair, visiting with the guests and nibbling her slice of cake, until she finally surrendered, exhausted.

"We need to toss the bouquet and get you back to bed," Aaron said.

Susan began to protest, but Alex chimed in. "Aaron's right. You don't want to set yourself back. You've been here far too long as it is," he said firmly.

Susan sighed, then agreed. "There're no single ladies to throw my bouquet to," she said, looking around the boardroom.

"Let me take care of that," Joan Torres interjected, signaling to Judy Young to join her as she exited the room. They returned almost immediately with a host of nurses in their wake. "These ladies would all love to catch your bouquet," Joan said.

They propped the double doors to the boardroom open, and Aaron wheeled Susan into position. He helped her to her feet, and she swung her arm over her head, releasing the bouquet in an arc that sent it sailing into the waiting arms of a divorced mother of three. The woman shrieked and everyone clapped. She hugged Susan. "Thank you, honey. I hope I find a guy as nice as this one," she said, winking at Aaron.

"I hope you do, too," Susan whispered in her ear before releasing her.

"Okay, my dear," Aaron said. "The party's over for you. I'm taking you back to your room. Doctor's orders."

———

Loretta Nash pushed Nicole's wheelchair toward the elevator on the second floor of Mercy Hospital. Nicole's first checkup since returning to Westbury had gone well, and Loretta was flush with happiness, oblivious to her surroundings.

Nicole pointed to a raucous group of people at the end of the hall. "Susan!" she cried, wriggling to get out of her wheelchair.

Loretta put her hand on her daughter's shoulder. "You've got to stay put," she said as she turned to look where Nicole was pointing.

There, at the end of the long hallway, was Susan Martin— resplendent in a bridal gown. The groom was helping her to her feet, and they were surrounded by a jovial group of women in hospital scrubs.

Loretta was about to wheel Nicole toward Susan when a shadowy figure crossed their path along an intersecting hallway fifty feet in front of them. Loretta hunched over, trying to make herself and Nicole invisible. She would recognize that portly frame and greasy pate anywhere. What in the world was Chuck Delgado doing at Mercy Hospital?

"What's wrong, Mommy?" Nicole asked.

Loretta put her finger to her lips and kept her gaze riveted on Delgado. He appeared to be in a hurry to go somewhere, carrying a sheaf of papers in his hand. He glanced quickly in the direction of the nurses, who were jostling for position to catch the bouquet. What she saw next chilled her like an arctic blast. Delgado stood, observing Susan Martin as she swung her arm over her head and threw her bouquet. He raised his right arm, holding it straight and parallel to the ground. He pointed his index finger at Susan, then brought his thumb down to meet his finger. He held his position, then threw back his head and laughed before continuing on his way.

Loretta shook her head. Had she really seen what she thought she had? She knew what that gesture meant; Delgado had taken aim with an imaginary gun and fired at Susan.

Delgado was rumored to be furious with Maggie Martin and anyone that had anything to do with his arrest. Would he seek revenge by harming Maggie or her family? Loretta knew firsthand what a vicious monster he could be. If Frank Haynes hadn't interrupted him, Delgado would have raped her last New Year's Eve.

She straightened her shoulders and began pushing Nicole's wheelchair down the hall toward the conference room. She'd let Nicole say hello to her sister on her wedding day and then take her right home. She needed to tell Frank Haynes what she'd seen, and the sooner the better. Frank would know what to do.

Chapter 54

Marissa and Sean Nash raced up the stairs to their apartment, with Frank Haynes trailing behind. Sean burst through the door. "Mom—guess what?"

Loretta stepped out of the kitchen and put her finger to her lips. "Shhhh … Your sister is taking a nap." She herded her two older children into the kitchen and motioned for Frank Haynes to join them. She smiled at him, and he felt the familiar jolt he always got these days when she did. "Okay, what?" she asked her son.

"We got to take Sally to the dog park after the movie," he said.

"And I got to hold her leash," Marissa chimed in.

Loretta nodded and gave Frank a quizzical look over the tops of their heads. Frank shrugged and looked at his shoes.

"So now you'll be wanting to get a dog, won't you?" she asked the two shining faces turned to hers. They nodded vigorously.

"Having a dog is a lot of work," she said. "You've got to feed them and walk them every day—especially when you live in a second-floor apartment, like we do."

"I'll walk him before and after school. I promise," Sean replied.

"And there's the matter of training, too. I've never trained a dog, and I don't have time to learn now. I told you we would consider it when Nicole's better."

"Mr. Haynes said that he'll teach us how to train him, and we can keep him at his house until you say he can come home with us," Marissa said, taking her mother's hand.

This time, Loretta did not smile at Frank. "We'll see. I'll talk to Mr. Haynes. You go to your rooms and start cleaning. They look like a bomb went off in them. I shouldn't have let you go with Mr. Haynes this afternoon, with your rooms in such a mess."

Sensing this was not the time to cross their mother, both children set out for their rooms without further comment. When they were out of earshot, Loretta turned to Frank.

"How's Nicole?" he asked.

"All of her test results were better than expected. She's not rejecting the kidney, and it's working beautifully."

"That's good news."

Loretta nodded. "What in the world were you doing, letting them hope that we can get a dog? I can't manage that right now."

Frank held up both hands. "I'm sorry, Loretta. I was out of line. But you should have seen them with Sally. They were so happy. I know how good Dodger has been for David Wheeler." He looked aside. "I remember how much it helped me when I got my dog when I was Sean's age." He turned to face her. "This hasn't been easy for them, you know. They've been scared about losing Nicole, and their mom hasn't had much time for them, either."

Loretta recoiled. "You think I'm neglecting them? I'm doing the best I can. You have no idea how hard this has been to do alone."

Frank Haynes stepped forward and put his hands on her arms. "I don't want you to have to do this alone. That's why I took them to the movies today. That's why I want to get them a dog and keep it at my house until you're ready to bring it home. It'll be good for Sean and Marissa, and it's something I can do to help."

Loretta leaned toward him.

"We'll all go to Forever Friends to pick out the dog. We'll get a small one, and you can have veto power. How does that sound?" he asked, pulling her to him.

Loretta rested her head on his chest and nodded.

"I have good news," he said softly, into her hair.

She pulled her head back to look into his eyes.

"Susan Martin got married today."

"I know. We ran into her at the hospital. Nicole got to see her in her wedding dress and say hello. Nicole said that her dress was the prettiest one she'd ever seen, and Susan told her she'd save it so Nicole could wear it when she got married. You should have seen them together, Frank. Those two have a magical bond." Loretta drew a deep breath. "I saw Chuck Delgado at the hospital, too. He did something that alarmed me."

Haynes' gaze turned to steel. "Did he come near you?"

"No. He never saw us. He had papers in one hand. Maybe he was there having some tests done, I don't know. Nicole and I were waiting for the elevator when I saw him down the hallway near where Susan was holding her reception. She was getting ready to throw her bouquet, and Delgado stopped to watch her. He raised his hand and pantomimed shooting her with a gun." Loretta demonstrated what she had seen. "He threw back his head and laughed, then proceeded on his way. It was really creepy."

"Did anyone else see him?"

"No. The hallway was deserted except for the commotion around the reception. He was a good fifty feet from them. Nobody else noticed."

"Did he see you?"

Loretta shook her head. "I was afraid he would, but he never glanced in our direction. We were at the other end of the hallway."

Haynes nodded, deep in thought. "Don't worry about it. I'll take care of it." He forced a smile onto his lips.

"How did you find out about the wedding?" she asked.

"Glenn Vaughn called to tell me."

"Why didn't they wait for her to get out of the hospital? They don't think she's going to die, do they?"

Frank shook his head. "No. Nothing of the kind. Glenn said that, after almost losing their happy future, they didn't want to wait any longer."

"That's wonderful, then. I've been terrified that she wasn't going to pull through. I'd never forgive myself if she didn't make it."

"Nonsense. None of that was your fault." He looked at her closely. He held his breath, then plunged on, into the question that had been plaguing his thoughts for weeks.

"How about you?" he asked. "Would you like to move forward into a happy future with someone? Can you put that creep Paul Martin out of your mind?"

Loretta leaned back and tilted her face to his. She nodded slowly. He bent as she stood on her tiptoes. Their lips met and held, and they both would have sworn that the lights flickered.

Frank Haynes couldn't feel his feet as he retreated down the steps and got into his car. They'd made plans to go to Forever Friends the next afternoon, and he wanted to stop in and look at the dogs available for adoption on his way home. Instead of heading to the shelter, however, his Mercedes turned toward Rosemont.

He pulled into the familiar clearing in the shoulder of the road that ran below the house. He hadn't been back since he'd decided to use his money to pay for Nicole's transplant instead of buying out Maggie's interest in the house.

He studied Rosemont's rear facade in the late afternoon sunshine. He shook his head in disbelief. Instead of feeling the bitter disappointment he'd expected, he was happy. Almost giddy, in fact. The house no longer spoke to him. It was just a house. He was impatient to be on his way. He had things he wanted to prepare for Loretta and her kids before their visit to the shelter—and later his house—when they brought the dog home. He should have food on hand. Maybe he'd fix them a meal. What did they like? What did he even know how to cook? He felt happier than he'd felt in his entire life.

Haynes started the engine and pulled away without a backward glance. He needed to stop at Haynes Enterprises to send an email to Simon Wilkens, and then he had a long list of things to do. His life wouldn't include Rosemont.

Chapter 55

Maggie and John walked through the back door of Rosemont as the grandfather clock in the foyer struck midnight. The excitement of the wedding had sustained them as they drove Mike to the airport for his flight. They'd talked about the wedding and relived their own ceremony on the drive home. But the busy day was catching up with them. They were fading fast.

"I'll take the dogs out and lock up. You go get ready for bed," John said. He caught her hand as she passed him and spun her into his arms. "You looked absolutely stunning today, Mrs. Allen. Have I told you that?"

Maggie snuggled into his embrace. "I believe you might have mentioned it. You look mighty handsome, yourself, Dr. Allen."

She reached up to kiss him. "I'll be asleep the instant my head hits the pillow. I spotted something stuck to the front door as we drove past. I'm going to bring it inside and head upstairs."

"It's probably an advertisement," John replied. "Why don't you leave it for tomorrow?"

"Maybe I will." Maggie yawned as she headed toward the stairway while John whistled for the dogs. She hesitated on the first step, thinking about what was on the other side of that door. But her exhaustion overcame her curiosity, and she wearily climbed the steps to the second floor.

They'd been in bed for ten minutes when John rolled over to her and propped himself on his elbow. "I can tell by your breathing that you're not asleep. Something's bothering you."

Maggie switched on her bedside light. "You know me so well, don't you? I need to see what's taped to the front door. I can't go to sleep without knowing. I'll just nip down to get it and be right back."

John threw back the covers. "Stay put, princess. I'll go get it. And if it's some stupid restaurant flyer, you owe me. Big time."

"You're my hero" Maggie called to his retreating figure. She listened to the heavy mahogany door open and shut and John's tread on the stairway as he made his way back to her. Was she imagining it or was he walking a bit faster?

"Here," he said, holding out an envelope. "This was taped to the door. It's addressed to you."

Maggie sat up and turned the envelope over in her hands. "This handwriting looks vaguely familiar," she said as she slid her finger under the flap and ripped the envelope open. She withdrew a sheet of paper, covered in cursive. "It's from Frank Haynes," she said, glancing at John before returning to the paper in her hand. She read it aloud:

Dear Maggie,

I want you to know that I have decided not to offer to buy out your share of Rosemont. Although I have long wanted to own Rosemont, my priorities have changed and I have decided to use my cash for other purposes.

We have not always seen eye to eye, but I know you love Rosemont and are a good and generous steward of it.

I am deeply grateful that Susan donated her kidney to Nicole and am glad that her kindness is not going to be repaid with tragedy.

I've told Simon Wilkens about my decision and instructed him to send you a promissory note. You can pay me the appraised half of Rosemont's value over the next twenty years.

Yours sincerely,
Frank Haynes

Maggie sank against the headboard and let the letter fall from her hands. "Am I dreaming this?"

John picked up the letter and read it again. "You're not dreaming."

Maggie threw her arms around his neck. "Rosemont is ours! Finally, completely, ours!"

The End

Thank you for reading!

If you enjoyed *Drawing Close*, I'd be grateful if you wrote a review.

Just a few lines would be great. Reviews are the best gift an author can receive. They encourage us when they're good, help us improve our next book when they're not, and help other readers make informed choices when purchasing books. Reviews keep the Amazon algorithms humming and are the most helpful aide in selling books! Thank you.

To post a review on Amazon or for Kindle:

1. Go to the product detail page for *Drawing Close* on Amazon.com.
2. Click "Write a customer review" in the Customer Reviews section.
3. Write your review and click Submit.

In gratitude,

Barbara Hinske

Just for You!

Wonder what Maggie was thinking when the book ended? Exclusively for readers who finished *Drawing Close*, take a look at Maggie's Diary Entry for that day at https://barbarahinske.com/maggies-diary.

Acknowledgements

I'm blessed with the wisdom and support of many kind and generous people. I want to thank the most supportive and delightful group of readers an author could hope for:

My incredibly patient and supportive husband, Brian;

My beta reader and book guru, Helen Curl;

My genius marketing team of Mitch Gandy, Jesse Doubek, and Jill Bates Wallace—thank you for always fueling my dreams;

My kind and generous attorney, Roger A. Grad;

The professional "dream team" of my editors Linden Gross and Jesika St. Clair, life coach Mat Boggs, and author assistant Lisa Coleman;

Matt Hinrichs for another beautiful cover; and

The Tooms family for generously allowing me to use their Texie as my Eve.

Book Club Questions

(If your club talks about anything other than family, jobs, and household projects!)

1. Where would you go on your ideal honeymoon?
2. Have you ever had to take a trip or attend a big event when you had to force yourself to ignore something upsetting?
3. How do you make yourself stop worrying about something?
4. What would you have done in Maggie's situation? Would you have told your children about the possibility of their having a half-sister?
5. Have you ever tried to talk your child out of doing something altruistic that might involve personal risk?
6. Have you ever splurged on a big purchase? Are you glad you did?
7. Have you ever lost a home you dearly loved?
8. Did you find happiness in your new home, and if you did, how did you do it?
9. What is the most memorable wedding you've attended?
10. What one, single piece of advice would you give newlyweds?

About the Author

BARBARA HINSKE is an attorney by day, bestselling novelist by night. She inherited the writing gene from her father who wrote mysteries when he retired and told her a story every night of her childhood. She and her husband share their own Rosemont with two adorable and spoiled dogs. The old house keeps her husband busy with repair projects and her happily decorating, entertaining, cooking, and gardening. Together they have four grown children, and live in Phoenix, Arizona.

Please enjoy this excerpt from *Bringing Them Home*, the fifth installment in the *Rosemont* series:

Chapter 1

Chuck Delgado yanked the cord on the mini blinds and opened his office window to the moonless night. The faint smell of gasoline from the row of gas pumps below wafted up to him on the second floor. His store below had closed an hour earlier, and he now had the place to himself.

Delgado raised the bottle of Jameson to his lips and took a long drink. He set the bottle on the windowsill and stared into the darkness.

Out there—somewhere—someone was trying to make sure that he was the only one charged with fraud and embezzlement against the Town of Westbury. He—Chuck Delgado—was going to be the patsy. He slammed his fist on the sill, sending the bottle of whiskey to the floor. It shattered into pieces at his feet, the pungent amber liquid seeping into the carpet.

Delgado cursed loudly and retraced his steps to his desk. He dropped into his chair, leaned back, and closed his eyes. His lawyer assured him that the state's case was weak, that there was no way he would be convicted of any crime. He wasn't so sure.

Delgado ripped open his desk drawer and rummaged for a pen and piece of paper. It was time to make a list of the people who had betrayed him. He'd deal with them if his attorney's confidence proved to be unfounded. If he needed to take matters into his own hands, he'd be ready.

Delgado wrote the first entry on the list: Maggie Martin. That do-gooder mayor was the one who'd turned the Town of Westbury against him. He paused for an instant, then smiled mirthlessly and resumed his task.

Available at Amazon in Print and for Kindle

Novels in the *Rosemont* series

Coming to Rosemont

Weaving the Strands

Uncovering Secrets

Drawing Close

Bringing Them Home

Shelving Doubts

Also by **BARBARA HINSKE**

The Night Train

And Now Available on The Hallmark Channel …

The Christmas Club

Upcoming in 2020

Guiding Emily, the first novel in a new series by Barbara Hinske
The seventh novel in the Rosemont series

I'd love to hear from you! Connect with me online:

Visit **BarbaraHinske.com** to sign up for my newsletter to receive your Free Gift, plus Inside Scoops, Amazing Offers, Bedtime Stories & Inspirations from Home.

Facebook.com/BHinske
Twitter.com/BarbaraHinske
Instagram/barbarahinskeauthor
Email me at **bhinske@gmail.com**

Search for **Barbara Hinske on YouTube** for tours inside my own historic home plus tips and tricks for busy women!

Find photos of fictional Rosemont, Westbury, and things related to the Rosemont series at **Pinterest.com/BarbaraHinske.**

Made in the USA
Middletown, DE
21 January 2021

32075595R00156